Silver Abyss

By K.A. Hill

Book Cover by Stephanie Forsythe @forsythefrontier_art

1st edition August 2023

ISBN 979-8-9889068-0-3 (paperback)
ISBN 979-8-9889068-1-0 (eBook)
ISBN 979-8-9889068-2-7 (hardback)

To Michelle, Stephanie, and Amber, thank you for humoring me every time I said I'm working on a book for the last fifteen years.

Chapter One

Tamantha hated today. She hated her brother for doing this to her. She hated her parents for making her go through with this. She hated what this day meant for her. She hated the Head of the Symvoulio, Leoline Baldwin, for standing in front of her. She hated to hate anything.

Leoline Baldwin took Tamantha's right hand and held it in his palm. Tamantha could feel the eyes on her back, two pairs of them belonging to her mother and father. She could feel the beaming grin on her mother's face without even giving a look to the petite woman. Tamantha Merope took a huge breath to ease away the anxiety.

"Your Royal Highness, Princess Tamantha Alexandria Celaeno Merope, do you accept the position as heir to the throne of the country of Sophia? Do you solemnly swear to protect the people of Sophia with your life? Will you take the throne upon King Alvyn James Merope's death, may he live a long life? Will you uphold the laws of the seven families till you die?" Leoline, the Head of the Symvoulio, asked of the young princess. She swore inside at her brother. This was all his fault. It was all his fault that she was standing here.

Tamantha Merope was not supposed to ever be standing here in front of Leoline Baldwin. She was supposed to be living the rest of her life in her brother's shadow, living her life as just another claim to the throne with her brother and whatever children he produced standing in her way. He had promised her that it would never come to this.

Nolan Merope broke his promise to his own sister. He just had to go and die with no children left to his name. He had a child with a mortal girl and not his own wife, but the child was not a pureblood or born into a marriage. He died.

"I will protect the people of Sophia with my life, and I shall take the throne upon the death of my father, King Alvyn James Merope. I will uphold the laws of the seven families and the Creator till my own death," Tamantha repeated the Symvoulio member's words. This was an oath that her own brother had taken when he was seven years old. He had stood here in this very spot in front of a different Head of the Symvoulio. Tamantha wasn't even a year old then.

Leoline slipped a ring onto Tamantha's right index finger. This ring belonged to every Crown Prince and Crown Princess since the beginning of the seven families' rule of the seven countries. "I now name you, Crown Princess Tamantha Alexandria Merope of Sophia." Leoline's words cemented the death of Nolan in stone. Nolan couldn't take the throne anymore. He was truly gone, and his sister had finally replaced what he once was.

The people in the ceremony hall applauded. Leoline directed her to face the crowd who had come to watch swear her oath to Sophia. Tamantha turned towards her watchers, taking a bow with Leoline towards them. They clapped once more.

Tamantha looked upon the face of her father. She saw the tears that had emerged on his face. He had a soft smile, but he knew what the ceremony truthfully meant. His firstborn is dead. His son would never grace the world with his presence once more. She then observed her mother's face. She was radiant with pride that her only daughter was now the crown royal and not Nolan.

Nolan wasn't her mother's son. He was the son of her father's first wife, who had passed away at the age of twenty-five, just like Nolan. Her mother never cared about her husband's first child. Clarisa Celaeno was not afraid to show it. When she married into the Merope family, she disdained the fact that another child had a claim before her own children will. The death of King Alvyn's first child was a blessing to Tamantha's cruel mother. It was a way to snake in her own claim to the throne since she was the seventh child in her own family. Clarisa Celaeno was once a princess of Thalassa. With Tamantha's oath to Sophia, Tamantha had no claim in the country of Thalassa.

The crowd was lined up around the surrounding walls of the ceremony hall. It was only a handful who attended, as this was not an official coronation for a queen. It was only a coronation for the crown princess. Her coronation for the position of queen would be a much grander ceremony with the majority of the country in attendance. She walked down the line, shaking her hands with each attendant.

First to shake hands with Tamantha were the members of the Symvoulio. There were seven of them. Members of the Symvoulio family dutifully stood behind them. Tamantha peaked behind Leoline Baldwin to meet eyes with Cole Baldwin. He had a huge grin on his face, brushing his shaggy red hair out of his eyes.

Cole had been best friends with Tamantha since his father took office when she was only four years old. Tamantha took a moment out of protocol to hug him in front of all to see. Now fifteen years later, the boy was greeting her with a genuine smile, whispering into her ear. "Congratulations, Tammy. You look beautiful in your dress." Cole was always such a tease. He is a year older than her, boyfriend of one of Tamantha's Guardians. Tamantha rolled her eyes at him, moving on to the next hands.

A few members of the royal families had come to see her ceremony, at least one from each family as representatives. Each person stood in front of the symbol of their family decorated in front of the hall. The Merope family symbol had a giant display at the back of the hall as this was the Grand Ceremony Hall of Sophia.

The Asterope family had sent their own crown princess to see the ceremony, although she was only five years old. Her father is the young king of Polemos. Tamantha resisted the urge to run her fingers through the small girl's long brunette hair. She allowed the child princess to shake her hand with eagerness. Nolan's wife was a lady of the Asterope family, but she didn't come to the ceremony.

All but one of the families had a member of attendance. The Alcyone, Celaeno, and Maia families had all sent someone who was at least fourth in line. The Taygete family had sent one of their lowest ranking family members. It was normal though. They resisted their duty to participate much in the customs of the seven families.

A hushed silence fell over the audience as she stood in front of the one symbol that was missing a representative. Tamantha dutifully placed her hand on the symbol, bowing her head in mourning in respect for the family that this symbol belonged to. The Electra family had not had a presence in over three hundred years. They were lost to the world.

Tamantha moved on to the aristocracy of Sophia. She greeted them all warmly. These were the dukes and duchesses who ruled over the numerous states of Sophia, the earls who managed the regions, and the barons who managed the towns individually. Each aristocrat bowed respectfully as she passed them by.

The final hands belonged to her cousin, her mother, and the king. First was her cousin, Lady Christine Merope. She is the daughter of King Alvyn's younger sister. She is now Tamantha's heir unless Tamantha has children of her own. Christine hugged her cousin instead of shaking the Princess's hand. The display of affection was surprising to Tamantha, but she placed her hands on her cousin's back.

She moved on to the next person who was waiting for her, her loving and doting parents. Her mother embraced her. She gave her words of encouragement, bestowing her affection upon her only child. Her father kissed her crown ring. "You will be a great queen someday, Tammy." His words meant everything to her, but she knew what being a queen meant. It meant her beloved father would no longer be here, just like Nolan.

Clarisa had always felt like she had failed her husband. She was never able to produce more children for him. His first wife would have most likely given him more children, but she died when Nolan was only two. Clarisa and Alvyn were married in an arrangement between the Merope and Celaeno family, a reinforcement of a peace treaty, a wife for the widowed King so the royal family would have more heirs. Her one child meant something to the Merope family. It gave her a purpose in having been forced to marry the King of Sophia.

By reaching her parents, it marked the end of the ceremony. She bowed to the crowd of people and left through the grand doors of the hall. She immediately headed in the direction of the west wing of the palace. Sophia didn't need her for the moment. She could enjoy the silence and peace of her bedroom. She could drop the facade that she was happy to be in this position.

When Tamantha entered her room, she looked at herself in the grand mirror on her dresser. She eyed the blue princess gown she was wearing. It was picked out by a member of the royal fashion committee. It was shimmering with diamonds embedded in a belt around the waist. The bottom half of the ball gown was tulle with glitter lightly coated onto it. She took the dress off first, causing her to shiver as the air licked her naked skin.

Tamantha then took off the princess tiara she was wearing. It was decorated in diamond and sapphire gems, the sapphire gems being the royal jewel of the Merope family. The crown originally belonged to a Merope princess three hundred years ago who had perished with the Electra family. The princess had been married to the Crown Prince of Electra at the time. The Crown Prince was the only survivor of the massacre, but he disappeared shortly after with no traces of where he had gone.

The princess studied her own face, noting the similarities to her own brother. His picture was taped to her mirror. She had the same icy blue eyes as her brother, except her eyes were bigger. The color of her eyes was common in the Merope family. Her hair however was a common trait to the Celaeno family, almost silver, blondehair. Nolan's hair was the dark brown that all males of the Merope family had. She loosened her hair from the decorative bun it was in, allowing her hair to flow down to the small of her back. Her pale skin turned even whiter in the harsh light above her dresser. Tamantha had full lips while her brothers were thin. Both of them had the same straight nose, the same high cheekbones, same as their father. She looked back at her trademark icy blue eyes.

Tamantha would always see her brother in her own eyes. She let out a shaky sigh, wanting to look away from herself. She felt it was the only way to latch onto her memories of him. She could never truly stare into a mirror without feeling the same blood as her brother run through herself.

The now Crown Princess walked over to her bed, staring at the short, elegant blue dress that she would wear to the ceremonial dinner. She wanted to wait a little longer till she joined the party, afraid of becoming the star of the show again. This was her day, but it wasn't really.

Tamantha took a moment to sit on a bench by the window, overlooking the gardens of the Sophia palace, letting the glow of the moonlight bathe her naked skin.

Tamantha looked up at the night sky. She admired the glowing monstrosity in the sky, watching its several tails float in the air. The tails shined with a rainbow light, shimmering as it moved quickly across the sky. Its glowing eye seemed to be looking in her direction. The people of Prota once thought of them as angels or Gods, but now they know it is just a creature that only appears at night. The latest name for these creatures is Architeuthis dux.

After slipping the new dress on, she went on her way out of her room, plastering another fake smile on her face. She was trying to keep from letting go the tears that plagued her every night since his death. Tammy was the last one to see him alive and the first one to find his dead body.

The late Crown Prince Nolan Alvyn Merope passed away on Anthesterion 17, 1038 at the age of twenty-five, leaving behind his father, stepmother, half-sister, and his darling wife, Rosaleen Asterope. His cause of death was failing to pass the Test of the

Lost One.

The Test of the Lost One had been an ancient tradition since the disappearance of their origin country of Prota seven hundred years ago. The test is administered by no one. It is a test created by the lost daughter of the Electra family. It was a curse placed on all pure bloods of Prota origins. Half-bloods will not feel the effect of this curse.

The girl was angry at her fellow people for leaving Prota without her. She was forced to stay behind by the Creator as punishment to the father of the girl. The lost daughter of Electra remains on Prota forever immortal, but forever alone.

This test's results are always random, pass or fail. Mathematicians have predicted a twenty percent chance of failure for all pure bloods, but the chance can increase or decrease for the royal families. The Electra family had a five percent chance of failing, while the Asterope family had an eighty percent chance of failing. The Merope family has a chance of forty percent. The test has plagued the Merope and Asterope families since the loss of Prota, forcing them to marry earlier than they would like. The Merope family lost King Alvyn's sister, his mother, and his own son.

On the twenty-fifth birthday of every pureblood, upon the twenty-second hour of their day, they enter the test, falling into a state of sleep. The dream can be pleasant or a nightmare. The one trapped in the test cannot be broken out of it. If it's a pleasant dream, they'll automatically pass. If it's a nightmare, the pure blood must pass the test by staying alive in the dream. If they die while inside it, they die in reality, the body completely stopping all organ function. No one can tell one how to survive it as each dream designed specifically to the person it is being conveyed upon. Survivors of it try to give tips to those who are approaching his or her twenty-fifth birthday, but they're long forgotten while in the dream.

Tamantha and Nolan went alone to their old elementary school at Sophia Academy, closed for the summer. Their Guardians were close by while they spent the last hours of Nolan's birthday together. Tamantha treasured Nolan dearly. They both talked of old times and the future. The hour was slowly approaching the time of the dream, but Nolan wasn't concerned. He felt confident he would survive, or at least that's what he told Tamantha. He always keeps his promises to Tamantha.

Nolan Merope was scared to death, burying it deep down under a sense of responsibility. He knew the day would be quickly coming to an end, and he wanted to stop it before it happened.

Tamantha squeezed his hand. Both of the young royals indulged in a little bit of drinking. Tamantha began giggling when Nolan made fun of her mother. He mocked Clarisa's tone of voice, telling Tamantha how she should act and look and to be better than that hooligan of a brother of hers. Tamantha knew that Clarisa would prefer it for Tamantha to be the Queen of Sophia, but Tamantha wanted the opposite. Tamantha wanted to be free of that responsibility, to not have to put up a front every time she goes outside her bedroom. She enjoyed solitude, preferring the company of those close to her. If Nolan passes his test, she'll be free from that burden.

Nolan's wife was at home, safe and sound. Nolan refused to include her in his last moments before he entered the test. His marriage was arranged by the Symvoulio and the Queen. Rosaleen was a lovely woman, but it wasn't his true love.

Nolan had fallen in love with a mortal girl named Melina while in high school. The girl became pregnant by him. When the Symvoulio and Tamantha's mother learned of this, they sent the girl away, forcing Nolan to never see his own child. Nolan would send presents and letters to Melina and his daughter in secret. He provided for them, so they wouldn't have to struggle without him.

Every time Rosaleen became pregnant, she quickly had a miscarriage soon after. The miscarriages always devastated her, becoming more depressed with each loss. Rosaleen was younger than Nolan by a few months. Nolan didn't blame her for her miscarriages. He gave her the love she needed as a good husband, but his heart would always belong to Melina. Rosaleen bore no heir for Nolan before his death, leaving his sister to be his heir instead of a child.

Tamantha talked about her excitement of going to Sophia University. It was an opportunity to be away from home, an opportunity to be away from the royal life. Nolan took a sip to that, telling her about his own adventures while he attended the university. The playful banter continued on until five minutes before the fateful moment.

"Tamantha, I want you to go outside." Tamantha wasn't shocked that Nolan didn't want her there. He was looking away from her. He didn't want her to see the pain he couldn't hide. He was always trying to be brave for his sister. Tamantha hugged her big brother from behind.

"I love you, Nolan." Tamantha tried to memorize how warm he felt, remember his smell, his height, his everything, just in case. She trusted her brother when he said he would live for her.

"I love you too, Tamantha. Now go."

Tamantha left the elementary school gym and entered the hallway where her Guardian, Siberius, was waiting. Siberius had been her Guardian, and he had been Nolan's best friend since they both entered this very same school. Siberius put his hand on her shoulder, giving it a gentle squeeze.

"Don't worry. When has Nolan ever broken a promise to you?" Siberius comforted the poor girl. The blonde princess nodded at the tall brute of a Guardian, but Siberius could see the tears that had already escaped her.

Minutes later, they heard Nolan's scream. Tamantha tried to rush in the door, but Siberius was holding her back. There was nothing she could do that would stop the nightmare. Only Nolan could pass through the nightmare on his own. He wouldn't wake up till he succeeded. The Guardians of the prince were waiting in the hallway. Nolan had commanded them to wait outside while the brother and sister enjoyed their last moments together.

The worried sister only heard silence now. Siberius let her go, assuming the test was over. The Guardian and the Princess only then noticed the distressed look on the faces of Nolan's Guardians. Their link to Nolan had been broken, which only meant he had failed. Tamantha felt her breath caught in her throat. He's fine, right? The gym doors closed behind her as she entered. Siberius swore out loud, rushing inside the gym before it was too late.

Siberius told her later on that he only wished he could have saved her from that memory that would forever haunt her. He wished he could have stopped her from seeing her brother lying on the ground face down. The only sound that could be heard was the princess's screams. Siberius admitted to her later something was strange about the way Nolan died. Instead of the usual face of peace that all those who failed display, he had a face of horror. He did not wish such a fate on his dear friend.

The pure bloods call themselves Eklektos, the chosen ones. Half-bloods would be called half-Eklektos. Most Eklektos tend to value themselves higher than any normal person upon the planet of Atlantis. They believed themselves to be the purest race among all the mortals beneath them. They called those mortals Anaxios.

Such pure bloods were sitting at the dinner tables of the Sophia palace. The Merope family did not believe themselves to be greater than any mortal as they are lovers of mortals, truly and forever. The Merope family's soul mates are thought to always be in the body of non-pure bloods, more so in the body of a mortal than a half-blood.

Tamantha sat at the head of the hall, taking the seat her father would always sit in. He had given her the seat only for today, a special treat just for his little girl on her special day. Her parents sat on either side of her, displaying smiles to whoever was looking towards their table.

The Celaeno family always considered themselves to be such pureblood. They looked down on any mortal who would cross their path. The Celaeno pride has always been the topic of concern in the Merope family as they were the exact opposites when it came to any mortal. Tamantha's mother would always hiss in annoyance when anyone would speak badly of her family. Her mother was also keen on bullying any Anaxios servant who had the misfortune of being near her. Tamantha's father frowned upon any of Clarisa's activities in the palace, his Merope side of him always shining through. Clarisa learned the hard way that she was not in the palace of Thalassa any longer.

The queen by marriage adored her own kingdom more than Sophia. She would always drag Tamantha on little vacations to Thalassa. It was a nation that comprised of islands and only islands. The best mode of transportation in Thalassa was by boat. Tamantha's relatives were always quick to jabber on about Tamantha needing to stop her Anaxios loving behavior. Her cousin, the first daughter of the Queen of Thalassa, third in line to the throne, had been chosen to represent Thalassa at Tamantha's ascension as heir.

The Taygete family was also an example of valuing themselves higher than any mortal. They value any animal above mortal life, a part of their direct ancestor's, Taygete, personality. Therion is a country with more animals than people. The country is mostly rainforests and grasslands. Therion is on the equator of Atlantis. It is always warm and always muggy.

The Taygete family didn't send their tenth in line for the throne because of the distance. They sent their tenth in line because they didn't trust the descendants of the other five sisters. Ever since the Electra family's demise, they haven't taken too kindly to be visiting any of their fellow royal families. They choose to rule Therion without the input of the other royal families, relying on their Symvoulio for advice. They choose their own Head of Symvoulio without an election in case a person is trying to barge in and press for indulgence in foreign affairs.

Tamantha could see the hesitation in the tenth in line Taygete boy. He was shifting in his seat, uncomfortable with the whole party. The Taygete family had no doubt instilled within him the three-hundred-year-old distrust that rose after much debate about who destroyed their allies, the Electra family. His dinner plate was still full. He was making no move to even take a bite of it. He was only thirteen years old.

The Maia family, however, was perhaps one of the most respectful of mortals. The Maia family always took care of their people, even allowing Anaxios to be on their Symvoulio. The Maia family rule over Paideeia, a country much like Sophia with different terrains up and down. It is the most eastern country of Atlantis.

The Maia family always remained neutral in any situation

unless they came under fire themselves. They belong to the oldest daughter of Atlas and Pleione, making them the motherly family. The queen of Paideeia sent her grandson, Kai, age twenty-seven, as a representative for the Maia family. Tamantha felt envy towards Kai. He survived his test, and Nolan didn't. It wasn't his fault though. Anyone from Paideeia had a low chance of failing.

The crown princess of Polemos was not so lucky. Almost all of her family was dead, and her own father was fast approaching his own twenty fifth birthday. It was normal for the Asterope family to rule young however, since many of their kings and queens had fallen to the curse. The little princess most likely already knew this, but she was too young to really understand it.

The Asterope family in general does not care for mortals. They are neutral towards them, more focused on their army. The Asterope family has the grandest army out of the seven, always ready for war should it occur. Wars were once a common thing and have popped up from time to time. Polemos was always on the winning side. Sophia has had its fair share of wars over time, mostly with Astrapi. Polemos hosts the Guardian Academy with their intense military training. Tamantha's mortal guards have been there just like any other Guardian of Merope.

Nous always picks the good side, no matter who is winning. It's a country that believes in the justice systems and innocent till proven guilty. The Eklektos of Nous believed themselves to be equal with Anaxios. Equality laws are valued very highly by the people of Nous. They fight for the laws only, no matter if it is good or evil. Nous is occupied by the Alcyone family. The sister of the King of Nous was chosen to represent her family today at the ceremony. She brought her own husband and children to attend.

The only missing representative came from a family who regarded themselves as gods to the people of Astrapi. They were above their own law, taking all the power. They even refused to have a Symvoulio like the other six. They were tyrants in their own way. The Electra family didn't deny their people rights of course, but the Eklektos and non-pure bloods would bow with fear and tremble before the feet of any royal who passed them by.

Now the Guardians of Electra rule over Astrapi with no heir in sight, ready to present the crown to the heir who is lost to them. It is unknown if there is anyone left from the Electra family. The only one the world knows of is the lost daughter who is stuck on Prota. People assume the Creator would know the answer to the Electra family's destruction, but She has not been seen in many years.

For now, the Merope family has acted as wardens of Astrapi, ready to step in if need be. The Astrapi government must follow their orders accordingly, for fear of destroying the treaty between Sophia and Astrapi. When the Electra returns, the Merope will gladly hand the reigns back over to them.

"There are so many things you will learn when you become Queen, my daughter." Tamantha broke out of her gaze to look at her father. There was a twinkle in his eye. His little princess grinned back at the king. This was a real smile, not part of the mask she is wearing today. Alvyn has always been affectionate with his children and would never stop until the day he dies.

The Mcrope family was known for their wisdom and intelligence. With this wisdom comes great curiosity and wondering. Tamantha was not as resourceful as Nolan was or her father. Her own great mind was not as refined as theirs was. She lacked in the government lessons that her own brother had received. It was always thought he would be King someday. Tamantha was still clever and able to analyze any situation. With plenty of lessons under her belt, she will be able to become a wise and just ruler. Most royals typically chose to attend the Academies founded upon the ideals of the Merope family.

King Alvyn rose from his seat, holding his glass in the air. "A toast to the Crown Princess, and may she rule Sophia with kindness in her heart."

"Here, here!" the audience responded, raising their own glasses.

One would think that a person in a position of power would be openly sociable, but Tamantha is not such a person, preferring to be completely by herself or to be alone with only select friends. She is supposed to make a speech, but she will not, a quiet rebellion to what was bestowed on her. Her path had been decided by her own blood, but she was never born to this role, only having it thrust onto her by tragedy. She hoped that in the next life that it would be very different. Nolan was lucky. He was free. She hoped his next life would be full of peace and love.

Soon, Tamantha will have a small taste of freedom, able to hide away in the stone walls of Sophia University, a chance to pretend things are still a little bit normal.

Tamantha returned the toast with a sip from her wine glass. It tasted like iron in her mouth, but she loved it. It was a welcome sensation that she hadn't had since the last full moon. Tonight was another.

The people of Atlantis worship only one God. She is the Creator of the world the people of Atlantis only know. All texts before Her have been lost to the void of time.

There are two races in the world of Atlantis, the Eklektos and the Anaxios. The Eklektos never age once they reach twenty-five. The Anaxios are considered mortals, even though Eklektos succumb to old age as well. The difference between Eklektos and

Anaxios originated from Prota. This trait of the Eklektos was created by the Creator.

Creator is the only title anyone is allowed to call the highest known being in the entirety of Atlantis. Her actual name had been lost in history as She had been rarely ever seen again since the demise of Prota. No one disdains Her for what She did to the original country. They only hate the person who caused Her anger.

The Creator was assumed to have been born to mortal parents more than two thousand years ago, but She was born different from any regular Anaxios. How She was born this way has never been discovered. It could only be summed up to be the gift of the Gods. She was born, but She could never die. She was born with the powers to heal anyone from the brink of death, but She could not bring back the dead. Everyone She had ever loved had died long ago.

It had been a thousand years since Her birth when She made the journey that would begin the Eklektos. She traveled the vast sea to the center of Atlantis. No one was ever able to trek to Prota due to the storms surrounding that would sink any ship that came near it. Her ship sunk, but She could reach the shore by swimming because She couldn't drown.

By entering Prota, the storms stopped as if it had been waiting for Her to be the first one. The Creator loved exploring the land that had never been touched. After a few years, she felt the same loneliness She did before coming to Her newfound place.

The Creator had powers that were unknown even to Her. From Her tears, two people formed, two halves of Her. It was a woman and a man, two souls created from Herself. She named the man and woman, Atlas and Pleione. Pleione had the Creator's ability to heal, and Atlas had the Creator's immortality. The two were soul mates and very much in love, giving birth to seven daughters. They were Maia, Taygete, Caleano, Alcyone, Asterope, Electra, and Merope. These daughters did not have the same powers as their parents.

Pleione passed on of old age, and Atlas came to the Creator and begged Her to bring back his beloved Pleione. The Creator could not bring the dead back to life. She however blessed Pleione's body and soul and promised that she would be reborn and always find Atlas in every one of her lifetimes from then on.

This blessing spread all over Atlantis, and it allowed everyone to find their soul mates again in another lifetime. It signaled all souls were subject to reincarnation. Whether or not this was because of the Creator, no one knows for sure.

Atlas then begged the Creator to allow him to be reborn himself. The Creator took away his immortality, and he passed on to the next life where Pleione was waiting.

People began to migrate onto Prota, hearing that this sacred land was now inhabitable and accessible. The seven sisters were chosen to rule over Prota, splitting it into seven sections between each sister. The seven sisters had families with the new inhabitants and would pass on the sections to their children.

After one hundred fifty years and after each sister died, She felt the despair of loneliness creeping up again because the remnants of the two people She created from Herself were gone.

She found another power within Herself. She blessed everyone on Prota with the gift of immortality as long as they remain on Prota. This immortality granted them the ability to never age after twenty-five just like Her, and they did not need to fear death. It would stop when they stepped off. She did this by cutting out Her own heart and placing it in a box in the center of Prota, infusing this blessing into it.

The people of Prota built a shrine around it, praying to it, praying to Her. They believed the Creator to be their God, unknowing the Creator was just born into the world like everyone else. The people of Prota did not know what She looked like, except for the royal families. She preferred this privacy instead of being worshipped wherever she would go.

There was a condition to this immortality. Whenever speaking to someone from the outside of Prota about this blessing, it was punishable by death to all, regardless of their heritage. Also, the outsider would be executed too to prevent the spreading of this secret.

The Creator eventually found Her soul mate among the people of Prota, meeting him at the docks of Prota when he first stepped onto the land. It took a thousand years for him to be finally born into Her life. She fell in love with him the moment their eyes met on that fateful day. The two gave birth to a daughter. This daughter's soul was created from the Creator's love for Her husband and soul mate. The daughter was Her only child, but it was Her most beloved creation of all.

The husband and the daughter took a fishing trip on the oceans around Prota when the daughter was only nine years old. The husband promised they would return safely.

Unbeknownst to the Creator, a member of the Electra family had been wronged. His wife had spoken of the blessing to an outsider and had been executed along with the outsider. The man was angry at the Creator and angry at this law. He wanted revenge. He knew of the Creator's family.

He watched the little family and decided upon how he would avenge his wife. He followed them out to sea on one of the Electra family's boats. His boat was much faster than the husband's, and he caught up to them. He waved to them with a sick smile, but they didn't realize anything was wrong. They had met this man before at one of the Creator's meetings. The husband and daughter trusted him.

The man boarded the boat with that evil grin on his face and took their lives, returning to Prota after he washed himself of their blood, carrying on with his day like nothing had ever happened. They were murdered during the night of a full moon.

The Creator worried when her family did not come back. She worried that something had happened to her child and her lover. She set out into the sea herself, coming upon the stranded boat in the middle of nowhere. She was struck with grief and sorrow. She had lost more people dear to Her, and they were Her most precious ones of all.

The Creator found a knife with the Electra family symbol on it. The wrath of the Creator began at the moment, furious that anyone from the seven families would have dared to commit this terrible crime against Her. She found the power within Herself to make Prota disappear. She would not destroy Prota as She treasured it, but She would make it impossible to find. She forced all to leave from Prota after discovering who the traitor was.

The Creator killed the murderer with his own knife and trapped his daughter onto the land with no escape. His daughter would be immortal forever, but she would be tragically alone. The Creator cursed everyone from Prota with a need for blood.

This curse would pass on to all Eklektos, affecting those with pure blood the most. Eklektos would crave blood upon the full moon, forced to drink from another to stay alive. They must feed on blood every full moon, or they will die upon the full moon's ending.

The pureblood Eklektos would never age in appearance at the age of twenty-five, but they would still die of old age just like any

Anaxios. The partial blooded Eklektos would still age after, but it would be slower.

Royal families must remain pure blooded to appease the Creator and not encourage her wrath once again. She wants the descendants of the seven sisters who would rule over the seven countries in Atlantis to suffer and never forget the crime committed and what was lost to all Eklektos. She made them rule each country with force, bonding them to their assigned place.

The kings and queens must be a pureblood in order for all Eklektos to continue living. It was the message bestowed to the last kings and queens on Prota, and it was passed on to every generation after.

Chapter Two

Tamantha exited the karavi with her Guardians, stepping onto the grounds where she would be spending the next four years.

The karavi shimmered away into the air, heading towards the University's karavi garage. The karavi was a floating carriage on land. Tamantha thanked her Celaeno ancestors for the mode of transport. They decided while traveling to each island by boat is the typical mode, but why not make it float outside of water? They worked together with the priestesses of the Creator's Temple to create this handy invention. They prayed to the Creator to give them this magic, and She did.

Gone were the days of carriages pulled by horses and boring boat rides. Now anyone can travel across Atlantis within a matter of days. Of course, the Celaeno royal family tried to keep this to themselves, but the other five families bullied them into sharing it with them and then the world.

Tamantha gazed upon the lavish brick buildings as she walked the grounds. They almost matched the architecture of the palace. Both were designed by the deceased Philip Merope, Duke of Rosebury, ancestor of Tamantha's very own cousin, Christine. The school was huge with several dormitories to accommodate the vast number of students. It was filled with many lecture halls and buildings to fit any student's major. It was founded by Duke Philip around the time of the Electra demise. It was created to give the people of Sophia the education every Eklektos, half-Eklektos, and Anaxios deserves, regardless of the race they were born into.

Tamantha was automatically accepted to Sophia University just by being born to the Merope bloodline, but she didn't want others to think she hadn't earned her place here.

This was Sophia University, a school based upon the Merope values of knowledge. The school was the most highly esteemed in the world, always boasting of their wide knowledge and extremely valuable education. People all over the country and all over the planet would try to get accepted into the school. The acceptance rate for Sophia University once accepted anyone who breathed many years ago, but now it only opened its doors very limitedly, of course with no discrimination against their origins.

The majority of spots belonged to Sophia citizens, but it had spots reserved for a thousand outsiders every year. Students were required to show academic excellence in their primary and secondary schools as well as work towards bettering their communities through volunteering. They also had to pass the exam to get into the school. The highest scores were generally accepted first, with the lower scores getting accepted based on merit.

Recently Tammy was attending Sophia Academy through preschool to her senior year of high school, another select school reserved for those who could afford the attendance fee.

By going to Sophia University, she would finally have the freedom she never had before, finally able to live in a dormitory like a normal person. The watchful eyes of the palace and her mother could not follow her here entirely without disturbing the students who attended. She would take what little she could get out of this opportunity with welcoming arms.

Tamantha could have been given her own dorm room by herself, but the Silver Oath ring on her finger said otherwise. She was the heir now. However, she was allowed to choose which Guardian would be in the other bed. Her Guardian of the same age would be her roommate in disguise. This Guardian is one of her best friends, Alessandra Aki. This arrangement was more favorable to her as it was it allowed her some comfort that she was not bunking with a complete stranger.

The Guardians were a select group of people who the Creator gave powers to, in order to protect those in rule. These Guardians descended from the ordinary guards of the first families. Anyone with these ancestors could become a Guardian, regardless if their parent chose not to. The Creator gave them a choice to opt out if they do not want to pursue the Guardian life.

Those who did pursue this path would spend their secondary school years at the Asterope Academy for Guardians, training and activating those ancient powers. They had more strength than anyone else in Atlantis, a strength designed to serve the royal families. They were more agile than most, braver than most. They always saved their charges from harm. They do not need to drink blood like the rest of the Eklektos, a gift from the Creator.

Guardians were automatically assigned to a royal through their own blood connection. They always remained within the families they originally served. No one chooses who they guard, not even themselves. It is chosen through their mind and soul after intense meditation to release the seal on their Guardian powers. They receive an image and a name in their head of who they are chosen to protect.

Alessandra Aki is a petite woman, almost a joke among the Guardians if she would be able to fulfill her duties to Tamantha at all. Despite her small body, she is one of the best fighters among the Merope Guardians, having defeated everyone in a duel at the Guardian Academy. Alessandra is not afraid to speak her mind and is always smiling, a truly happy person. She got the lucky draw when she discovered her charge would be her own best friend.

Alessandra's father was an ordinary Anaxios from Paideeia, but her mother was a Guardian in Sophia. Her mother met him on her travels, following her charge who was Christine's mother. Alessandra chose to continue the Guardian line within her family, while her three brothers did not want to follow that path.

Siberius Gagnon had hoped it would have been Nolan as they were best friends. He was slightly disappointed to learn he would be serving the prince's little sister instead, but he gladly carries on with his duties for his charge. Siberius has been by Tamantha's side since he turned eighteen. He's almost a giant compared to those around him. His stature puts fear into his enemies. He, however, is a big softy at heart, afraid to touch anyone as he thinks he may hurt them.

Siberius traces his roots to the main Guardian of the first king of Sophia. His ancestors always became the General of the Guardians in Sophia. His mother is the current General. His own bloodline makes him the Captain of Tamantha's Guardians.

Tamantha has five other Guardians who have connected to her. The greater the family members' place in line to the throne, the more Guardians are assigned to them. Her father has fifteen, and her cousin only has three. Her brother had nine. Some Guardians have been chosen to guard the lesser Merope who are farther down the line and only share the same blood. It's rare for them to take to a weaker blood Merope as Guardians usually link to those most in power. Those charges could, in theory, barely even fit the definition of a half-Eklektos after the line has been thoroughly mixed with Anaxios blood.

Tamantha's mother had Guardians from her family, only three though. Tamantha had her Merope Guardians because her position of power was higher in the country of Sophia, making blood connections from the Merope Guardians automatic and Celaeno null and void. If she traced her position in the Celaeno's line for the Thalassa throne, she would be at least fifteenth in line behind her six Aunts and Uncles and their children.

Crown Princess Tamantha already felt the eyes watching her as she strolled to her dormitory. The students already knew she would be coming here, the recent ceremony fresh in their minds. She was the proper age to begin college. She wondered if this happened to Nolan too.

Tamantha was unsure of herself, feeling the anxiety slowly rising with every step. Could she really be the next queen? A princess always has to put up a front as she holds the country on her shoulders.

These people would watch her grow and would see her take over. They want to believe and have faith that she will take care of them. She would never let them see the truth. She won't show them that she never wanted any of this. She could not let them know she was scared that she was Sophia's doom.

She sighed in relief as she crossed the arches of the Pleione dormitory, named after the soul born from the Creator. There was also an Atlas dormitory.

Priority females would live in the Pleione dormitory, and priority males would live in the Atlas dormitory. Priority was based on rank. Diplomats from other countries and the royalty would live here. It was not uncommon for a person in line for one of the seven thrones to attend Sophia University.

Children of Symvoulio and children of the aristocracy would typically also live here as well if they were not already from the capital of Sophia, Kyrios, the place Sophia University is based in. Students who have the choice to live at home usually take it, not wanting to give up the luxuries they are used to, or some don't want to pay for the high room and board fee.

People who have high grades have a possible chance to place into the Pleione and Atlas dorms, but only the very few are lucky enough when spots are open. Tamantha's other best friends, Sara and Davin Fletcher, twins, were ordinary Eklektos who are instead residing in the lesser dorms. She would have to pay a visit to them if they are not permitted entry to visit her.

Tamantha looked up the stairs, eyeing the many floors above them. This was going to be her home. She could feel the excitement creeping in. She felt freedom dancing across her shoulders. She could try to pretend she was ordinary here. She was ready for this new adventure.

"Tammy!" A voice cried out from behind Tamantha. She knew it was her redheaded puppy dog of a best friend.

Alessandra turned around quickly to clothesline him. He fell backwards onto his back, struggling to breathe from his throat being almost crushed in. One almost forgets the petite girl has the strength of a rhino.

"Sorry, Cole," Alessandra whispered. She helped him up and gave him a kiss on the hand. Tamantha couldn't help but stifle laughter as Cole melted into a puddle of embarrassment. People were staring. Students carrying their stuff off to their assigned room gazed at the couple.

"I missed you, Al. How are you, my darling?" Cole pulled Alessandra into a hug and kissed her several times on her cheeks, neck, and forehead. Alessandra hid her face under her jet-black hair.

"I've got a job to do. Stop it," Alessandra told him, pulling away and returning to her charge's side. Tamantha tilted her head with curiosity. "Don't forget your manners, Cole. All crown royalty must be bowed to when in their presence, even if it is only a head bow." Tamantha frowned, having not noticed this had been already going on when she stepped onto the campus.

It was a rule of Sophia University. Tamantha is currently the only one with the title of Princess or even Prince to live on school grounds at the present moment. The last one was Nolan three years ago. Cole made a humble bow with his hand on his chest and his other hand out wide. "Apologies, Your Royal Highness."

"Cole, enough with the formalities. You don't have to do that. I exempt you from the rule," Tamantha ordered, reminding herself to send a letter to whoever made this rule and tell them to shut it down. Cole stuck his tongue out and approached her. He wanted to go with them to their dorm. Siberius stared down at Cole, although he was only three inches shorter.

"'Sup, Siberius?" Cole had already noticed the glare. Siberius was just doing his duty, but he returned the fist bump that Cole presented him. Siberius already trusted him, and Cole did hold ranking as the son of Head of the Symvoulio.

The group of four went upstairs to Tamantha and Alessandra's new room. Cole already had his room set up as he has already been here for two years and being in the Atlas dorm allows him to reserve the same room. His room was only a single bed, unlike Tamantha's current situation.

The palace of Sophia is in Kyrios as it is the capital of Sophia, but Tamantha made a deal with her mother to be able to live on campus like a normal student. This was before Nolan passed away.

The queen decided she would allow Tamantha to live on campus for one year, but then she would have to return to living in the palace. Tamantha was not allowed to live alone. Tamantha was Crown Princess now, so she will figure out a way to change the deal if she decides she likes living in the dorm. It would be like pulling tooth and nail with her mother though. The first thing she had to do to make this happen was to make sure this year went as smoothly as possible.

Alessandra made Cole sit on her bed. She began decorating her side of the room with dozens of posters of famous Guardians and technique boards. She also put two wooden sticks on the wall to rest her sword on. It was directly next to her pillow in case of an emergency. Cole tried to steal Alessandra's sword from her belt, but she quickly shut that down and flicked him on the forehead.

Tamantha wondered when she would get a chance at love like this. She was destined to have an arranged marriage if she didn't find an Eklektos on her own. She had to keep the bloodline alive as there were only three living pureblood Merope alive that could care for the throne, her father, her, and her cousin. Her cousin was attending Sophia University as well, starting this year, but she was going to live in an apartment that the family owns close to the campus.

Cole is a pureblood, but he will most likely marry Alessandra if permitted by his father. It was, however, normal for Baldwins to marry Meropes. Baldwins somehow always won Symvoulio positions, and these were voted positions. They were a long bloodline dating back to Prota, having served the Merope family even then.

Tamantha did her own decorating for her portion of the room, throwing up a painting of bouquets of assorted flowers local to Sophia and photos of her and her friend. It almost looked like an ordinary girl was living here.

The plush comforter from Thalassa and expensive sheets from Paideeia said otherwise. The Pleione and Atlas dormitories have the highest room and board for a reason. The room wasn't even like the normal dorm room. It was double in size, almost triple, and the ceiling was at least twelve feet high. They were also decorated with the finest furniture that money can buy. It was a room fit for royalty.

"They're having a welcoming party, Tammy, for all the freshmen this year. You should go. It will be a lot of fun, a lot of stuffy old professors thought," Cole suggested. He started stroking his chin like he had a beard. "Hm, yes. This wine tastes positively luxurious if I must say so myself." He faked holding a glass and taking sip from it.

"Sounds boring and so not my thing," Tamantha groaned. "I will probably be forced to go anyways. A princess has her duties." She said the last bit in her mother's tone of voice. She was born into the wrong life this cycle; she was sure of it. Cole stood up from the bed and started shaking her hand with both of his.

"So nice to see you here, Your Royal Highness. You look stunning in that dress of yours. May I tell you boring stories that you don't want to hear." Cole was hunched over like an old man, his face down to Tamantha's height, five foot seven.

"No, thank you, but I'm sure you will still tell me." Cole returned it with a furious nod up and down, twenty times in three seconds. Alessandra stood on her bed, holding her arms out like she was about to give a speech to the public.

"Quiet down, ladies and gentlemen. We have a royalty in our presence, the future queen of Sophia! Doesn't she look radiant? I'm sure she would like to give a few words!" Alessandra motioned Tamantha to come up and join her, prompting a middle finger in her direction. "Well, screw you too. Can we vote for a new queen please?" Siberius clasped his hand over his mouth in a gasp. He didn't make a joke of this like they did.

"I vote for Siberius to be the queen!" Tamantha screamed, pushing the giant to Alessandra's bed. "He would look wonderful in a tiara!" Siberius shrugged her off, shaking his head, tired of this facade. She forced one of her many tiaras on top of his head anyways.

"I will be outside, Tamantha," Siberius said, taking his leave from the room, walking out with the tiara still on his head.

Siberius would probably spend a couple hours standing outside her door. Tamantha wondered how students will react when they see this giant man with a tiara on his head. Two of her Guardians are already posted in the building besides Siberius and Alessandra, and the other three were patrolling the grounds of the University with the help of the hired guards.

"He's no fun," Cole retorted, tipping his hat off to the intimidating man. Tamantha began laughing out loud, the first time in a while. "Thank you. Thank you very much. I'll be here all day."

"Please don't." Tamantha bit her tongue after the words escaped her, but Cole just grinned at her, that goofy grin that makes anyone smile. "Should we go find Sara and Davin, or let them come to us?" Cole shrugged. They were friends, but not best friends to him. He enjoyed the company of his girlfriend and his princess the most.

"I think let them settle in and see what they do," Alessandra said as she placed a picture frame of her and three brothers on her desk. Cole followed Alessandra all around the room at the heels of her feet, waiting for her to snap and possibly use a sword sheath on his head.

The welcoming party would consist of what Cole and Alessandra just insinuated, a professor or president of the school inviting her to come give her own message, and everyone coming to greet her. She would pretend she never even heard of it.

There will be invites sent out to all of the new students this school year. It would be her first time appearing publicly after becoming Crown Princess. The ordinary people would be excited for a ball to dress up and dance while the high-ranking crowd could talk about how great their life is. She'll probably try to burn the invite if the Guardians don't catch her with the matches. She swears some of them are on order to report everything she does to her mother, even though they are sworn to secrecy by their client. Her mother would come here and drag Tamantha if she had to.

A knock on the door put Alessandra on her toes, close to the sword just in case, but trying not to seem too cautious. She still does have a job to do, regardless of her friendship status with the princess. Siberius opened the door and cleared his throat. "The prince and princess, Davis and Sage, would like to join in." Tamantha snorted, and Cole busted up laughing. Siberius messed up their names on purpose because one of them probably requested to have the made-up title as a greeting.

"We're so special, they placed us in the Norm Dorm," the voice of Davin called out behind Siberius. Tamantha let them in, quickly embracing Sara. Davin nodded his head once at Cole and gave Alessandra a thumbs up for her awesome skills, having noticed her pull the sword off the wall when the siblings walked in.

Sara was a little taller than Tammy's shortest Guardian, but still shorter than the princess. She had gorgeous brunette hair that always seemed to have the perfect curls. Her face was heart shaped and the rest of it matched the nature of the shape, a truly beautiful face. She shared the same green eyes as Davin, the color of a leaf just born on the bare trees in the beginning of spring. Davin was the same height as Cole, towering over all three girls. He had dirty blonde hair, not quite as light as Tamantha's.

"Tammy, your security detail is mean. He doesn't like us because we don't have a title, so we made him give us one," Sara told her friend, leaving the hug.

"He's being a sore butt. Probably because he is surrounded by college students, and he hasn't gone to college in three years and forgot what fun it was. Please continue on Guard, Siberius, with the tiara," Tamantha teased. Siberius rolled his eyes and left the room again, tiara still on top of his head.

Alessandra tapped Davin on the head with her sword sheath. "No Norm Dormies allowed. Get out." Tamantha pulled Alessandra from behind into a hug.

"Why can't we all just be friends?" Tamantha nudged Alessandra into her boyfriend's arms. Cole squeezed the Guardian and put her in a corner.

Davin pulled out an assortment of sticks. "Let's play a game. The game of Death." This was a game teenagers and young adults like to play. It's a game to predict who will die first and how, going in order, and it has to be a little bit realistic. It's morbid, but it blows time. It gets very interesting, and you can see who has the sickest mind.

The five friends each grabbed a stick. Whoever gets blue dies first, and whoever gets red gets to decide how they might die. The rest who draws blank sticks will watch. The red and blue do rock, paper, scissors to see if the blue stick will succumb to the given death. If the blue wins, they get to keep playing. It continues till the last one is alive, proclaiming him or her the king of Death.

Alessandra held out her hand, showing the blue strip on the stick. "Ouch," Alessandra hissed. Her chocolate eyes searched from person to person, waiting to see who her murderer would be.

Sara held out her hand after looking at it. Red. "I think you will die in the line of duty with a knife through the heart. Your mother will be proud, but your father will mourn the loss of his only daughter," Sara said, her prediction probably correct or maybe not at all. Sara and Alessandra stood in front of each other, playing rock, paper, scissors. Sara, scissors. Alessandra, paper. Alessandra squealed in distress and fell backwards on her bed dramatically, pretending she had been stabbed.

"What a way to go. The world thanks you." Sara dodged the pillow thrown at her.

"Next," Davin said, throwing out an uncolored stick. Tamantha drew a red stick, and Sara drew a blue one. Sara groaned, awaiting her fate.

"What is your order, Your Royal Highness? What is my execution?"

Tamantha thought for a moment. "Someone ties your shoes, and you trip into a see-through floor and break it," Tamantha proclaimed. Sara stuck her tongue out as she got into rock, paper, scissors formation. Tamantha threw out a rock, and Sara did the same. A draw. One more try. Another draw or blue winning would keep Sara in the game. Tamantha threw out another rock. Sara screamed as her scissors were smashed. Sara joined Alessandra on the bed.

Cole began fake crying, mourning the loss of the two women,

particularly his girlfriend. "Here lies a woman who never got to live her life because she liked her job too much," Cole sang, writing on her gravestone. "She forgot about her boyfriend." Alessandra ignores him, clinging to her fellow dead girl.

Cole gestured for the next stick picking, probably hoping for a blue. He indeed pulled the blue stick, and Davin pulled the red one.

"You're going to stab yourself on accident through the leg, stabbing right in the artery, while walking behind one of Tamantha's Guardians because their sword just happened to be in your way," the blond-haired boy stated.

"Siberius, how could you!" Siberius grunted outside in annoyance. Cole draws scissors, and Davin does paper. Cole is still alive. "I made it to the hospital, and my father decides not to sue the Guardian for reckless sword wielding."

Tamantha draws the blue this time. Cole draws the red. "You die of an aneurysm after dealing with the bullshit of the world. The final straw was when the country requested diamond toilets for all." Tamantha busts up laughing at his words. Coles wins, sending Tamantha to the bed with the other women. Alessandra pulls Tamantha onto Sara and her laps.

"Don't worry, my queen. We will take care of you as you await the next life," Alessandra sweetly suggests. Tamantha shakes her head. She would like a quick passage to her reincarnation after this.

Davin curses as he draws blue, and Cole throws his hands in the air in victory with the red stick standing out against his already red hair.

"You will work as an accountant for the rest of your life, and you catch your wife cheating on you. Her boyfriend, however, stabs you," Cole offers. The men fight it out. Both start with paper.

Then Cole brings out rock, and Davin loses with scissors. "I'm the king, baby!"

Chapter Three

Tamantha breathed out a sigh of relief as she slouched into the booth of the Blue Moon restaurant. The Blue Moon was one of the posher places on the campus and usually came with high costs. They would be away from the prying eyes of the public here.

Alessandra threw her book bag into the corner. They had just finished their first week of college. "That professor is a pain, saying there will be an essay almost every week. It's just a history class! He can kiss my derrière," the Guardian said. Alessandra jabbed her napkin with a fork.

Siberius was sitting in the booth behind Tamantha, taking the time to have his own lunch but careful not to interfere with the princess's personal life.

"He was alright for a history professor. I just wish he would go a little in more depth to the origin story of Prota, or maybe what the Creator's old name could be," Tamantha replied. Alessandra shrugged, bored already of the class.

"Where the heck is the waiter?" Alessandra exclaimed; her fork ready to stab the unknowing victim who made her wait for food. She always got a little angry when she was hungry. Alessandra was happy though, even if she didn't show it now.

Alessandra had been at the Guardian academy the last four years and being linked to her best friend allowed her to be with her friends again, instead of stuck with the Guardians that trail the King.

Tamantha took the fork from her and set it down in its proper position next to the knife and spoon given to Alessandra. She pinched Alessandra's cheek with a grin. "You can be patient, or you can sit with your partner instead," Tamantha threatened, gesturing to the man sitting innocently behind her. Siberius grunted at her, pulling up his menu so to avoid being noticed.

"I didn't know a princess could be so controlling," a deep voice said from behind her. Tamantha didn't recognize the voice, turning her head back to peek at him. A man around her height stood with his pencil and paper, a short apron around his waist.

Tamantha held her breath when she saw his eyes. They were a sharp silver, almost blending in with the white of his eyes. He had medium length dark hair on his head, almost touching his shoulders. He made a formal bow with his hand on his chest. "Pleased to meet you, Your Royal Highness. I am Athan, and I will be your waiter today." Tamantha was speechless.

Alessandra looked back and forth at them. "I will have a pastrami sandwich and fruit please," she ordered, interrupting Tamantha's stare. Tamantha turned back to look at her Guardian.

Tamantha didn't understand why his silver eyes mesmerized her. She had never seen this eye color before, and she has met a lot of people.

"I'll have the turkey sandwich with extra veggies, and can I get a bowl of tomato soup also?" Athan nodded, writing it all down on the notepad. Athan made sure to get Siberius's order as well, knowing this tall and lean man was part of her crew. Siberius placed his order.

Tamantha watched as Athan walked away. Tamantha squeezed her napkin. "Oy, Tammy, don't rip it," Alessandra poked fun. Alessandra noticed the sudden nervousness within her best friend. "Are you okay?"

"Sorry," Tamantha muttered, putting the napkin back on the table. She straightened her back and resumed the proper form a princess should take. "Did you see his eyes? I've never seen that color before."

"No, I haven't either. I'm sure he's just from a different country or something," Alessandra offered. Tamantha had met people from every country in Atlantis, and this was definitely not a trait of someone from another country.

"Maybe." Tamantha pulled out the class textbook for her Ancient Atlantis History class. An old map of what the world looked like before the Creator appeared. The world had been just one giant continent at one time.

She fingered it open to the first page, reading the first paragraph:

"The history of the world before Prota has been carried for many generations through oral traditions and old paintings. The written word did not appear until Prota became a country. The most common oral tradition passed down through the people of Atlantis is the light disappeared, and the sky closed above them. The ground cracked as a giant earthquake roared. People believed it was the end of all they knew of Atlantis.

"Then the gods deemed the world whole and gave them the sun. It rises for half of the day and sleeps for the rest. Some countries before Prota would worship the sky beings who floated in the sky at night, glowing rainbow lights. Some would sacrifice to the large sky beings to have their crops be bountiful."

Athan walked out of the kitchen with short hair, carrying

their food. Tamantha was suddenly confused by the missing hair length. "Did you cut your hair back there?" Tamantha noticed the knot in her stomach had gone away when this short haired Athan walked in. Maybe she had just liked longer hair.

Athan raised an eyebrow and shook his head. "I am not Athan. He's my twin brother. I'm Clayton," the different man told her, a little bit of anger in his voice. Perhaps he was used to being mistaken for the other twin. He left their table quickly, returning to the kitchen. He had the same stunning silver eyes as his brother.

Alessandra started to laugh at Tamantha's confusion. "That was unexpected." Tamantha frowned, proceeding to eat what she ordered.

"Did you ever feel like this with Cole?" Tamantha wondered.

"I think I thought he was very annoying with that red mop on his head. It took years to feel like he was more than just a friend," Alessandra told her. She stuffed her face eagerly. The hunger induced anger dissipated, and the sweet Guardian had returned.

Tamantha looked up when she saw the real Athan walking around. She felt like her breath had escaped her body again.

"I don't know what's wrong with me. I can't deal with this right now. I've got to focus on school," Tamantha mulled over, knowing it was stupid to feel attraction towards an ordinary waiter. He wasn't so ordinary, however. Something told her so. She could feel her own body gravitating towards him.

Tamantha stared at the red envelope she took out of her mailbox, passing it over to Siberius to check for any possible traces of poison. He pulled a spray bottle of clear liquid out of his jacket, perfuming it once after he opened it. Nothing happened, making him hand it back to her.

Assassinations were rare as the royal families were beloved by the people. From the moment Atlanteans are in school, it is taught to them that the existence of the seven royal families is what makes the world stay whole, to protect them from the doom placed by the Creator if anything happens to them. Some think all seven families must be alive to keep the end of the world from happening, but some think as long as at least one family is alive, then the world is safe. The Electra family is missing after all. There is a rumor that maybe the last prince had a descendant, but most assume the Electra family's role in the seven families applied to the Lost One on Prota.

Tamantha slipped the card from the envelope, cueing a frown to grace her face. It was an invitation to the Welcoming party. No doubt every freshman had received one, but she noticed a letter was also in the envelope. She was hesitant to open the letter, feeling there was a hidden motive in it. Alessandra checked her own mailbox, finding the same red envelope. She opened it and only found a card.

"You are cordially invited to be a guest speaker at this year's 300th Welcoming Party. We hope that you will accept and inspire this year's freshman. Signed, the President of Sophia University" Tamantha read it out loud. Alessandra snorted, suspecting it would be entailed in the red envelope. Siberius took a strong stance as noble girls passed by the princess. Each one bobbed their head at her royal highness. She recognized Christine in the crowd. Why was she in the Pleione dorm and not at home? She noticed the silent guard trailing behind ten feet. She pulled her cousin away.

"Your ladyship," Siberius announced, bowing formally to the second in line to the throne. Lady Christine nodded her head back.

"What are you doing here?" Tamantha asked, curiously looking over her cousin's shoulder at the group of ladies waiting for her.

"I made some friends in my classes. They're daughters of some dukes and earls," Christine explained. Tamantha grinned, glad that Christine was socializing with others, not very surprised it was only nobility she chose to hang out with.

Christine was okay with being around Cole, but she turns up her nose around the ordinary Eklektos and anyone beneath them. It was just how she was raised, easily influenced by her aunt, the Queen. Tamantha didn't mind. It was common for these attitudes to be around, regardless of the Merope family's mortal loving tendencies. Christine brushed back a lock of her dark hair, a feature that resembled Tamantha's late brother. Tamantha felt a sharp pain in her heart as she thought of him. Christine was all she had left besides her father. The Lady was important to the Princess.

"Well, make sure you come visit me sometime. I miss talking to you," Tamantha remarked, taking Christine's hands into her.

"Yes, Your Royal Highness. I will," Christine squeezed her cousin's hand, returning back to her new group of friends. Tamantha watched as she turned the corner. Christine is a princess as she is in line for the throne, but she was given the formal title of Lady Christine, Princess of Rosebury and chooses to endeavor in the future duchess life. Her father is the Duke of Rosebury.

Christine was dressed more properly, wearing a knee-length skirt and formal shirt. She was more of a princess than Tamantha. Tamantha was standing in the hallway with a tank top and ripped jeans, dressed like a common girl, barely recognizable as the crown princess. She turned on her heel, walking to the elevator to return to her room. She didn't like having this role, but even she would accept the destiny given to her. She would take this country on her family's behalf with graceful rule.

The Crown Princess adorned a red gown, simple but elegant. Alessandra wore her guardian uniform as well as Siberius. Their swords were at their sides, ready to be used at any moment's notice.

Cole was standing outside her bedroom door, offering his hand out to the princess to escort her. They almost seemed like a couple, but they were not. He would be her date at the Welcoming party. Alessandra didn't mind. She loved the red-haired boy and trusted him. It was all formalities. Such was the life of the Guardian, forced to be a piece of jewelry for the royal family to lug around at parties and balls.

"Good evening, Your Royal Highness."

Tamantha curtsied to him. "Thank you for accompanying me, Lord Cole."

"My pleasure." Cole guided Tamantha out of Pleione Hall to the ballroom located on the campus. Most freshman entering the building were wearing semi-formal attire. The nobility did the same as Tamantha and Cole, dressing themselves in attire that set them apart.

The people in the ballroom all stood and bowed when she entered. Cole raised her hand as they trailed further into the ballroom, causing the crowd to part for them. Tamantha displayed a humble smile. Cole was raised to be a gentleman with his parents believing he would take her hand in marriage someday.

Lady Christine had the opportunity to opt out of the Welcoming Party, using her status as the King's sister's daughter as an excuse for not needing to go. She stated her beloved cousin should be the center of the Welcoming party.

The crowd resumed its' chattering, having taken in enough of the royalty that was so close to touch, but they would never dare to.

The glaring eyes of the rest of Tamantha's Guardians sat in positions along the walls and stage. The normal guards were standing watch outside with one of her Guardian's barking orders at them.

The President stood at the stage, issuing a speech about how great it was to see such a booming class, and he expects them all to be the very best the university has to offer.

Tamantha looked happy as she took the cue to join the stage. It was a facade, but she would learn to wear this strange mask.

"Good evening, ladies and gentlemen. I hope you've had a great start at Sophia University." Cheers erupted from the crowd. "As you may know, I am a student at Sophia University as well. I hope the next four years will be wonderful and filled with friendships that you will cherish for a lifetime. I may be the future queen of Sophia, but I will not only be queen. I would be a wife, a mother, a sister, a friend, an acquaintance, just like all of you will have some role in the future.

"Your bonds with your fellow man will really be what you carry with you, regardless if you complete the four years or drop out. I hope that you all find the path that you are destined to be set upon. May the Creator bless all your dreams."

The large group of freshmen applauded.

Tamantha walked off of the stage into her barrier of Guardians, safe and untouched. She let out a sigh of relief after finishing, but now she knows she must mingle with anyone who approaches.

There was a section roped off for the nobles and VIP to give them space from the commoners. She entered the red roped fence. Everyone inside rose as she entered and gave a bow or curtsy. Some felt flustered being so close to the princess, and some felt it was normal.

A couple of the Guardians sticking to the walls of the ballroom, merged with the red fence, a closer watch on their charge.

Tamantha eyed Davin and Sara sitting off to the side in the special reserved area. She strolled over to them with her entourage in tow. She had specifically requested that they gain entrance to the VIP section as her special guests. It was her bargaining chip with the President to get her to do the speech. Cole gave Davin a fist bump, and Tamantha gave Sara a hug.

The nobles in the section were used to seeing the twins around Tamantha as most of them attended Sophia Academy as well. The sons and daughters of aristocracy would respect any and all of Tamantha's friends, a token to get in the princess's good favor as they too would be ruling their own little pieces of Sophia.

The twins were of ordinary birth, born to a wealthy man from Astrapi and their mother died shortly after giving birth. The circumstance of her death is unknown as her passing was sudden.

Their father paid good money to get them into Sophia Academy, assuring they would have automatic entry into Sophia University. He wanted the best future for them. The twins had been taking care of each other while staying in the dormitories of the Academy as their father rarely came to visit. He felt the money spent was enough to tell the twins how much he loved them. However, no one believed the two had any real status.

The party began their dancing with the VIP having their own private dance floor. Tamantha stood next to Siberius, listening as the nobles and rich students came to greet her. She would hold out her hand out to them and allow them to kiss her hand. They bowed and curtsied, saying their hellos, and then they would twirl away.

"I need a drink," Tamantha whispered to her trusted Guardian. She sent Alessandra off to go dancing with Cole. They were in a private area. She could let it slide. They rarely got to play the part of boyfriend and girlfriend.

Tamantha walked over into the bar, eyeing the liquors on the shelves. "What will it be?" Tamantha recognized the smooth honey voice from last week. He reached out his hand toward her, and she placed her hand in his, receiving a gentle kiss on her Silver Oath ring. She avoided staring into his silver eyes again.

"Athan, you're working here too? Is the shorter haired version of you here as well?" Tamantha asked. Athan laughed, probably heard complaints from his brother about the princess's mistake. Athan nodded, gesturing his head to man who shared his silver eyes. Clayton was serving drinks, but he glanced at the bar with a frown.

"What will it be, Your Royal Highness?" the stranger asked.

"Anything to get through this mess." Tamantha was burying the anxiety deep down in her stomach. Athan smirked, proceeding to make a cocktail that would make her forget her troubles. He placed the green colored drink in front of her. Siberius took it before she could grab it. He sipped it for her, passing it back to his charge. "Thank you, Siberius."

Athan stared up at the tall brute of a Guardian, slightly intimidated. "I wouldn't poison it," Athan defended himself.

"No, but someone else might," Siberius retorted. "You never know who might also be waiting for a chance to slip something into her drink." He gestured to the roped off section full of aristocrats. Not all can be trusted. Tamantha waved him off.

"It would be nice to have an excuse to leave," Tamantha said, downing the drink quickly with no regrets. She didn't care what was in it. She'll call it the Misery liquor, snorting at her inner joke. Athan raised an eyebrow at her silent thoughts painted across her face. "So why are you working at this fine, esteemed institution, good sir?"

"I am working on my Master's in Ancient History, and my brother over there is a little late to the game. He is a freshman as well," Athan explained. Tamantha nodded, slightly paying attention but also staring into her empty glass.

"I'm sorry but be a dear. Another one?" She raised her cup to him. He nodded. It was his job after all. He brought back the cup, handing it to Siberius first, receiving a huff from him. Siberius passed it onto her. "Thank you both. What part of history are you focusing on?"

"The beginning. Prota, the Creator, before She existed, and Atlas and Pleione." Tamantha smiled genuinely.

"The truest mystery of the world, where is She? Who is She? What is Her name even? How did she create two souls?" Athan's face strained a little, trying to think of it.

"If I ever know her name, I will let you know," Athan stated, earning a glass raise in cheers from her.

Clayton walked up to the bar, placing his tray of empty glasses on the counter. He did the required bow, but he barely looked at her. "I need more drinks, Athan. These higher ups are heavy drinkers," Clayton noted, swinging his hand around. Athan ignored his remarks, maybe as respect to the royalty in their presence.

Tamantha shrugged, putting her now empty glass back on the bar.

She started giggling. "Even she is one, too?" Siberius glared at the shorter haired brother.

"Is there always an evil twin and a good twin? It must be Davin that is the evil twin," Tamantha said under her breath.

She jumped when Clayton slammed his fist on the counter. "I don't want to hear that from the likes of you." Clayton was practically fuming, and Siberius now had his hand on his sword, ready to pull it out at any other spontaneous outburst.

"Your Royal Highness, I think it would be best if we return to Guardian Alessandra and Lord Cole," Siberius suggested, more like ordered. Tamantha stared at her empty drink.

"I apologize, Clayton, is it? I don't know what I might have done to receive such treatment, but I'll take my leave now. I hope to talk to you another time, Athan. I would love to hear more about the ancient history." Tamantha received bows from the pair as she parted. Athan seemed annoyed at his brother.

The alcohol was setting in. She could feel it. She pulled Davin from the sidelines, noticing he was on his lonesome. His missing sister was flirting away with a random boy. She would entertain him and make him dance with her. He has a girlfriend, but she was at a different university.

Princess Tamantha watched as the crowd around her blurred, plastering a sloppy smile on her face. She would have to thank Athan. He made good drinks.

Davin practically held her up while they twirled around the floor. Alessandra and Siberius shared a look, communicating their worry over her. Cole touched her midback, making sure she was okay.

The Guardians dragged her away from her boozy activity to a place where she would be unnoticed. The people could not see her like this.

The last time she was drinking like this was when she lost Nolan.

A single tear slipped from her pale blue eyes before she fainted.

Chapter Four

Tamantha opened her eyes to see the twinkling stars of the night above her. Her head was lying on someone's lap. She reddened as she remembered the darkness that overtook her while enjoying the party away with her beloved friends. How many people saw it? She still felt the effects of the drink.

Athan left the ballroom to bring her glass of water. "What was in the drink?" Siberius questioned, crossing his arms on his chest. Athan winced, obviously not knowing what he was talking about.

"I think she was just overwhelmed, Siberius. Nothing to do with the drink. She barely ate anything since lunch time," Alessandra offered an explanation.

Siberius's lips turned downward, dropping his hands at his side with frustration. He had tested the drinks himself. There was nothing wrong with them. "Sorry," Siberius grunted to the bartender. The silver-eyed boy shook his head at him.

"It's okay." Athan placed the cup in her hand when she sat up. Cole stood up from his seat, having done the task of keeping the princess comfortable. Alessandra sat down next to her royal highness, rubbing her back. Tamantha turned around to barf into the fountain she was sitting on.

"How long was I out?" Tamantha rubbed her lips with the handkerchief that her best friend handed to her. She nodded her head to Alessandra.

"Only an hour. Some of the party has died down. Nobody saw you go down except for us and this guy. Sara went back to her room as she was hysterical. Davin escorted her," Alessandra said, pursing her lips at the vanishing twins.

Tamantha sipped the clear liquid, hiding her anguish. She thanked Cole for his help, slowly standing up. Alessandra tried to stop her, but Tammy ignored her.

"I'll have to excuse myself to the President. I would like to end the night," Tamantha ordered. Athan watched her curiously, amazed how she could bury something like this. "Thank you, Athan, for the Misery drinks. It gave me the reason I was looking for."

Athan raised an eyebrow at what she labeled them he mixed for her. "Right. Well, I have to return to the bar. I hope you will be okay. Let's talk about that ancient history next time we see each other." Athan left to go back inside the ballroom.

Tamantha waved briefly, feeling awkward about the events.

Tamantha looked herself over, checking for any remnants of puke. "I guess we will have to go back into the belly of the beast. Shall we, Cole?" She held out her hand to him.

The redhead nodded, keeping his thoughts about the situation to himself. He glanced over at his girlfriend, wondering if any jealousy was rising. She did have to stop dancing with him after all. He would make it up to her on her day off.

The star couple proceeded into the ballroom once again. The crowd didn't stop to bow this time. They were too busy enjoying the night. Tamantha's eyes scanned the room for the man who forced her to give a speech. She located him talking amongst a group of professors, joining their conversation.

"Thank you for the evening. I enjoyed the party," Tamantha told the President. He made the professors bow to her.

"I hope you have a good night, Your Royal Highness. I hope we have another chance to have you as a guest speaker." She would rather not. He received a bob of her head from her as she turned away to hide her dislike. She linked her arm with Cole's, hoping they could make their way out of the building as quick as they can.

Everything slowed down around her as she saw a figure zooming through the crowd. The genetic copy of Athan was approaching her at rapid speed. Siberius was distracted, signaling for the Guardians to take their leave with her. Alessandra also noticed what the princess saw. Cole looked behind at Alessandra, not realizing the situation. What could Clayton possibly want?

The evil twin stood in front of Tamantha, offering her purse to her. "You left this behind, Your Royal Highness." Something seemed off about him. She reached out her hand to him to take back what she lost.

What is she doing? She felt the need to run. This wasn't the same angry, disgruntled server she had seen before. He was someone different. She saw the glint of something metal in his other hand too late.

Charcoal black hair appeared in front of her, trying to grab at the hand, but he was too fast. A gasp of air came from the petite woman.

Tamantha's eyes bulged wide open. A scream escaped her mouth. "No!" Tamantha felt Cole's hand tighten around hers. Clayton realized he failed, running away at insane speeds. Alessandra fell backwards into Cole and Tamantha, catching them off guard and knocking them to the floor.

A knife was stabbed into her heart.

"No. No. No!" Cole stammered, trying to do something, blood covering his hands.

Tamantha was shaking, obviously in shock. Siberius screamed out at the Guardians to go after the attacker, with a couple of them surrounding Tamantha, Cole, and the dying Alessandra in a protective barrier. The crowd was forced back away from the vulnerable princess. Tamantha tried to come up with a way to save her best friend. She let out a weak cry.

"I'm sorry, Tammy. I failed you. What a shit Guardian I am," Alessandra whispered, life slipping away from her. "I think I'm going to die, aren't I?" Tamantha shook her head, trying to deny it.

The object plunged into Alessandra Aki was silver, one of the deadliest metals to Eklektos. Alessandra gasped air.

Siberius was frantically trying to get the medics to come faster. The Guardian Academy trained him for healing his charge, but not for wounds like this.

"Cole, I love you." Alessandra touched Cole's cheek. He was losing his mind, unable to save her. Her hand dropped to the floor.

"Al, please, Al!" Cole cried out, pulling her hand, trying to get her to touch his face again.

Medics, who came too late, checked her pulse as a duty, but there was nothing there. The Guardians began to pull Tamantha away from Alessandra, needing to get her to safety. She tried to claw them away and to get back to her best friend. All she could do was scream.

Assassinations were rare, but they do happen.

Tamantha sat on her side of the room, hugging her knees and

staring across at the empty bed. Another piece of her heart had been stolen from her.

They still had not found Clayton. He disappeared without a trace, and his brother was no help, having no idea where he went or why he did it.

The funeral was beautiful. It was in the final resting place for the Guardians of Merope. Her ashes were placed in a stone case on the wall, etched with her name and the years she was alive. Alessandra's mother was unable to let go, kneeling knees in front of her daughter's grave. Losing her broke her mother. Her brothers were no different, and her father sat on one of the chairs away from them, hiding his own grief, ready to be the rock that his wife would need. He would put his own sadness aside.

Alessandra was awarded the Sophia Medal of Honor post-mortem for sacrificing herself in the line of duty. The family didn't want their medal. They wanted their daughter and sister back.

Tamantha attended the funeral, feeling completely numb. Cole didn't go. He wanted to say goodbye to her in his own way. Siberius came in full uniform with his fellow Guardians to honor Alessandra. The queen even showed up to it as thanks for saving her beloved child.

A daughter lost to save someone else's daughter.

It had been weeks since the murder of her own best friend and Guardian. She couldn't stop feeling like she could have saved Alessandra. She felt so weak and powerless. Why was she the stupid princess? Why did she have to put other people's lives at risk to protect a stupid seat? Tears escaped her. She grabbed a pillow and screamed into it. This is why her mother told her to never get attached to the Guardians. They were expendable.

A knock at the door spooked her. She didn't want to speak to anyone. The world didn't exist outside this room. She ignored the intruder.

The same noise came again. Tamantha lay on her bed and turned towards the wall to feign sleep. The nuisance came inside anyways. She didn't care who it was. They need to go away.

"Tammy," a redhead hummed. She winced. He sat down on the bed next to her, staring at the same spot she was focused on before. "I don't know what I'm going to do." She grunted in response, choosing to avert her eyes to the ceiling.

Tamantha had missed classes in the last few weeks, choosing to grieve in peace. She was given such a chance when her brother died, and she took as much time as she could get. Cole had done the same, but the two had refused to see each other since that night. Both felt significant guilt and couldn't look each other in the eye. They were grateful that attendance wasn't mandatory except for final exams.

She sat up, staring at the blaring red on his head, the only bit of color she had really observed in a long time. She dropped her head to let her pale blonde hairbrush against her bare legs. "You know my mother called? She told me to get over it. Typical," Tamantha muttered. Cole put his hand on top of her head, ruffling her golden locks that she inherited from the bane of evil.

"The Queen is always one for keeping appearances. Hiding away like this annoys her," Cole remarked, used to Tamantha's mother's wonderful tight grip on the rules of society. "I would dare to insult her, but Siberius is outside the door, probably listening in." Cole coughed when he heard a thud outside the door.

Tamantha chuckled and then swallowed it down, believing she shouldn't be allowed a moment of happiness after taking away his. "We have to eventually rejoin the living world whether we like it or not." Tamantha nodded, trying to hold back the tears. She rested her head on his shoulder, and he wrapped his arm around her.

"First my brother, and now her." Tamantha was barely understandable as her voice muffled into his shirt.

"I think your mother might send your cousin in with a full suit of armor to get you out of the room. Let's get some breakfast, Tammy," Cole comforted. He was feeling worse than her. He was hiding his pain, using Tamantha to release it. She relented, clasping her hand in his. He dragged her out of the room after she got dressed properly. She put on a knee length pencil skirt and a blue sweater, fit to make her mother proud.

Tamantha's meals had been sent up to her room in the last few weeks. She had the option to use the cafeterias, cafes, or restaurants. Siberius chose what she ate to make sure she lived, bringing her partner to her when it was time to feed.

Tamantha ignored the crowd of students who were doing their required bowing, but she could see the look of pity behind their stiff manner. She wouldn't accept their sympathy. They didn't really care. It was like asking someone the question how you are, and the answerer would share equal uncaring with the word fine. She didn't notice how much she was leaning on Cole.

An entourage of three Guardians and an extra guard were following the princess around, a barrier of protection after the recent events. She would normally only be followed by two Guardians, but Clayton had yet to be caught. Precautions must be taken. Even Cole had two guards following him, protection for the son of the Head of Symvoulio.

There was no doubt in her mind that the rumors would begin to arise that she and Cole are dating or engaged now that his girlfriend was out of the way. She waved that thought away, angered by it.

The walk to the Blue Moon seemed long, but she was happy to relax into the folds of the booth. She didn't feel uncomfortable about the two men sitting in the booths before and after hers, nor the two men standing in front of the exits from the booth. Cole was just as used to it as her.

Her breath hitched when she caught the eyes of Athan looking at her. He was a waiter here after all, regardless of what his brother did. He approached her table, prepared to do his job.

A hand was placed on Athan's chest. A low growl came from Siberius's throat. "I must ask you to not serve Her Royal Highness and to send someone else instead." Athan didn't feel phased by the threat under the Guardian's tone.

"As you wish," Athan obeyed, bowing to Tamantha and looking for a server to replace him at the booth. She felt a little bit of panic seeing the same face as Alessandra's murderer, but she felt saddened that he would be alienated because of what his twin did.

"No, Siberius. He can serve me," Tamantha spoke up with a small voice.

"Your Royal Highness, it is out of the question. He may be in league with that Clayton boy," Siberius muddled, not willing to let his charge be in danger again.

"I order you to allow him to approach the table." Tamantha stared him down from her seat. Siberius nodded, signaling Athan to come back.

Cole was piercing him with glaring eyes, taking in the image of the killer's face. He was restraining himself from grabbing a fork to get revenge.

"I apologize for my Guardian's behavior. I'm sorry that what your brother did has repercussions on you. You are not your twin." Athan looked down at the ground for a moment. She wondered what he was feeling. His face displayed no trace of emotion. She placed her order for breakfast as did Cole begrudgingly. He stepped away to bring the order to the kitchen.

"I don't trust him. I can't. Not after what his brother did to Al," Cole said, choking a sob back. "We don't even really know him."

"I understand. We don't, but he did nothing wrong himself." Tamantha searched for him in the room, watching him when she found him. He was the good twin, right? She couldn't help but see his innocence in all of it.

"I just don't feel comfortable. I'm sorry, Tammy." Cole placed his head down on the wooden table. She brushed her hand through his fiery hair. She didn't blame him. It was typical for the victim's family and friends to put blame on the people the suspect was related to. They are just as much as a victim in this situation.

"We can't ever know unless we give him a chance," Tamantha remarked, letting her moment of grief dissipate for the time being. Athan returned quickly with the food, giving it to the guard taste testers first. "Athan, have you heard anything at all from him?" He shook his head.

"He disappeared, and I don't know what made him even do it. It's not like him. He may be an ass, but he would never try to act violently," Athan explained. Athan averted his eyes to look for a distraction. "If I knew where he was, what loyalties do I have? To the crown or to my flesh and blood?" Tamantha accepted this. A princess may be assumed to put her life on the line for the country, but what would she really do when it involved someone she loved? Cole was twisting a napkin with his fingers.

"I am aware that you were raised by your Uncle? He is a Guardian for King Bassett," Siberius spoke up, looking at a notepad. Was he really interrogating him here and now?

"Yes, he took us in after our mother passed away. King Bassett is one of my dear friends," Athan revealed, his age close with the King's. Tamantha raised an eyebrow.

"I had never seen you before at court in Polemos before," Tamantha wondered.

"I am not of noble blood. My only connection is my uncle as my own father didn't choose that path." Tamantha bit into her pancake casually while listening.

"Both of your parents are dead?"

"Yes, my father died of cancer, and my mother," he paused, his face straining a bit as he tried to recall it. "I can't remember what happened to her. They never told me."

"How sad," Tamantha responded. She stared at the meal in front of her, feeling a wave of nausea. Tears welled up in her eyes, but she wiped them away before anyone noticed. She felt that maybe she could find out that piece of information. "May I ask you another question? Did you and your brother train at the Guardian academy?"

Athan had a look of disbelief that the princess was so instinctive. "I did, and Clayton did also. Strangely however, neither of us received someone to protect. We passed all the tests, but when we went to get our call, there was nothing."

Tamantha looked at Siberius. "Is that normal?"

Siberius nodded. "Some Guardians' charges are not born or already dead. It could be the case for those two." Tamantha pursed her lips in wonder, trying to understand the mystery. She remembered the speed Clayton was moving at, how quickly the blade was coming at her. Clayton must have had the Guardian powers. Does Athan also? If so, why do they have no client? You can't activate the skills without receiving the call, right? Something was weird about all of this. She wanted to figure it out.

Cole stood up from his seat. "I'm sorry, Tammy, but I can't stay here anymore," Cole muttered, walking away from the table without waiting for a word from her.

"Cole!" Tamantha called, frowning at his distasteful departure, but she knew why. "It's alright, Athan. He's having a hard time. We all are."

"It's okay. I deserve it," Athan mustered. "I must return to work, Your Royal Highness. Maybe we can continue this conversation another time." He bowed and left her alone with her three Guardians and an extra guard to hover over her while she ate breakfast.

She finished it quickly, leaving a significant tip, and she wrote a note, leaving a specific whisper to contact her on the telecrystal. Siberius debated with her whether that was wise. She ignored him, wanting to hear more about the boy with moonlight eyes. He intrigued her. Her mother would most likely sum it up to being another plaything for her, but Tamantha would say it differently.

Tamantha pondered entering the Atlas Hall to visit Cole after he left, but she could feel the watching eyes of students walking to class or going back to their rooms. If she went through those doors, rumors would spark that the princess was seen going into the boy's hall. Maybe she had a hidden boyfriend or lover.

Siberius stood behind her, looking down at her pale blonde hair. "Your Royal Highness, if I may say so, you both need each other right now." Tamantha jumped. She was surprised that Siberius would ignore the rules and scandal. He was right.

Siberius was close to Alessandra as well. She was best friends with Cole and Tamantha since they were young children, but he was also best friend to the late Prince Nolan. He had watched the three grow together. His heart was broken over the loss of his new partner, happy to watch her become such a brave Guardian for her size. He had seen her scores and rating. She was one of the best. All because she wanted to serve her best friend, and she wanted to continue to be around both of them for the rest of her life.

Alessandra was lucky, assigned to someone she cared for. Siberius regretted not being there for Nolan, but he already accepted the charge given to him. He knew it was destiny that she was put together with the princess. She would have hated to have been the Guardian for Lady Christine or King Alvyn, but she would do her duty like he does. He would support their charge.

Alessandra died so the princess could live. He would honor whatever Tamantha chose to do for Alessandra's sake. Her mental health was just as important as her physical wellbeing.

Siberius lightly pushed on her back. Tamantha cleared her throat. "I don't need your permission, now do I?" Siberius grinned, overjoyed to see a little bit of her coming through the cracks. Tamantha clicked on her heels, making the guards at the entrance of Atlas Hall open the doors for her.

The men in the hall were shocked to see her walk in. "Thomas, stay here," Siberius barked at the extra guard. The extra guard almost whimpered at the big scary Guardian, the future general of the Guardians. He was a fairly new guard, recently transferred for Tamantha's attendance at Sophia University.

"Yes, sir." Thomas marched over to the other guards, standing with them. These were guards assigned for Atlas Hall and its patrons, plus a couple for the son of the Head of Symvoulio. They seemed intimidated by a royal guard joining their watch of the hall. Tamantha only thought of this new guard as very strange, but she never associated much with the guards, only seeing him guarding outside Pleione Hall. She couldn't figure out what made her want to put a ten-foot pole between her and this guard.

Tamantha glided across the hallway towards the stairways, attracting the attention of the people living in Atlas Hall. They were all getting a glimpse of what was rumored to be the most beautiful woman in the world, at least the most beautiful out of the seven royal families. Siberius rolled his eyes as he walked in front of her with the other two guardians behind the princess.

There were whistles and calls as she passed the middle floors, surprised to see a girl in the boys' hall. Was this how nobles and the upper class really acted in their own private spaces? Some of them shut up when they realized who it was, and others ran away to hide in their room for fear of scolding from the princess or the Guardians. Tamantha smirked at their shame.

As she reached the top floor where the most esteemed guests stayed, she felt a sense of dread. "Siberius, I will enter alone," Tamantha ordered. Siberius shook his head.

"I will open the door first," Siberius announced. She knew there was no room for argument.

"Fine," Tamantha gestured her hand to the door to Cole's room. He had no roommate. He was all alone. There was only silence coming from inside.

Siberius opened the door, peeking in to check for any intruders, only noticing Cole laying on his bed. Tamantha walked past the giant, making him shut the door and leave her to be with her grieving childhood friend. "Cole?" He groaned back at her, staying put on the bed. "I'm sorry. I shouldn't have asked so much like that."

"It only makes me angry. It makes me want to get revenge. She shouldn't have had to die. These brothers show up out of nowhere, and she is gone forever," Cole spoke into his pillow.

Tamantha sat next to him on his bed, petting his hair. "I'm scared of what I might do. I can't live without her."

"She was your soul mate, Cole. You will see her again in another life," Tamantha remarked, knowing the Creator had designated for souls tied together to find each other eventually. She wondered selfishly when she would find hers, but it didn't matter now. One half is always in deep mourning when the other half dies.

Cole turned around to look up at the great beauty sitting next to him. "I'm sorry, Tammy." Tamantha didn't understand why he was apologizing. His eyes were growing heavy.

"Hey, you big idiot." She poked his cheek lightly, trying to keep him awake. A small smile etched onto his face. "Cole?"

Cole fell into a deep slumber with her fingers running through his hair. She admired his peaceful face. She wondered how much sleep he got over the last few weeks. He must have been driving himself mad with sadness and worry.

Tamantha stood up from the bed, looking around his room. It was an exact copy of hers, except it only had one bed, one desk, and was the perfect single.

Her eyes centered on the photos on his dresser. There was a picture of his family with his mother, father, his sister, and little brother. His resemblance to his father was uncanny. His sister looked more like the mother, and the little brother was a combination of both parents. She bit back the tears when she saw a picture of Alessandra and Cole together, so happily in love.

She remembered taking the picture for them. It was an amusement park in Thalassa, a venture with her Celaeno cousins to bond a little. Alessandra had taken a vacation from Guardian Academy to join them. Sara and Davin had also come with. The couple had been arguing that day about how she'll never have any time for their relationship. They didn't know how wrong they could be. The call she received would create the best opportunity for them to be together.

Tamantha stared at the picture of all five friends, a picture taken at Cole's twentieth birthday. On the twentieth birthday of anyone following the religion that worships the Creator and the idea of reincarnation, a ceremony is performed. A priestess will spend a week before the birthday meditating. The result is a symbol tattooed onto them, and it belongs to the birthday person's soul. These symbols are recorded to keep track of all the lives, so people can reflect on what they once were in a past life and learn from those experiences.

Cole had done the ritual. His tattoo is etched on his wrist. It was the choice of the person to find out what they used to be, but he never did so. He was waiting for Alessandra to do it, so they could look at the histories together.

Soul mates are easy to find among records because they usually have some sort of connection in their many past lives. Sometimes in person, it is easy to recognize who your soul mate is, but in some lives, they could be a person only passing by in a crowd, a brief encounter, going on with their lives.

Cole and Alessandra had already known the answer to that. Alessandra attached herself to him since they were young children. Cole would whine about the girl he had become friends with, spitting out that girls were gross. He still cared deeply for her even at such a young age.

Tamantha walked over to the sleeping man, staring at the tattoo on his right wrist. She felt the urge to trace the edges of it. She kneeled next to the bed and pulled his hand toward her. He didn't wake from his morning snooze. She felt odd about it, putting it back on the bed gently.

She turned away towards the windows, looking out onto the grounds of the University. It had a wonderful view of the surrounding forests with a glimpse of the ocean off in the distance. She wanted to visit the beach again someday soon, to feel the sand gather between her toes. She almost wished to be swept away by the waters to the deep blue, but she wouldn't give up.

Tamantha searched around the room once more, nosing in his business. She focused on his desk, noticing a glass of water on the table. There was a bottle of medicine next to it. She picked it up, surprised by how light it was. She turned it to read the label, immediately dropping it on the ground. "Cole?" Tamantha whispered, kneeling down next to his bed. She started to shake him.

Cole's chocolate eyes fluttered open. He moaned and smacked his lips from sleep. "Sorry, I must have fallen asleep." She felt the worry in her heart dissipate, letting a small bit of relief trickle in.

"Why is the bottle of sleeping pills empty?" Tammy asked, wondering where the contents of the bottle had gone. She remained on alert, wondering if she should call Siberius in. Cole's sleepy smile fell short, swiftly sitting up. He put his head in his hands.

"I'm sorry," Cole muttered.

"Quit saying sorry. What happened? You didn't take them all, did you?"

Cole shook his head, eyeing the trash can next to his desk. "I thought about it. I couldn't bear the pain anymore. I feel like I've been torn in half, but I couldn't give up like that. She wouldn't have liked me trying to follow her. I dumped them all down the sink." Tamantha stood up and faced the window, not letting the gentle beam on her face be seen by him. He was okay.

"I apologize for going through your things. I was scared something might happen to you. I love you, Cole. You're my best friend, stupid," Tamantha said, letting her grief escape the high brick walls of her mind. He came up behind her and wrapped his arms around her, warmth enveloping her.

"I know." Cole and Tamantha spent the next few hours learning how to say goodbye to the strange, tiny woman who took a piece of their hearts with her.

Chapter Five

"Your Royal Highness, my name is Elsabeth Gagnon. I am your new Guardian," the woman with blue hair spoke, kneeling before the princess in her bedroom.

"Gagnon? You must be Siberius's sister," Tamantha remarked, glancing at the towering beast. He was less than pleased to see his sister here, probably expecting her to connect with the King or Lady Christine. He might have even expected her charge to not even be of the living world.

"The General of the Guardians has assigned me to replace Guardian Aki. I will be your new live in protector. I hope we will be on good terms and that I can please you, Your Royal Highness. Princess Tamantha, may I assume my role as your Guardian?"

Tamantha reached her hand out to the newcomer, burying the feelings that were rising up at the mention of deceased best friend. Elsabeth took the princess's hand gently and kissed it delicately, sealing the bond between Guardian and the protected.

Elsabeth rose and bowed to her new captain, her brother. "I will follow your orders, Captain Gagnon."

Siberius looked pleased to be able to boss his little sister around, but there was a little tension. As another Gagnon,

Elsabeth has the possibility of taking away his position as Captain and future General. This was determined by the General as well as their charge. He was on edge about who their mother would favor more. Tamantha, however, had the final word as the future Queen.

"Your Royal Highness, shall we proceed to your class?" Siberius suggested, putting formal rules off until later.

Tamantha's class today was ancient history, a favorite of hers. She would hear stories about the Creator and the two souls that emerged from her being, Pleione and Atlas. She wanted to know more about who the mystical woman was, how she made the world that it is now. Her other classes were politics, Sophian literature, environmental science, and ethics, but none of these interested her as much as her ancient history class. The past would always fascinate her more.

The moment Tamantha arrived at her class, her fellow students and the professor rose and bowed at her presence, another rule set by Sophia University's council.

Regardless of her stature, it was the teacher's responsibility to grade her with fairness and based on her efforts and intelligence. There was no special treatment for nobility, not even the Crown Princess. They would only receive the respect that their title demanded, such as bowing for the higher nobility, most importantly her.

Tamantha raised her hand to signal them to sit down. She winced at the screeching of chairs shifting as they returned to their positions. She eyed Sara in the audience, choosing to take a seat next to her.

Elsabeth trailed behind, reluctantly looking at Sara suspiciously. Tamantha could hear Siberius behind her, explaining that Sara is okay with them. It caused Tamantha to shamelessly grin to hear how important Sara was to her.

"Hello, Tammy," Sara hummed, resting her head on her hand with boredom. Unlike Tamantha, it was not nearly as fascinating for Sara and was labeled as nap time.

"Class, today, I will not be teaching the lesson. Instead, it will be one of our graduate students." The door to the professor's office opened and in walked a man with familiar silver eyes. "This is Athan Wright, and he will be giving the lesson. I will be in my office if he needs me to assist him."

Tamantha almost dropped her pencil at his appearance. Sara was less than amused due to his relation with the one who took Alessandra's life, but she would give him the benefit of the doubt.

Elsabeth was reaching for her sword at his resemblance to the almost assassin, but Siberius grabbed her hand. "He is not the killer. Cool it."

Athan was looking up at Tamantha's desk, flashing a smile up to her after he did the required bow. "Thank you, Professor Williams. I will be giving the lesson today. As the professor already said, I am Athan Wright. Today's lesson will be about the Creator and Her existence before Prota was found." Tamantha was more than pleased when she heard this, straightening her back a little more to show she was listening intently. "I know Professor Williams gave a lesson about the war between the three nations, dating back a thousand years before Prota's indoctrination as a formal country. This is slightly related to that."

Tamantha zoned out a bit, waiting for the bit about the Creator.

He promised her a name. When would that day come? She was sure her father already knew the truth about the Creator. It was bestowed to the leaders of the nation to know the real background behind the world, but this was something Tamantha would probably not have access to for another forty years when her father would likely pass.

"It is theorized the Creator came from the country called Sigontaro, a former combination of Sophia and Astrapi. Her parents might have been of noble birth, or they might have been two people from a lower class. It does not matter what class She was in, does it? She was an ordinary woman with a marvelous gift." The students in the classroom nodded with approval. Many belonged to the religion that worshipped her.

"What was this gift, and where did it come from?" a skeptic from the audience questioned.

"We do not know where it came from, and we don't even know if She was born with it or developed it slowly over time. What is important is the first power that She was revealed to have. The Creator was immortal from birth. She seemed to stop aging at twenty-five, a trait that the pureblooded Eklektos have inherited from their origins. They are not immortal like the Creator, but they do stop aging in their outward physical appearance.

"The only one who also had true immortality like the Creator outside of the gift given to those on Prota was Atlas, a soul that came to be along with Pleione."

Athan met eyes with Tamantha for a brief moment, averting it to look at the other students.

"Many believe it is a gift from the Gods to create a Goddess on earth. We do not call Her a God, however. We only call Her the Creator because we do not truly know if She is a God, but we know Her as the Creator of Prota. How people choose to worship is up to the individual. Can we ever really know what She is or if Gods even exist? We only know what has been recorded in history, and no magic book can ever prove the truth about how the world came to be or who She is."

"Are you of the faith, Mr. Wright?" a curious student asked.

"I do not know what I am. I only know what I have learned from my experiences. The Creator is a mysterious woman who we can only know the truth about from Her own lips, but alas, She is in hiding forevermore till she chooses to come out. Maybe She isn't even alive today."

Tamantha heart panged a little at that thought. She had a feeling the last piece of what Athan said could be true. Somehow, she could sense the woman that everyone prayed to was no longer in this world.

"The Creator had lived for a thousand years before She became the woman that we know. The powers She has could just be a genetic mutation, but it probably is more spiritual than that. Everyone in this room is destined to find their soul mate someday, even if it's a brief brush of a shoulder on the street. Is a destined meeting even a real thing?"

"Could you be my soul mate?" a female student squealed, earning a light blush from the presenter.

"We don't ever really know. The Creator didn't even meet Her supposed soul mate till long after She made Prota. Within those thousands of years before that moment, where was She? Did She explore the world, and did She meet the same soul mate long before? The Creator is in very little of recorded history before Prota and even after. We believe She is the daughter of mortal parents, but is that true? Was She really born, or did She just appear? The important thing about learning history is to ask the right questions and to not believe everything you hear."

Tamantha had once wondered who her soul mate might be or what her past lives were like, but it wasn't important to her any longer. She was going to be betrothed to a person chosen by her mother if she didn't find her own pureblooded love.

"If She was a prevalent figure in the world before Prota existed, we would have to know her name to find true records about her. The Creator passed on stories about her own life to people in Prota. We know that she had a family before when she was in her youngest age. They were lost to the great plague that led to overthrowing the Sigontaro royal family. None of her known children had the same gifts as she did, so it is not genetic, or at least, it could be recessive. The Creator is known to be a traveler, and she lived in several places throughout the thousand years before. She may have been running for her life quite often. To have the gift of immortality would attract unwanted attention by kings and peasants alike."

Elsabeth sat on the bed across from Tamantha, maintaining a soldier-like pose and stoic face. "Guardian Gagnon, you don't have to be so stiff. Here. Your name is Elsabeth, right? Hello, Elsabeth. I am your roommate, Tammy." The Guardian swallowed a lump in her throat.

"Hello, Your Royal Highness. I am Elsabeth," the blue haired girl stated, trying to fight back the rules and regulations beaten into her by the Guardian Academy.

"You can call me Tammy or Tamantha. We're going to be living together, so we need to become friends. Can I call you Elsa or Beth?" the princess asked, keeping a calm nature to lure in the girl.

"Beth."

"Alright, Beth. How old are you? Where were you born? Do you have any friends?"

"I am eighteen years old. I was born here in Kyrios. I don't have any friends. I was too busy with my studies," Beth stammered, nervous about acting so casually with her charge.

"Do you know what you do as my roommate and Guardian? You're in disguise as a normal student." She paused, pushing back the creeping grief. "Even Guardian Aki had to assume the role, but she and I were already good friends. We're going to be close, so the Guardian speak will be reserved for only formal events, alright?" Beth nodded.

"Tammy, may I ask who your friends are?" Tamantha smiled.

"There's Cole, the red headed dude, and there's Sara and Davin. Both are twins from Astrapi, but they've lived here their whole lives. There's also Chris, you know, the Lady, but she and I don't spend much time together." Beth listened and took all the information in. "They can be your friends too. I'm sure they'll like you. The blue hair is quite a conversation starter." Beth grabbed a strand of her mane subconsciously, looking at it.

"It's my favorite color, and my mom hates it. She said it's not proper for Guardians to have such un-uniform like dye. She can get over it." Tamantha giggled, imagining the General of the Guardians freaking out over seeing her own daughter running around with vibrant hair.

"I like it," Tammy remarked. "Did you always want to be a Guardian?"

"No, I didn't. My mom said it would be a disgrace if a Gagnon isn't a Guardian, so she forced me and enrolled me into the Academy," Beth groaned.

"I know how that is. My mother has her claws sunk in to make me do whatever she wants, but I guess that's what happens when we have such high-profile mothers. I know my mother is probably plotting out a betrothal and potential suitors. She'll be calling for me soon. Ever since my rise to heir, she's had a wide grin on her face, ready to groom me for Queen."

Beth never imagined the Queen could be so pushy. The Queen had Guardians from her own family, so they didn't have to report anything to the Sophia General. The Queen is seen as a graceful and kind woman with love for her child and stepchild. Only the people around her see her true colors, but that's to be expected from a Celaeno woman.

"The General doesn't have any planned betrothals for me, but she does expect a lot out of me and Siberius. We represent the family, so she has little spies to whisper what her children are doing. She is ready to yell at us if we make a mistake," Beth described.

It was a starting point for them to bond over. They share crazy mothers. Beth felt a little more comfortable now in the presence of the Crown Princess, and she was looking forward to calling Tamantha a friend.

Chapter Six

Tamantha stared out the window at the night sky, seeing the shimmering glow of the full moon. The creatures in the skies glowed in the moonlight, gracing the sky as they floated across. She could even see the gigantic blob creatures some people called a whale grace their presence.

It was that time of the month for pureblood Eklektos, the need for food that didn't appeal to normal people. She envied Anaxios and the half-Eklektos and their innocence.

If a pure blood doesn't feed, they die. It's a curse. Eklektos, who planned to pass on to their next life, used this time for that, but she heard the death is painful. She's heard rumors that they shrivel up and bleed out from every pore in their body.

Tamantha had seen an Eklektos die before. Another student forgot to feed, and she died in the cafeteria at the Academy. They tried getting blood to her, but it was too late. It was wrong. How can anyone forget when it's such a pivotal time for all of them?

There are news reminders constantly around the full moon, so no one could forget.

The mortals romanticize it, saying the bite could make

anyone Eklektos.

There is such guilt that the Eklektos might possibly kill the one they are feeding from. The Eklektos might not be able to stop and might drain them. There are news reports of Eklektos who drained their partners, and sometimes it's on purpose.

The partner is usually someone in a contract with the Eklektos they are giving to. They get paid to do it and get the drug-like effect of pleasure and numbing. The bite has a slight venom to it.

Siberius is off to find Tamantha's contracted partner, one assigned to her since she began to react to the full moon. Sometimes it is around puberty, or it can start even earlier. Tamantha started feeding when she was around four years old, extraordinary for any Eklektos to do so. She's always been able to feed and unhook when she was done. She never went so far to kill her partner. The partner's written contract keeps her from speaking about her exchange with the princess.

The Guardians were so lucky they didn't need to do it. It was the will of the Creator. It was rather convenient really. Most Guardians had fed before they became connected to their charges, and people who can become Guardian, but never do, must continue the pure blood ritual.

Sara and Davin would go to the house of their partner instead. They didn't have to be protected because they were not important. Most ordinary Eklektos would do the same because it was their need for blood, and the partner did not have any obligation to come to them unless written in the contract.

Because Cole and Tamantha were high profile contracts, the partner must be picked up and brought to them. These partners are monitored by doctors and checked for any illnesses or possible contaminations to keep them from being poisoned or sick. The royal partners were heavily cared for and were paid a large sum of money, more than the standard for ordinary Eklektos. The money was enough to keep them living without even need for a job to sustain their lives. The names of the partners are kept out of record, so they don't become targets for assassination attempts.

Beth sits on the bed, working on her homework. She peeks from the corner of her eye at the mystical woman. Here alone in the bedroom, she is only Tamantha Merope, not her royal highness. She didn't miss the process of having to take a partner for blood lust. This was her first time without it.

Tamantha eyes her telecrystal when it glows and hums. Cole was done already. What was taking Siberius so long?

"Let's go have some coffee, Beth," Tamantha called, already fetching her jacket. Beth was about to protest but knew better. Tamantha needed to feed, and the partner was not here, causing her to be more anxious and worried. A break would be best.

"Alright," Beth agreed, calling on her telecrystal to other Guardians and the extra guards.

Tamantha was rarely seen without Siberius, but the substitute captain would coordinate the protection detail. This used to be Alessandra's job. It would have been passed on to a more experienced Guardian, but based on Beth's parentage, it was naturally put into her hands. A General's child will be given special classes at the Academy to handle the operations of an effective Guardian team, even if they don't connect to the heir, an exceedingly rare occurrence. Siberius and Elsabeth had an older sister leading Nolan's Guardians, but she retired when he passed away. She had hopes of becoming General, but those died with her charge.

Three Guardians were already positioned outside the door, waiting to lead the princess to wherever she wanted to go.

Tamantha passed them without a word, choosing to keep mute. Coffee probably meant Tamantha's favorite restaurant on the grounds of Sophia University. Beth stood dutifully by her side.

Tonight was cold, and the university's streets were almost bare. Most Eklektos were in their rooms, enjoying the feeling of being drunk on blood. The Anaxios knew it was a special time and feared secretly that some Eklektos would ravage them.

Tamantha hugged her jacket to her, the air fogging with her breath, relieved to finally reach the warmth of the Blue Moon. She searched the customers and workers, looking for a familiar face. She found the silver-eyed waiter taking orders at another table. She went over to a booth immediately, trying to not draw attention, but it was kind of hard with the giant guards trailing behind her. Beth sat in front of her, resuming her homework with her sword between her legs.

Athan approached the table with pen and paper in hand. "Evening, Your Royal Highness. How is the full moon treating you?" The manager didn't care if he was making conversation with the princess instead of his job. It would be rude for him to interfere with the princess and whatever she chooses to do. It would earn a harsh growl from the Guardians, especially Siberius if he was here.

"Just coffee with a lot of sugar and cream, please. It's going okay. Siberius hasn't brought the partner to me yet, so I didn't feel like wasting anymore time waiting," Tamantha remarked. "Did you feed yet?" She knew that Athan had trained to be a Guardian, but it seems he was never assigned to a charge for some reason. Did that mean he still needs to feed?

"Honestly, I have never had to feed." Tamantha raised an eyebrow. He was Eklektos wasn't he?

"Aren't you a pureblood?" Tamantha questioned, curious

why that was possible.

"I am, I think. My uncle told me my mother was, but it's just unusual. My father is also an Eklektos, but we never felt that urge to feed, never grew the incisors. I think it might have to do something with my mother," Athan explained.

"Do you remember your mother?" Athan nodded.

"She was beautiful and kind. I have her eyes. We don't have any pictures of her, so I only have my memories to rely on."

"No pictures? Nothing?" Athan shook his head.

"I don't even know who her parents are or if they're even alive. I wish I knew more about her. I tried to find records, but I came up with nothing." Tamantha was beginning to forget her worries about tonight, listening to him intently.

"What was her name?" Tamantha asked, slyly trying to hide her own mission of helping him. Beth was on edge, listening to the conversation. She didn't approve of Tammy's plotting.

"Athanasia. Her married name is Athanasia Wright, but her maiden name is unknown to me," Athan said, obviously named after his mother. "I'll get your coffee, Your Royal Highness."

"Call me Tammy. We've talked enough," Tamantha said, earning a glare from Beth. Normal students had to be formal when speaking, and Tammy just added him to the okay list. Her words are the ultimate. He gave her a weary smile, afraid of Beth's sword. He walked away before he could get stabbed.

"Forgive me, Tammy, but I don't think that's wise. His brother tried to assassinate you," Beth hissed, earning disapproving looks from the other Guardians.

"He's not his brother, and I know how it feels to be looped into the same circle because of your siblings or parents. I know you do too," Tamantha explained. Beth looked down at her homework. She was always compared to her brother and her sister, and she would hear about it and be judged if her mother did something wrong. "Get to know him. I'm trying."

Elsabeth's telecrystal began to glow and hum, making the other Guardians straighten up like the caller was in the same room. "Yes, Si? Alright, we will bring her." Tamantha already knew what it was, standing up out of the booth. She was anxious to rid the empty, burning feeling in her stomach. Athan returned with her coffee.

"Sorry, I have to go. Thank you though. I'll see you around, Athan," Tamantha stated, handing him payment for the coffee she didn't drink. Athan nodded and gave her a gentle wave. He watched as the royal entourage left the Blue Moon, a longing seen from her departure.

Tamantha was back in her own room fairly quickly. The Guardians could barely even keep up with her. "It's about time!" Tamantha exclaimed, almost about to throw a tantrum. Feeding was a very testy time for them, angered very easily. "Good evening, Cadence. How are you today?"

"I'm good, Your Royal Highness. I'm ready whenever you want to start," the woman stated. She was much older, in her middle ages almost. She had been around since Tamantha began to feed at a young age, hand selected by the king and queen.

"Her medical records are clean. The royal doctor just checked her yesterday, so it is okay to begin," Siberius said, skimming through the notes the doctor had left with her.

Cadence sat down in a chair in front of Tamantha, used to the process. Tamantha had already sunk her teeth into Cadence when the partner suddenly began to cough. The princess stepped back, wiping the trickle of blood from her mouth. She had to wait. The blood tasted good on her tongue, familiar with her partner's red liquid.

"I'm sorry. My throat must be dry. Could I get some water?" Cadence requested. Beth fetched some water from the bathroom.

"Are you alright, Cadence?" Siberius asked, required by the rules. "She had seemed fine when we went to get her." Cadence nodded her head, taking the drink from Beth and instantly relieving her parched throat.

"I'll be fine. Just give me a moment," Cadence said, still coughing.

"Call the doctor, Thomas," Siberius ordered the extra guard. Thomas ran out to find the campus doctor specific for Pleione wing. "Tamantha, did you take any blood?"

Tammy nodded. "Only a small bit though when I bit into her." Siberius frowned.

Cadence's coughs got worse. Siberius pulled the princess away and put her on the corner of her bed. Tamantha heart sunk, wondering if something was going wrong.

If a partner is sick, it can be passed on to the feeder. The name of the partner was hidden in records, so they couldn't be poisoned and pass it on to the feeder.

Cadence was a mother and wife, receiving a significant income from her role in the full moon. She had watched Tamantha grow, still seeing the four-year-old child within her. Cadence had started out in her early twenties. Tamantha had been to her wedding and met her babies.

Cadence started choking and wheezing, coughing up blood into her hands. Blood began to leak from her nose. "Oh Creator, I'm going to die," Cadence whispered. "I'm sorry, Tamantha." She fell forward in her seat onto the floor. None of the Guardians bothered to pick her up, more concerned with the princess.

"Someone help her!" Tamantha cried, shocked by what was happening. Tamantha didn't know what to do.

The doctor ran in. "What's going on here?"

"She suddenly started coughing, and now this," Siberius explained.

"Did her royal highness drink any blood?" Siberius grimaced.

"Yes." The doctor reached into her medical bag, fetching out a black liquid.

"Make her drink this now. She will puke, but it will stop her from absorbing anything," the doctor ordered, kneeling next to Cadence to check her out.

Siberius dragged Tamantha to the bathroom and handed her the vial. Her ice blue eyes cringed when she tasted the strange liquid. She instantly threw up into the closest drain, the sink. Beth helped hold back her hair.

"Siberius, what am I going to do? I need to feed," Tamantha stated after she finished puking out her dinner as well. Siberius shook his head, fetching out his telecrystal.

"Stay in here." Siberius gave his sister a look to not let their charge out.

"Beth, is she going to be okay?" Tamantha had known this woman for most of her life.

"I don't know, Tammy," Beth said honestly. Tammy fought back the tears.

After a few minutes, Siberius opened the door. "Your Royal Highness, let's go out for a little bit, okay?" Siberius used his huge body to shield her from the mound on the floor covered up by a sheet.

Tamantha covered her mouth to choke back the sobs and nodded, heading towards the door to the hallway. She listened to the conversation between a Guardian and the doctor. "Was she sick or poisoned?"

"We have to wait for an autopsy. We're lucky the princess

didn't ingest more." Tamantha wouldn't grieve for her partner like she did for Nolan or Alessandra. She would feel sorry for her family and plan to send them condolences.

The princess and her cavalry returned to the Blue Moon they had left only less than an hour ago. Athan bowed, curious why she was back. She slumped down in the familiar booth, choosing to lay down in it. "Is everything okay?" She perked up at the familiar voice.

"Is your brother around?" Siberius growled.

"I haven't heard from him or seen him since that incident," Athan said in a monotone, tired of being asked about him.

"Clayton Wright?" Siberius pressed.

"I have only one brother, and no, he's gone missing. Believe me. I want to find him too," Athan retorted. "Would you like your coffee again?"

"I want one Anaxios fresh and warm please," Tamantha muttered from her position on the seat.

"I will see what I can do. Anything for you folks? Do you ever eat or drink on the job?" Athan joked. None of them were in a joking mood and were eager to take revenge for their fallen comrade even if he didn't do it. "Tough crowd." Beth stared at her new friend, worried.

"There's a dead body in my room, and I'm hungry," Tamantha whined, sitting up in her seat. Athan felt sympathy for her and was slightly shocked. She would never age past twenty-five, but she had to drink blood to stay alive. Obviously, she didn't kill the partner by overdrinking. Something else happened.

"I will contact the General for an immediate temporary partner. The full moon ends tonight," Siberius said, trying to calm the hungry princess. The last note did little to help her worries.

"I'm going to die," Tamantha groaned, laying her head on the desk. Siberius stepped away from the booth to make the call on his telecrystal to his mother. A protective barrier was put up around her booth and even outside the doors of the Blue Moon. Most of the customers had been driven out if they were finished, and no one else would be let in.

"Waiter, bring some soup and a grilled cheese sandwich for her royal highness," Beth requested. Tamantha nodded. She just puked her guts out. Athan left the table quickly, hurried by the direness of the situation.

"Why are you interrupting the business?" the manager spoke up, standing in front of the guards with his arms crossed on his chest.

"You will be compensated for any losses. There is an emergency, and her royal highness must be protected. You don't need to know any more information," Beth explained, standing up from the booth.

"I don't care if I get compensated. If the princess can just waltz in here and shut down my restaurant, then it's bad for business. Customers don't want to worry about getting kicked out because she's hungry," the manager argued. He was fuming.

"This has never happened before, and her royal highness has come here to eat many times without having the business shut down to accommodate her. When it is a state of emergency, the crown must be dealt with first." The Guardians were staring down at the short little manager. "Besides, this restaurant is on school property. It must follow all university rules, including shutting down and serving only a single customer if there's a danger going on." The manager threw his arms up in the air and stomped off into the kitchen, almost running into Athan who was holding a tray of food.

"Hurry up with that order, and make her go away," the

manager hissed to his poor waiter. Athan ignored him. He had been to the Guardian Academy and knew the protocols that went on behind the scenes.

Athan set the tray down on the table, receiving a taste test from Beth since Siberius was not here. "Still didn't poison it." Beth glared, piercing him with mental daggers. Beth slid the tray across the table to Tamantha, who greedily dug in. Tamantha motioned for Athan to sit.

"I want some company that isn't my pack of guard dogs." The guard dogs were less than pleased by her denouncing them, but she was slowly declining in sanity with the closeness of the full moon ending. She knew she wouldn't die, but the impending doom was weighing down on her. Emergency partners were always around. There were even companies in the telecrystal handbook for Eklektos to whisper if their partner is missing or died. The Guardians wouldn't simply go to the extent of hiring a company like that.

Athan pulled up a chair and sat down, knowing the Guardians wouldn't let him sit across from or next to her. "So what happened?"

Tamantha swallowed the piece of grilled cheese in her mouth. "Well my partner just died all of a sudden from some mysterious disease, or maybe she was poisoned. I bet these guys are thinking you have something to do with it, but you have an alibi. You were here when she was picked up, talking to me." She said this more to make the Guardians aware that he couldn't have poisoned Cadence, or at least she hoped so.

"Did you feed?" Athan asked, concerned.

"Barely, but they gave me magic throwing up juice. Now I'm okay, sort of. You're lucky you don't have to deal with it."

"I wish I had something just to have some mental stability

about who I am," Athan mused. Tamantha looked down at her food.

"Sorry."

"It's okay." Athan was watching her, studying her features.

Siberius returned to the table, growling at the waiter's presence. "The General is on her way with a replacement," the towering Guardian explained, still keeping an eye on Athan.

Tamantha finished her food. "Where will she meet us?"

"She will come to us," Siberius stated, closely looking at his sister for a reaction. He could see her fidgeting in her seat. He was enjoying it. Tamantha started to notice it too.

"Your mother is coming. Your mother? Your as in plural," Tamantha giggled. Beth's face started to turn red with embarrassment. She wouldn't say anything though. "Well at least it isn't mine." Tamantha had a stupid smile plastered on her face.

"Is your mother really that bad?" Athan asked Tamantha.

"No one truly knows my mother. She's a bitch," Tamantha retorted. She started laughing uncontrollably. She was losing it.

"Your Royal Highness, don't speak of her majesty in that way. She has her spies," Siberius reminded, looking at the bunch standing in the Blue Moon around the table. The princess was still cracking up. Athan raised an eyebrow.

"You're from Polemos, right? You're buddy buddy with King Bassett? Did he have spies?" Tamantha questioned, trying to choke back the laughter, drawing closer to insanity.

"Bassett is a young king. He probably has less of a network to obtain discreet information. You know he has a birthday coming up?" Athan explained, reminiscing about his times with his old friend.

"Yes, I do, but there's no big birthday bash this year. He's turning twenty-five, and he's an Asterope," Tamantha mentioned, watching Athan despair over that fact. Tamantha felt bad for the way she was speaking, but she just felt all jittery and funny. "Sorry."

"I know the mortality rate for their family. Are you okay?"

Tamantha nodded, feeling ashamed of her behavior. Athan reached over to pat her on the hand, but Siberius grabbed his wrist in a flash. "Just trying to comfort her."

Siberius let go of the arm, making sure the strange boy kept his distance.

Tamantha looked up when she heard the sirens. She could see the bright lights flashing outside the window. Athan was removed from the table and made to go away with the extra guard Thomas escorting him to the other side of the room. Tamantha stood up from her booth, impatient to get the show on the road.

The General of the Guardians walked in with an Anaxios following behind. This was an Anaxios hired to be temporary relief for the royal family if something should happen to their permanent partner.

"General!" Siberius announced, causing all Guardians to salute her.

"Stand down. Siberius, have someone sent to help clean up the body," the tall woman ordered. The General approached the princess and kneeled down in front of her as well as the food. "Your Royal Highness, I'm sorry for your misfortunes. You may feed whenever you like. This Anaxios has been untouched."

Tamantha greedily bit into the Anaxios, a man of her height.

The General turned to her daughter while the princess made with her full moon desires. "Elsa, how are you, my darling?"

"I'm fine, mom," the blue haired girl replied.

"Is your brother bossing you around much? I know he loves this little treat of powering over his little sister. You let me know, and I will deal with him." She looked at her daughter's hair, holding a strand. "You still haven't changed your hair."

"Her royal highness has not asked me to do so and does not mind it." The General frowned.

"I don't think you will be impressing the Queen tonight then." Tamantha was too busy hungrily drinking to hear that last bit.

"Queen? Queen Clarisa? The mother of the Crown Princess?" Beth questioned, feeling a bit happy to hear her new friend would be suffering like her.

Tamantha finished, blood dripping down her chin. She pulled back and looked at the door when she heard it open.

In walked the tall, beautiful, blonde-haired wife of the king, and she was looking straight at her daughter. "Her Majesty, the Queen!" her Guardian announced.

Athan was shocked to see the Queen so up close and personal, watching from the sidelines. He did the appropriate required kneel on his right leg, bowing his head down. Everyone also did the same except for the princess.

"Oh, no," Tamantha whispered. In her state of shock, she forgot how bloody her mouth was. Clarisa gave a graceful smile as she strolled over to her daughter, but her eyes showed her disapproval.

"Hello, my dear. You should clean up. Don't need anyone to think you have bad manners," Clarisa scolded. Beth handed a napkin over to her charge, trying not to be noticed by the queen.

Tamantha wiped her face and ignored the Anaxios who was being dragged away. "Hello, mother." Clarisa's smirk did not reach her eyes. Tamantha gave her mother the obligatory hug, kissing her mother on either cheek.

"I heard about what happened and asked the General if I could tag along. I was worried about you." Tamantha knew her mother probably had other motives.

"I'm fine. Cadence died though. I feel bad for her," Tamantha said briefly, looking down at the ground.

"Well, I am glad you're okay. You must visit the family and tell them how sorry you are. She was of great service for many years for my little early bloomer." Tamantha eyed Athan in the corner. Clarisa focused her eyes on Beth, glaring at the vibrant hair. "You must be her new Guardian. Hello, Elsabeth." She looked like she was going to tear Beth's hair from her scalp, but the queen wore a perfect mask. "What lovely hair." She was saying this with the upmost sarcasm.

Beth bowed respectfully to the queen, ignoring the obvious orders hidden. "Good evening, Your Majesty," Beth acknowledged. "Thank you."

"Mother, why don't you meet my friend?" Tamantha requested, knowing she would piss off Clarisa. She motioned for Athan to come over, earning a nod from him. Clarisa's Guardians made a good barrier with a hole for Athan to see through. "This is Athan Wright."

The moment she heard the last name of the boy, the smile plastered on her face faded away. This man was related to the one who tried to hurt her precious heir. "Delighted."

Athan bowed. "Your Majesty."

"His uncle is a Guardian to King Bassett, and Athan is also very good friends with him," Tamantha boasted, trying to put him good light. The queen would not ignore the fact that his brother was responsible for the failed assassination as well as maybe tonight.

"How wonderful. I must let King Bassett know I met you. He probably has much to say," Clarisa said through her wide teeth.

"Yes, I have known him since we were both children," Athan

explained.

"How wonderful. Are you a pureblood?"

"Excuse me?"

"Eklektos, my dear. My daughter is not to converse with the lowly Anaxios and half-bloods. It is much below her to do so," Clarisa retorted, earning a scowl from her daughter. She wouldn't argue with her mother though to avoid making her even more mad. She, however, came from the Merope family. She will talk to the non-pureblooded if she so chooses.

"I believe I am, or at least that's what my uncle told me."

"Do you feed?"

"No."

"Then how can you be an Eklektos?" The queen practically lifted her nose in the air, refusing to continue this conversation with the Wright boy. "You may leave." She was making him exit the Blue Moon with her Guardians happily forcing him out.

"Don't be rude, mother," Tamantha pleaded, watching the silver eyed boy leave the restaurant.

"I will not associate with their kind," Clarisa snorted. It was hard to believe she was a mother, since she looked like she wasn't a day over twenty-five. Didn't all Eklektos look like that?

"Why are you here? I know you wouldn't come rushing over here if you know I'm alive. You didn't when Alessandra died," Tamantha reminded.

"I truly love you and care for you. If I know you're okay, then I don't need to worry. The Guardians will protect you at all costs. As a queen, I have many duties." Clarisa pondered on these so-called things to do.

"Uh huh. Can we get down to business?" Tamantha raised an eyebrow at her strange mother.

"Child, you have not been answering my calls on the

telecrystal and been ignoring my requests for meetings. Why not come when I know where you are and know I can corner you?" She was ready to reveal the real reason. "As you know, you are the Crown Princess now. We must find a suitable husband. I want you to come to dinner next week on the day of King Bassett's birthday. We will toast to him, and then you and I will go over the potential suitors, your father not included."

"Do I have a choice to refuse?"

"Of course not. I will have Siberius bring you around dinner time. I'll make him force you into the karavi. Please be dressed nicely." The queen was preparing to leave once she knew her mission was over.

"Hey, mom."

Clarisa paused, feeling her motherly love kicking in. "Yes, dear?"

"Have you heard from Nolan's wife at all? I haven't since the ceremony."

"No, she ran off to grieve in private. She's no use to this family anymore anyways. She never became queen, so she lost the title of crown princess when it passed to you. The Lady Rosaleen can return her own family if she wishes to." Tamantha couldn't see behind the perfected mask, a skill she probably would never be able to master. "See you next week, Tamantha."

The room kneeled to her as she left, captivating the people who could gaze at her.

Chapter Seven

Tamantha dragged Cole to dinner with her parents. She didn't want to face her mother alone, and she thought maybe she could distract her mother for the night away from the idea of marrying her off.

"How are you, Cole?" King Alvyn asked, genuinely concerned for him after his loss.

"I am good, Your Majesty." Cole was hiding his pain. It was hard for him still even though it had been a couple of months since her abrupt departure.

"Is school going well for you? Keep in touch with your parents?" Cole nodded.

Tamantha tuned out of their conversation, trying to ignore the look her mother was giving her. Her mother had a mischievous grin on her face. It was probably a bad idea to bring the Eklektos with the last name of Baldwin, a common source of spouses for the Merope family. She was shaking her head constantly without figuring out where her mother's off smile was directed at.

Siberius and Beth were standing off to the side in formal

uniforms, required when working in the palace. Beth was enjoying the princess's anguish a little too much. She knew her own mother was just down the hall and would hope to avoid her door.

Tamantha was downing the glasses of wine a little too quickly to try not to think about the conversation coming after dinner. Clarisa was not going to give up on her plans, and it would not be avoided by the princess.

The King raised his glass to end the dinner. "May King Bassett have a delightful twenty-fifth birthday and not be taken by the Lost One. May he reign for many years," Alvyn toasted, earning a raise of the glass from the rest of people at the dinner table. Tamantha gulped down the red liquid.

"Alvyn, why don't you and Cole go discuss the games while my baby and I catch up?" Clarisa hummed. The King didn't see any reason to argue, leaving the room with the Head of the Symvoulio's son.

Tamantha was about to make a run for it, but Clarisa had already grabbed her hand and held it, hiding the fact that she was squeezing it really hard.

"You are so beautiful. Any man would have you," Clarisa mentioned, pulling the princess to Clarisa's private lounge.

"Mama, I don't want to. I have another six years before my twenty-fifth birthday comes up. I don't need to be making babies right this moment," Tamantha bargained. Her mother wasn't having it. She forced her child to sit down in the golden cloth seats, holding a binder.

"The crown needs as many heirs as possible. Besides you, there is only your cousin to take the throne. I would rather it passes down from my blood, meaning you need to get married and start making me some grandchildren." A twenty-five-year-old looking grandmother would seem so strange, but it was normal for Eklektos, just like it was normal for her mother to almost look her age.

"Mama, I would rather not be cattle," Tamantha suggested, trying to butter her up by calling her mama.

Clarisa opened the binder and started flipping through the pages. "Thank you for bringing that Eklektos boy. The Baldwins always have handsome men in their family. Wonderful genes I hear. He is definitely at the top of list."

Tamantha rubbed her forehead in disbelief. "Mother, he is my best friend. I am not marrying my best friend."

Clarisa overlooked that fact, continuing her search through the book. "Oh, there are so many noblemen around your age, Sophian and other nationalities." Tamantha could hear her giggling like a schoolgirl. She glanced at Beth and Siberius, begging them to put her out of her misery. "It's a shame you can't marry heirs. Your cousin is looking rather fine, but of course, he is my dear sister's future king. There's plenty of fish in the Eklektos sea besides him."

Tamantha was disinterested in whatever her mother was going to offer up. "Mama, can it not wait another year?"

"No. We need to make a list of suitors and notify them of their eligibility, so they can ask to court you. Cole Baldwin can be one of them." Tamantha sneakily reached for the binder, about to rip out of her mother's arms, but Clarisa was quicker, turning away with the book of men.

"What if I wanted to marry a woman?" Tamantha coaxed.

"That's fine as long as a few blood heirs are given to the throne," Clarisa said. Tamantha knew it was futile. She begrudgingly sat next to her mother. If she didn't have any choice, she would at least pick the ones she likes better. "Here's the second son of a Duke. He is your age, and he likes to go outdoors. Wouldn't that make him bit of a risk if some hunter accidentally shot him with an arrow?" Tamantha shrugged, pointing out a few that she would care to give a chance.

"How about that son of the President of the Astrapi?" She knew that one would get on her mother's nerves.

"You are not going to marry an Electra guardian. Who knows if the Electra royal family will ever make an appearance again? If they don't come back, that son will become the next President of Astrapi. The people always vote them up," Clarisa explained. They were beneath her. Guardians don't belong in the royal family.

"Alright, if you throw Cole Baldwin in there, then I want to throw this normal guy in the contestants," Tamantha chose, pointing at a picture in the book. It was a picture of Athan. Her mother was burning with rage. She tore Athan's page out of the book and threw it in the trash. "I'm surprised that was even in there."

"I asked my assistant to compile a list of eligible bachelors with heavy stress on noble blood, but of course, she serves the Merope family. You Meropes don't distinguish between the classes and would be happy to marry an Eklektos from the streets." If only the country knew her mother spoke like this. Tamantha shook her head. "That guy might not even be an Eklektos. Plus, his brother tried to kill my precious little girl." Clarisa faked some sobs. Tamantha wouldn't fall for it.

"Hey, mom. Have you heard of a woman named Athanasia?" Clarisa looked up from her task at hand, staring at her daughter's ice blue eyes. She seemed to know the name.

"Why do you ask?" Clarisa was hiding something, but Tamantha knew no prying would get it out of the woman. The queen was known for keeping her secrets.

"Athan doesn't know where his mother came from. He said her name was Athanasia. He couldn't even find records on her," Tamantha mused, thinking about how to get that kind of information. There was an archive within the palace, and Sophia was known for the vast knowledge they have obtained. Almost everything within history is stored within the archives, except for top level security.

Tamantha was almost shocked when she saw her mother stand up from the couch and pick up the crumpled ball of paper with Athan's name on it. "I will consider him." What did her mother recognize about that name?

"Mom, who is Athanasia?" Tamantha was surprised at her mother's actions. The boy was a normal citizen, yet he received approval from the classist queen.

"That's something you will have to find out when your father is gone. That won't be for many years," Clarisa disclosed, returning back to her mission to have grandbabies. Tamantha knew her mother wouldn't talk about the subject anymore past this point. "That means Cole Baldwin is in the pool too." Tamantha cringed. Cole was going to be making fun of her when he received the letter.

The mother and daughter spent the next couple of hours going over the possible men who could try for the crown princess's hand. Clarisa decided to retire for the night, having drunk too much red wine. She would send out the letters to the chosen bachelors tomorrow. Tamantha went to Cole and her father, seeing them still in full conversation over who would win the next nest. They probably wouldn't stop for another hour. She would likely spend tonight in her room and go back to the university in the morning.

Tamantha left the king's lounge, not caring for their

argument on which team was better. Cole was lucky. People who disagree with a king would be frowned upon, but as Tamantha's best friend and as the son of Head of Symvoulio, Alvyn had known Cole since he was a baby.

Tamantha's two main Guardians stood dutifully behind her. The rest of the Guardians were on their own posts or off for the night. The Guardians wouldn't care where she went inside the palace as long as she stayed inside of it.

"Let's go the archives," Tamantha requested, already walking towards it. Siberius didn't seem to approve.

"That boy's mother is none of your business. You heard her majesty," Siberius protested, staying put.

"It doesn't hurt to look, Siberius." Tamantha would go there whether he liked it or not. Beth was smirking at her charge's rebelliousness. She was starting to enjoy having the princess as a friend.

"Let's go, Tammy," Beth announced, making sure no one was around to hear her speak informally. The halls were almost empty as it was bedtime for most people. Tammy grinned, grabbing the blue haired girl's hand, and putting more speed into getting to her destination.

The archives were full of shelves and the ceiling was fifty feet above them. Ladders and stairs were necessary to reach the higher shelving. It would take years to search for a specific book or record, but that was what the archivist was for. She instantly knew where anything you wanted was. Almost everything in history was recorded here, and almost every book ever written was in here.

Tamantha had liked to spend many hours here when she was a child, just reading for as long as she could. She would hide away from the queen here, and the king would read to his little girl. Nolan and Tamantha would fight over a book if they both wanted to read it, or Nolan would pick out a book he thought his little sister might enjoy. The last thought brought some tears to her eyes.

Tamantha approached the desk. The night archivist was on duty, looking up from a record with her tiny glasses. The night archivist took a moment to register who had made their presence here. She scrambled up straight and bowed, almost hitting her head on the desk. "Your Royal Highness!"

"Hello," Tamantha replied sweetly, giving one of the graceful smiles her mother was famous for.

"How may I help you, Your Royal Highness?" the archivist questioned, looking at both of the formal guards.

"I would like to find a record please. Athanasia Wright."

The archivist nodded. "One moment please."

Tamantha watched as the archivist went into the back office to look up the location. Beth was amazed by the vast library, itching to look around. "Go ahead, Beth. I'll be fine. Your brother is here." Beth took the opportunity, avoiding her brother's eyes. She was gone in a flash. "Let her have some fun, Siberius. You've been my Guardian for too many years to count. You barely even take a vacation." Siberius grunted in response. He was remaining formal while he was in the palace, realizing who could come around the corner.

Tamantha stared at the large portrait of her father above the archivist's desk. It was made shortly after his coronation. He didn't look different at all from the picture, the same man, slightly changed by the stresses of kingship. If he had been Anaxios, he would be grey haired from all the work it takes to run a country. Alvyn is a wise king and benevolent ruler. The people trust him and adore him. He only came into power fifteen years ago. The crown was passed to him from his grandmother.

His mother passed away from the Test of the Lost One and only retained the title of crown princess. The Crown Princess Juliette had three children before her death. King Alvyn was not the original heir. He had a brother born before him, just like Tamantha. The brother had been in a boat accident with his wife and child. All three were killed, leaving her father as the heir. There was also Alvyn's younger sister, but she died of the same thing that killed their mother. Tamantha's grandfather, the father of the king, is very much alive, although he chooses not to be involved in the family. He did his duty and will send birthday cards and make a few calls every now and then. He had only been forced to marry Juliette and happily found another wife.

Tamantha was displeased to be in the same situation as her grandmother. She would be forced to marry someone she didn't want to just so she could secure the bloodline. In all likeliness, it was probably going to be her best friend who she has to string into unwanted marriage. The red head probably sensed it was coming since Tamantha had no romantic relationships with an Eklektos.

If she died at the age of twenty-five, her spawn would have to take the throne from her father. It was what the Test of the Lost One did to the royal families, force them to act on the insecurities. As much as she didn't want to be in this position, she didn't want to have her own children go through the same thing.

Tamantha waved away the thought, focusing back on the situation at hand. She would try to find love among the bachelors so that it would not be an uncomfortable arrangement between her and whoever becomes the future crown prince.

The archivist finally returned to the waiting princess, staring up at the towering man. His size was always intimidating to anyone who got close to his charge. "Yes, I found the records for Athanasia Wright. Unfortunately, Your Royal Highness, these records are sealed, and you do not have the authority to access them." Tamantha stood there dumbfounded that these words came from the archivist.

"The records are sealed? What do you mean I don't have the authority to access them?" Tamantha demanded. She wanted so desperately to unlock the mystery for Athan, even though she was probably doing this for her own selfish reasons. She did want to help him really.

"I'm sorry, Your Royal Highness, but only certain people have the jurisdiction to obtain sealed records. You are on a priority level, but you do not have the necessary level to read them," the archivist explained, trained on what the rules are for these situations.

"Who would have access over a Crown Princess?" Tamantha couldn't comprehend this. She thought back on her mother's reaction to hearing the name. Something was serious behind whoever this woman was, and she would have to try hard to get even a snippet it seems.

The archivist clasped her hands in front of her, maintaining the proper and polite stance that the archivist must hold on to her job. "I do have permission to at least tell you who can see the records. The only ones who can go into them are the General of the Guardians, the archivists of this library, and His Majesty, the King."

Tamantha would ask her father, but he was not keen on giving away top-level secrets to even his own daughter. Why would the identity of this woman be kept away from the public and even her?

"It seems up until fifteen years ago, the children of the king or queen would have had also been able to gain entrance to things like this, but unfortunately, upon his coronation, King Alvyn chose to change the priority levels on the record of Athanasia Wright. The King's word is law. Is there anything else I can help you with, Your Royal Highness?"

"No. Thank you, madam." Tamantha turned on her heel away from the archivist, annoyed with her father and the woman who was only doing her job. Siberius whistled for his sister like she was a guard dog, and she instantly appeared. "Sorry to cut your tour short. I will bring you here another time." Beth mouthed that it was fine. Tamantha was making a direct beeline for her father's private lounge, and he was most likely still there with the red-haired bachelor.

"If he doesn't want you to have access to it, Tamantha, then leave it be," Siberius pleaded. "He must have his reasons." Tamantha was stunned that he broke his formalities in the palace, something so unlike him.

"I want to at least try to ask him why," Tamantha told her gentle Guardian. Tamantha proceeded with her purpose, going around the Guardians to see her own father. She knew he was in there because the king's protective detail was wherever he went. The Guardians bowed as she breezed past them. She nodded her head in acknowledgement.

"Hello, sweetie," Alvyn called, enclosing her in a hug. Cole waved from the big chair, enjoying the luxuries befitting a king.

"Daddy, can I ask you something?" Beth and Siberius were outside. Her Guardians were not allowed in here like they were let into the queen's lounge.

"Yes, you may by approval of the King!" her father announced. He had a dopey grin on his face. She could tell her father had been drinking with Cole, having too much fun with hanging out with another guy.

"Alright. I want to ask about a woman named Athanasia

Wright," Tamantha asked, realizing her mistake when the smile on his face dropped. The name was not kind to his ears.

"You will have to wait until I drop dead." The king was adamant in his answer.

"But why? Why is there so much secrecy? I am the crown princess for Creator's sake!"

"Athanasia is a woman whose identity is to be sealed and never opened unless necessary. Why are you even asking?"

"What is she the queen of freaking Astrapi?" This was a phrase quite commonly used to call someone out for acting special.

"How did you know?" The king started laughing at his joke. "No, seriously. She isn't, and if I ever need you to know, I will allow you to find out. For now, leave it alone."

Tamantha sighed and looked down at the ground. "I was asking for my friend, Athanasia's son, Athan Wright." The King scratched his chin.

Tamantha relaxed when she felt the warm hand of her father on her head, stroking her hair. "Her son will have to find out on his own, and you can't try to interfere with it." Tamantha bit her lip. She tried, and she knew it was over.

Tamantha opened her eyes, staring at the ceiling of her room, unused to being here. She would get dressed and go to breakfast to appease her mother. Then she would grab Cole and make a run for it before she can get tortured more by the woman who gave birth to her. Beth yawned loudly when Tamantha left her bedroom, causing the blue-haired girl to choke with surprise.

"Good morning, Your Royal Highness," Beth hummed, straightening up before some queen walked by.

"Yes, it is," Tamantha chimed, linking her arm with her

Guardian. She didn't care about the Guardians needing to be in uniform in the palace. She just wanted to get out of here. "Let's finish up this little visit and go back home." Beth smiled in return, glad to hear Tamantha calling their little humble abode their home.

The Guardians outside the dining hall bowed to the princess. She removed herself from Beth's arm when she entered the room.

Tamantha was confused when she saw the solemn looks on her parents' face. "What's wrong? Did Grandpa die?" Tamantha joked. The king motioned for her to sit in her seat. Cole was already there, sharing the same expression as her parents. "What is it?"

Her father spoke. "Honey, King Bassett Asterope passed away."

Chapter Eight

Tamantha entered the room in her blue ball gown, noticing the stares from the crowd. She felt uncomfortable being here, but it was part of these ceremonies. A representative must be here.

It was always Nolan who stood in the spot she would take. The royal families only sent their crown princes and crown princesses to represent them in coronations. She had been at the funeral for King Bassett as well, paying respects to the Asterope family. His funeral was only a day ago with a crying child marching behind the carriage carrying him. Today was her day. She was only six years old. Her birthday was last month; the last birthday she would ever spend with her father.

"Crown Princess Tamantha Alexandria Merope of Sophia," the herald of Polemos announced. The Temple of the Creator was full of people, and they bowed to the ice blue eyed princess. She moved down to her spot in front of the Merope family symbol.

She saw Crown Prince Koichi waving to her. She acknowledged him with a gentle nod. She clasped her hands in front of her, feeling the tiara digging into her head. She would do her role in the ceremony, and it was her first time ever doing so.

King Bassett had passed away from the Test of the Lost One as many Asterope family members do. They have the highest mortality rate, and this outcome was to be expected. King Bassett's father had also died from it when King Bassett was only seven years old. The Asterope royal family marries off much younger than the rest of the families with such heavy assurances weighing on them. He was married to a Polemos noble lady at the age of fourteen. They gave birth to the Crown Princess of Polemos when they were nineteen. His wife died of childbirth, and he never remarried, leaving him with only one sole heir.

The Asterope family typically rises to power at a young age. The longest reigning Asterope to actually live past twenty-five was almost a hundred years ago. The youngest ever Asterope king was only two years old. Advisors would help raise the country and teach the young queen or king. They would cram it into them and be left alone to rule once they turn fifteen. Today was the formal coronation for Crown Princess Luvina Marie Asterope of Polemos. She was off in another room, waiting to be guided in.

"Such a shame they have to be crowned so young," her cousin chimed in. Tamantha peeked at him. He was Crown Prince Cedrik of Thalassa. It had been a while since she had seen him, not since her mother forced her to go on vacation with her Celaeno relatives. She chose to be silent, not willing to engage in any talk before the coronation began.

"Don't interrupt the ceremony, young man," the crown princess of Therion advised. It was a rare appearance for the highest-ranking family member of Taygete to be here. Their distrust for any of the other royal families was evident. The Electra family had been their allies and would still be if they ever appeared again.

Cedrik rolled his eyes at her, turning his eyes to his cousin.

"Hello there, Tammy. How do you get more beautiful every time I see you? Must be the Celaeno genes," Cedrik remarked, grinning slyly. Tamantha said nothing back, although she felt warm from his comment.

The Alcyone crown princess almost slapped her own forehead in embarrassment. She was around the same age as her mother. She was the sister of the King of Nous. Her brother was married to a man, making it difficult for him to produce a blood heir. He chose to allow his sister to take the throne when he dies instead. He enjoyed adopting children into his own family, although they would never have a chance for the throne, regardless of parentage. She agreed with the Crown Princess of Therion that Cedrik needs to shut up.

Tamantha glimpsed at the Asterope symbol. There was no heir after today. There were no siblings and no children to succeed after Crown Princess Luvina.

Nolan's wife had eligibility still, but it was up to the Symvoulio of Polemos to choose who would become the next Crown Prince or Princess. Her sister-in-law was the daughter of King Bassett's uncle, but she was missing even now and had not extended her wishes to attend the coronation. There was something unusual about Rosaleen's disappearance, even though she still sent letters to friends and family.

"Please rise for the Crown Princess Luvina Marie Asterope of Polemos!" the herald called, causing the people in their seats to stand up. The five representatives remained seated in the chairs. Luvina was still their equal till they put the giant crown upon her head.

The six-year-old entered in a gown designed for this ceremony, gold with jewels and long sleeves. She wore a red robe around her shoulders, trailing behind her. It seemed almost heavy for the small girl, but she carried it well with the chosen Ladies of her court holding up the robe for her. Her face seemed almost too adult. Her advisors had probably instructed her on how she should express herself. She shared the same chocolate eyes as her father, a beautiful brown that captivated the audience.

Luvina's advisors stood by her side in formal garb meant for the coronation, each wearing a black robe around their shoulder. Luvina had sixteen Guardians bound to her, all of them stood on either side of the procession, walking forward with it. The Guardians wore a red uniform with the Asterope symbol on it. The choir was singing praises to the Creator for this blessed day.

The Head of the Symvoulio of Polemos stood at the end of the long aisle, directing the Crown Princess to come forward. The little girl followed his orders, and her advisors, ladies, and Guardians marched in the same stride, staying at the exact same pace as her.

The tiny princess reached the end of the long walk, standing in front of the one who would perform the ceremony. "All may sit now." The audience shuffled back into the pews. Tamantha watched Luvina take a deep breath, thinking no one would notice. "We are gathered on this day, the twenty-third of Thargelion, to elevate Crown Princess Luvina Marie Asterope of Polemos to Queen of Polemos. May the Creator bless this day and make it holy for Polemos."

Tamantha wondered how long it would be until she was in the same position as Luvina. She most likely had many years before her father would die and pass the crown to her, and it might not even happen if she succumbs to the Lost One.

"Crown Princess Luvina Marie Asterope, please kneel," the Head of the Symvoulio directed. This was not the same as the ceremony to accept the position of heir. This was a ceremony to declare her the ultimate ruler of a nation. Luvina got down on both knees, almost being pushed down by the heavy garb she was made to wear. "With this crown, you will be our ruler and sovereign. You will be our protector. You will use your power to maintain the rules of the land and enforce them. You will uphold the faith of the Creator even if no one else believes. You will inherit the wills and beliefs of the people of Polemos. Your Royal Highness, Crown Princess Luvina Marie Asterope, do you promise to follow all that is required of you as the Queen?"

"I promise to do so," Luvina said. An amplifying crystal had to be pinned to her dress so the crowds could hear her small voice.

"Will you always honor this oath till the day you die?" She is a child that already has to face the fear of death.

"Yes, I will." More deep breaths came from Luvina. There was so much pressure on a girl who just wanted to enjoy her childhood.

"Please remove the robe placed on her shoulders," the Head ordered to Lords and Ladies chosen to do so. The heavy red robe was removed, causing Luvina to stagger a little. She straightened up before anyone saw it. "Dress her in the white robes, please." The same Lord and Ladies rolled out a silk white robe with the Asterope symbol enlarged on the back, much lighter for Luvina. They placed it on her shoulders. The Head of the Symvoulio picked up the large crown from an assistant.

Tamantha was sure this one would knock the small girl over.

"I now crown you, Your Majesty, Luvina Marie Asterope, Queen of Polemos!" the head announced for all to hear. He placed the crown upon her head, almost too big to fit on her head. The new queen did not stumble, rising to her feet. "Please sit upon the throne of your ancestors where every king and queen of Polemos has sat." The little queen sat down in the grand throne. "May the representatives from the seven families come forward?"

That was the cue for the five crown princes and princesses to do their role in this ceremony. Tamantha stood up from her mini throne, approaching the focus of the coronation, followed by the other four. Each one kneeled down in front of the queen. Tamantha began first, "the Merope family acknowledges your ascension." She put a hand on her heart.

"The Maia family acknowledges your ascension," Koichi stated, crossing his arm over his chest.

"The Celaeno family acknowledges your ascension." Her cousin did the same as her and Koichi.

"The Taygete family acknowledges your ascension."

"The Alcyone family acknowledges your ascension." Both of the middle-aged crown princesses put their hand on their hearts.

"The Electra family would acknowledge your ascension," the President of Astrapi, a representative for Electra since there was no other, stated this from the crowd, standing up and putting his hand on his heart.

"The Asterope family acknowledges your blessings," Luvina responded, copying their moves. The Head of the Symvoulio gestured for the family representatives to return to their seats, and they followed his orders.

"With the blessing of the Creator and Her children, I present to you her majesty, Luvina Marie Asterope, Queen of Polemos," the Head of the Symvoulio declared to the world. All in the audience and even the heirs of the other countries stood up and bent forward to bow to the new queen. Her Majesty rose from her seat and was guided out of the Temple of the Creator. She was being escorted to the Asterope palace with a grand parade where the coronation ball would take place.

"Her royal highness, Crown Princess Tamantha Alexandria Merope of Sophia and Lord Cole Baldwin, son of Lord Leoline Baldwin!" the royal herald yelled into the ballroom. The audience clapped to their presence.

Elsabeth and Siberius were directly behind Tamantha in their formal uniform with the flag of the Sophia nation embroidered onto it with the sigil of the Merope family also on it. Tamantha wore the same gown she wore to the coronation. Cole had not been at the coronation, barred from doing so because he was not a Polemos noble.

Cole took Tamantha's hand and guided her down the long stairs with the red carpet, the color of the Asterope family. He brought her into a safe open spot for her to stand with him. The herald called out the name of more royalty and aristocrats. Tamantha had told Cole about her mother's plan, but she did not say he had been included in her mother's plotting.

"Her majesty, Queen Luvina Marie Asterope!" Anyone who was sitting automatically rose. The ladies curtsied, and the gentlemen bent forward, including the royalty who are now beneath her.

"Such a shame King Bassett had to go like that," Cole muttered to Tamantha. She nodded in agreement, remembering the expression on her brother's face. They never got to wake up from that nightmare.

"Thank you for coming to my coronation and to the coronation ball. I am greatly pleased to see so many familiar faces here and to see so many who will support me in my future years as Queen. I will not fail you as Queen and will live up to the expectations set before me," Luvina said, speaking into an amplifying crystal. This was her coronation speech. It was short and simple. She was only six years old after all. Tamantha wondered how many times she had rehearsed it with the advisors until she could articulate all the words correctly. The crowd applauded the new queen. "Let the festivities begin!"

The orchestra began to play the music created there in Polemos. The dance began first with the queen and the crown heirs with their dates. A Guardian was chosen to be Luvina's dance partner, and it was quite sweet actually. Cole was already well trained in the proper ballroom form as he was used to them because of who his father was. He was always chosen to be her date, even though there was no romantic feeling between them.

Tamantha placed her hand on his shoulder and her other hand in his hand. Her arms were gloved up to the elbow in white silk. He put his other hand on the small of her back. She already knew the rumors were sparking that this was likely the boy she would marry, and they were probably right. Tamantha stared into Cole's brown eyes.

The princes and princesses, along with the queen, danced to the song dedicated to the Creator. The couples twirled with the queen in the middle with her Guardian. They moved in a circle around her, sticking with their dates. The ball gowns on the ladies shimmered with the ballroom lights. It was a dazzling show for anyone watching.

Tamantha took her eyes away from Cole's for a moment, her eyes caught on someone in the crowd. It was a familiar silver eyed man that she knew.

The dance finished, and the partners curtsied and bowed to each other. Tamantha and Cole returned to the safety of her Guardians. She saw the queen from the corner of her eye, making her rounds to greet her guests. She was still wearing the giant crown.

Tamantha halted when she found the familiar silver eyed

man lurking in the corner away from the rest of the crowd. Tamantha should have known Athan would have been here. He was King Bassett's friend after all, and he probably had some presence in the little queen's life.

Tamantha directed her group towards him. Athan had already been watching her from a distance. Elsabeth and Siberius made no comments on it. They were in a high formal mode and would not reject any of the princess's ideas unless it compromised her safety in anyway.

Athan bowed to his newfound friend, glancing at Tamantha's arm linked with Cole's. "Your Royal Highness, what a pleasure. I didn't think you would find me," Athan commented, not taking his eyes off the elbows.

"Of course. I enjoy our friendship, Athan. I was wondering if I would find you here. She is your friend's daughter after all," Tamantha mentioned.

"Yes, she is." Athan was still staring at the arms being linked. "Your Royal Highness, may I ask you for a dance?" Tamantha permitted it, taking his hand and leaving Cole by himself.

The next song began, and for some reason, Athan already knew how to do the dance. "Where did you learn?"

"They teach you in the Guardian Academy. It's supposed to help when our charges request us to dance with them, but I have none, now, do I?" Athan explained. Tamantha understood.

"I'm sorry about your friend's death, Athan, truly." Athan gave a weary smile.

"Thank you, Tamantha," Athan replied. "You look lovely as ever." Tamantha grinned.

"How sweet," Tamantha giggled.

"I thought his death would bring out my brother. He was just as close to King Bassett as I was. If he doesn't even come out of hiding for this, then something must be wrong. Something happened to him," Athan considered, obviously wishing his brother would just come home, even if it meant seeing him in chains.

Tamantha didn't know what to say and looked down at the floor, looking back up to see Athan's eyes fixed on hers. Silver meets ice blue. Athan was leaning forward.

Athan stopped, close to her face. "They are right about what they say." Tamantha felt her face burn bright red at the closeness. She felt herself being pulled away by a smaller hand.

"Thank you for the dance, Athan. There are more people who would like to dance with her royal highness," the blue haired girl told him, bowing for a brief moment. She brought Tamantha back to Siberius and Cole. The Guardians looked displeased. Cole was holding back his laughter.

"What?" She had a dazed look on her face. Cole couldn't stop himself and burst out in chuckles. Tamantha pursed her lips and glared at him. "What's so funny?"

"Oh, nothing," Cole hummed. There were a few ladies in the room eyeing the date of the Crown Princess.

"You should go dance with some of them, Cole," Tamantha suggested, sending him away for his rudeness. Tamantha turned her nose up.

A man cleared his throat behind her. Tamantha twirled around.

"Hello, my wonderful cousin," Crown Prince Cedrik hummed. He was practically breathing on her face. Tamantha blushed.

"Good evening, Cedrik," the princess replied.

"May I be accompanied by the most beautiful woman in the world for a dance?" Tamantha smiled sweetly, noticing the

Celaeno pride radiating from her cousin.

"Yes, you may, Cedrik," Tamantha responded, taking his hand. Siberius and Beth watched from the sidelines.

"You are astonishing, my dear. We never thought our cousin would become the future Queen of Sophia. You make our family proud. Well done," Cedrik commented. The two danced to the newest waltz.

"It wasn't an easy rise. I lost someone I loved," Tamantha muttered, averting her eyes to something else in the room.

"Yes, it was a tragedy that your brother was taken by the Lost One. That girl does the worst things to the kindest people," Cedrik reflected, taking Tamantha's hand and guiding her whirling in front of him. "You know, it's such a shame the two of us couldn't be together, or we would make the world quake at the might of us ruling our two countries together." Tamantha pursed her lips.

"I'm sorry, but that is the way things are," Tamantha replied, ending her dance with a curtsy. Cedrik grabbed her hand before she could walk away. He kissed the back of it.

"May we be together in our dreams." Cedrik left her standing there, baffled.

Tamantha returned to her pair of Guardians, already seeing Cole back. "Did someone alert the world of my mother's crazy plans?"

"I think it is the way it is. They all know you are coming closer to that age with no romantic prospects. I wouldn't be surprised if a few other men will try to dance with you," Beth commented.

"Don't leave my side, Cole," Tamantha requested, wrapping her arm around his elbow.

"But darling, the girls! I want to flirt with the girls," Cole whined. He needed to have fun. It was the first time he felt okay after Alessandra's death.

"Fine." Tamantha crossed her arms in front of her and pouted. Tamantha watched him immediately straighten up his posture. He was peering behind her, seeing something small but big. Tamantha turned around, curtsying when she saw who was in front of her, the star of the ball. "Your Majesty." Cole, Siberius, and Elsabeth followed her direction and bowed as well.

"Hello, Crown Princess Tamantha. Thank you for coming to my coronation. I hope you are enjoying yourself," the little queen stated. It was obviously scripted by the advisors.

"I am pleased your coronation went so well, Your Majesty. I hope your reign is long and prosperous," Tamantha said, giving a genuine smile. She worried for the small child, a country weighing down on her tiny shoulders. She knew everything would be okay though. Polemos was already prepared for this with systems in place to protect the monarchy and their rule.

"Thank you for your kind wishes. You are very pretty," Luvina giggled, blushing for being out of line. Tamantha bent down to her level, placing her hand on the girl's shoulder. She would have put it on top of her head, but there was a fairly large crown on her head blocking her from doing so.

"You are gorgeous and so much like your father, Your Majesty. Oh, the crown princess of Nous's son looks like he wants to have a dance with you. Why don't you go?" Tamantha suggested, watching the six-year old's face turn more red.

"But boys are yucky!"

"They won't be forever," Tamantha reminded, glancing at the men in the crowd. Athan had disappeared. "Just go and try to dance with him. It might be fun!" Luvina peeked at the Nous prince and clasped her hands together. Luvina's Guardians were approving of it.

"Okay!" Luvina sang, approaching the boy. He was

stammering and surprised. He was the same age as the little Queen, maybe a little older. Tamantha watched the two children dance together with the Nous prince accidentally stepping on the Queen's foot. She didn't mind. A child would still be a child.

"That was sweet of you," Beth commented, grinning at the princess's embarrassment. Tamantha just shook her head at her, making Beth return to Guardian duties. Tamantha set herself on a mission, to find Athan Wright in the ballroom full of strangers. It wasn't hard to find his set of eyes.

Tamantha glided across the floor, searching for the silver-eyed boy. She wanted to talk to him and tell him what her father said. He never called her on the telecrystal, so she didn't have his whisper. She felt eyes on her as she tried to see where he was.

Tamantha could see Cole in the distance, flirting with a Paideeia duchess and trying to get her to dance with him. The duchess giggled and responded to his flirting, but she was a little scared to dance with him. He was Tamantha's date after all, the one the herald called together with her. The duchess met the princess's eyes, asking for approval. Tamantha nodded, turning her attention back to her own goal. The duchess happily accepted Cole's request for a waltz.

The Guardians could sense what Tamantha was trying to do, restraining themselves from telling her it is a bad idea. The blue haired girl rolled her eyes, while Siberius held no expression on his face.

The curious girl stared at a door, leading out to the gardens. She walked towards it, prompting Siberius to talk into his telecrystal. Two other Merope Guardians appeared, more protection for the Crown Princess in case something happens outside. She picked up her dress, walking outside. People would notice her missing presence.

Athan was laying back on a fountain in the center of the gardens, staring up at the night sky. His suit was getting crinkled by his relaxed position.

Tamantha approached him, standing where he could see her. He sat up and cocked his head. "Are you following me, Your Royal Highness?" Athan questioned, smirking.

"Yes, I was looking for you. I wanted to talk to you," Tamantha mentioned, sitting down next to him. The Guardians had distanced themselves to give her privacy, but they were watching all entrances and exits to the garden and keeping a close eye on Athan.

"Well, shoot." Athan was staring into her ice blue eyes with the mesmerizing silver. She had to avert her eyes for a moment to stop herself from becoming lost.

"There are records for Athanasia in the library in the palace."

Athan looked stunned. "Did you open them? What do they say?" He was excited to finally find out something.

"I'm sorry. I couldn't. My father put a high priority seal on them. I can't even read it," Tamantha muttered, feeling sorry for not being able to help him.

"Why? What is so important about my mother to keep her a secret from the world?" Athan asked, more to himself than her.

"My father said you would have to find out on your own. He told me to stay out of it. I wish there was more I could do." Tamantha stared at her feet.

She was surprised when she felt arms around her. Her eyes were wide open, and the Guardians had obviously noticed, a couple of them itching to pull their swords out. "Thank you, Tamantha." Siberius put a hand up to make them relax.

Athan was only hugging her. What he did next made her skin turn red.

He kissed her on the cheek.

"You're welcome. If I can help anymore, I will gladly do so. My father is hiding something about it from me too, and my mother knows Athanasia somehow," Tamantha replied, trying to ignore the fact that he kissed her cheek. Athan was smiling, really smiling.

"And I will do my best to help you find the name of the Creator," Athan promised. He let go of her, sensing the danger of the pack of guard dogs. They were glaring at him. "I pissed them off I think."

"They're just doing their job. It's okay," Tamantha reassured him, giving her Guardians a look to back off. "I know at least that your mother is important if my mother and father won't tell me. We can find out things about her somehow. We just can't give up. I mean I told my mom to throw you in the bachelor pool, and she said no. Then she gladly added you when she heard about your mom."

"Bachelor pool?" Tamantha realized she had talked too much, putting her hand on her mouth.

"I, uh," Tamantha stuttered, trying to pretend she didn't say anything. Athan crossed his arms on his chest, grinning widely. She bit her lip, thinking of some kind of distraction.

"Tamantha, what does that mean?" Athan was laughing.

Tamantha took a deep breath. "My mother is gathering a list of suitors, and I added you to it. I think you're most likely one hundred percent Eklektos if my mother is giving you a chance." Athan's lip turned into a thin line.

"Well, then, I will do my best to win your heart," Athan joked, being more egged on by Tamantha's shyness. She put her face in her hands and groaned.

"Your Royal Highness, I think you should return to the ball.

I think some people will be missing you," Siberius called, gesturing to go back inside. Tamantha sighed, getting up from her seat on the fountain. Cole was standing at the door, looking at her.

"I'll see you around, Athan," Tamantha muttered, waving to the silver eyed boy.

Athan seemed lonely when she faded off in the distance, returning back to laying back on the fountain. The stars were shining tonight, and they now missed the faint glow that once occupied the seat next to him.

Chapter Nine

"Princess Tamantha drank my wife dry! I want justice for it! I want the world to know that she is a monster!" Tamantha stared at the image on the wall projected by one of the Blue Moon's telecrystal in the corner of the restaurant. The news was displayed on it. Wild eyes turned to her. She was confused why he was telling lies. One of her Guardians went over there and tapped it to play a different frequency. A comedy about an Eklektos and Anaxios married couple is now playing.

"Oh, for the love of the Creator!" Sara hissed, knowing the truth. Tamantha wanted to run. She didn't do it. Cadence died from other causes. She hadn't even asked Siberius what happened to the Anaxios.

"I don't know, Sara. I'm sure it will get fixed," Cole told the petite girl. Sara shook her head, downing her coffee.

"I'm late. I have a date!" Sara stood up from the booth.

"A date? With whom?" Tamantha chimed in, curious about her best friend's love life.

Sara hid her face behind her hair, almost squealing with delight. "Oh, he's this boy I met in my math class. He's really cute!

He's from Astrapi just like I am! He's the nephew of the President of Astrapi, and oh my Creator, I just can't get over him." Sara was giggling and in love. Tamantha smirked, happy that her friend might have found someone.

"I hope the date is wonderful!" Tamantha gave her friend a hug. "Go! You don't want to be any later!" Sara nodded, picking up her homework and throwing it in her book bag.

"I will make sure to tell you how it went." Sara ran out the door, looking back for a moment with a wide grin.

"It's so sweet how our babies grow up," Cole sobbed, faking it. Tamantha shook her head at him and sat back down, sipping her coffee. She had too much homework, but the news was starting to distract her. "I wonder what her brother thinks of him."

"If she's going, then he must have given him a chance," Tamantha commented. Beth was silent in the corner, focused on her homework. It was surprising she was taking school so seriously. Tamantha put her hand on Beth's book. "What did you want to be if you didn't become a Guardian?"

"I wanted to be a doctor," Beth quietly said, staring at the hand on her book.

"A notable career. Do you still want to do it?" Tamantha was honestly curious about what Beth really wanted. She was forced into the Guardian career by her mother.

"I do. If I could, I would go for it, but once you are a Guardian, you can't just quit. When the charge is in need of help and calls for us, the Guardian can sense it and has too much of an urge to save them," Beth explained, taking the book back and closing it.

"I think you should do it if it's what you really want to do. I won't be around forever, and I don't want you to regret your life." Tamantha opened up the book again. "I support you whole-heartedly." Beth bit her lip and tried to block her charge from seeing her tears. She used the sleeve of her jacket to wipe them away.

"Thank you," Beth whispered. Tamantha smiled, turning her attention to the big brother.

"What happened to Cadence, Siberius?"

"I received news about it, but I would rather you not be concerned with it until we figure it all out, Your Royal Highness," Siberius deflected, glancing at Athan who was doing his job as a waiter. Tamantha connected the dots. It probably had something to do with Clayton. She wasn't ill then. She was poisoned.

"Do you really think it was him again?" Siberius remained silent.

"Your Royal Highness, while we were away at the funeral and the coronation, someone broke into the archives. A file was stolen," Siberius was trying to change the topic. He probably just made it worse.

"A file? You don't mean the one I asked about?" Tamantha questioned. Cole raised an eyebrow.

"What file?" Cole wanted in on the conversation.

"I was researching something for Athan. I didn't find anything though," Tamantha muttered, biting the end of her pen.

"Yes, Your Royal Highness. That file has gone missing. The General hasn't notified the King yet, and she's waiting till more information comes up. It has to be a staff member, a Guardian, a guard, a maid. We don't know yet. All people who were working in the palace that day are under investigation." Siberius was relaying all this information.

"And if you can tell me so much about this, why can't you tell me what happened to my partner?" Tamantha was a little pissed that things were being kept from her.

"The Queen has asked the General to keep you out of it,"

Siberius mentioned. Tamantha wasn't really shocked. "I think the Queen had an idea that this might happen." He nudged towards the crystal in the corner. The Eklektos and Anaxios couple were fighting about why they don't just use the Anaxios to feed on the full moon, since it would be much cheaper. "She wants to handle the press release about the details."

Tamantha shook her head, turning her attention the silver eyed boy. Someone had taken the file about his mother. It has to be someone who knew about their conversations or someone who knows Athanasia Wright. She wouldn't tell Athan, not yet anyways.

"By the way, Tamantha, I got a very interesting letter from your mother. I haven't opened it yet," Cole stated, waving an envelope around. He wanted to take the conversation off of the boy related to his girlfriend's killer.

"Don't open it. I swear it's junk mail," Tamantha announced, trying to snatch it from him. He was too tall for her to reach it from him. Beth covered her mouth to hide the laughter, causing the princess to glare at her.

"To Cole Baldwin, son of that one guy on a plush seat," Cole began to read. Tamantha looked around the room, hoping no one is listening in. He ripped the envelope open as loud as he could. "Dear Cole Baldwin, I cordially would like to announce that you are eligible to court the Crown Princess, Tammy." Cole winked at her. She groaned.

"Please don't read anymore," Tamantha begged, too embarrassed for him to go on. She could see Siberius was enjoying it.

"My daughter is at the age where she is ready for someone to take her hand in marriage. I hope that she will find love in you," Cole read on. "You were right. It's junk mail." Tamantha nodded quickly, still trying to take it from him. "Tamantha, will you marry me?"

"No." Tamantha had the letter in her hands and started making a run for it.

"Oh, my Creator! That woman just stole my mail! That's a federal offense!" Cole yelled. Tamantha didn't look back. She gasped when she met with silver eyes.

Athan took the letter from her hands and returned it to Cole. "I received the same letter." Cole did not look happy about that.

"Let the best man win," Cole challenged. Tamantha put her hands in her face.

"Oh, Creator," Tamantha huffed, leaving the Blue Moon without a word. Siberius and another Guardian were behind her, along with Thomas, the extra guard.

Beth ran out, still stuffing her bag. "Give me a little more time, Your Royal Highness."

"Sorry, I was busy trying to not die from my mother's pushiness."

Tamantha stared up at the giant tree in the middle of the university. She wondered what Nolan would think about this. He'd probably tease her and tell her to ignore her mother. He would want her to be living her life.

She also reflected on what Alessandra would think about the position her mother forced her to be in. She might have to marry Alessandra's boyfriend. Would she have approved?

She didn't notice she was on her knees. She didn't notice the tears falling.

Tamantha sat on her bed, staring at the projection from Beth's telecrystal on the wall. She could hear the telecrystals humming and clicking. There was glowing and flashes of light in the background. It was a press conference, signed off by her mother.

"On the fifth of Thargelion, Crown Princess Tamantha's partner passed away. We have done our investigations and done an autopsy on Cadence Oscar. A blood test was run, and it concluded that she was poisoned shortly before she arrived at the place of her royal highness's residence. The propaganda that her royal highness fed from the partner and drained her is untrue. The palace is in the process of compensating the Oscar family for the loss of their wife and mother. We will answer any other questions in a short moment," the Speaker for the family announced.

Tamantha felt a little relieved, knowing she does not have to go out into the world and worry someone will think the wrong thing. There will most likely be people who think it is a cover up, but at least the truth is out.

"We have determined who poisoned Cadence Oscar. As many of you may remember, her royal highness was attacked in the beginning of Elaphebolion. We never released to the public the name of her attacker until we felt our own manhunt has come across no answers."

Tamantha put her hand over her mouth. It would solidify who they were after, and it would possibly put Athan into danger.

"The nephew of an Asterope Guardian by the name of Clayton Wright attacked her royal highness, and she was left unharmed. One of her Guardians was killed in the attempted assassination." His picture floated on the screen. His face made her remember the blood and holding Alessandra as she faded into the next life. She remembered the pain Cole faced and how close he came to giving up.

Tamantha was spooked when her telecrystal started glowing

and vibrating in her lap. Beth reached for it, but Tamantha already answered it even though it was an unknown whisper. "Hello?" Tamantha heard a crack in her own voice.

"Tamantha, I need help," the voice asked. Athan's face was looking back at her.

"Athan?" Tamantha wondered, glancing at the blue-haired girl standing over her. Beth tapped her own telecrystal and stopped the projection.

The voice took a deep sigh. "Tamantha." She felt her heart drop and pull back up again. "There's a bunch of angry people in the restaurant. They think I did it."

"Are you alright?" Tamantha worried for him.

"Yes, I am for now. Did my brother really do all this?"

"I'm sorry, Athan." Tamantha faltered. "Listen, I'm going to send some guards to help you, okay?" She motioned for Beth to let Siberius know. Beth moved quickly.

"Okay." Athan paused for a moment. She could hear his breath heaving. "He's never been like this. I can't believe any of it."

"Athan, sometimes the people we love are hiding the deepest secrets and are someone else completely," Tamantha comforted, not sure how to help him.

"He called me," Athan muttered. Tamantha's ice blue eyes widened.

"What?"

"He kept saying, 'I didn't do it. Please tell them it wasn't me.' How do you believe that when you watched him stab someone?" An object was hit on the other line.

"Why didn't you tell anyone about this?" Tamantha looked at the blue haired girl who was about to take the telecrystal from her.

Athan frowned as he stared back at her through the

telecrystal. "He's still my brother, and I feel like something is very wrong.

"I know," Tamantha whispered, laying back on her bed and staring up at the ceiling. She should feel angry and vengeful at the man who killed her best friend. All she could do is stay on the sidelines and let others figure it all out. She just wanted to know why.

"Tammy, we're sending some of the guards to help him. Please end the call," Beth pleaded.

"Did he tell you where he is?" Tamantha asked, trying to gather her own clues.

"No. Can't you guys track the whisper from the telecrystal? I can give it to Siberius. I just want him to come home."

"I will ask Siberius."

A door was opened and shut. "Hey, you guys. Thanks for coming. They're here, Tamantha."

Tamantha smiled with a sigh of relief. "Good."

"I will let you know when I'm safe. Thank you so much, Tammy. I really owe you," Athan praised. She felt a little sad when she heard the beep, signaling the call had ended.

"Tammy, until Clayton Wright is found, it's probably better for you to stay away from Athan," Beth explained with remorse. "It's for your own safety, Tammy. A lot of confused people will try to hurt him. We will have some guards assigned to protect him, but please do what I ask."

Tamantha agreed to it. He was a boy she barely knew. He was a boy who was related to the wrong person. He was the boy with the silver eyes.

"Silver eyes," Tamantha muttered, thinking deeply. Beth raised an eyebrow and sat down in front of the princess on her bed. "Do you think silver eyes are ever mentioned in written text?"

"I don't know. I've never heard of it, Tammy." Tamantha made a mental note to check out the archives. Surely that wouldn't be cheating. Athan's mother has silver eyes. Maybe it runs in the family.

Tamantha rubbed her finger on her telecrystal, thinking of phrases she could search for. She decided on silver eyes' historical presence. She traced the words on her telecrystal, getting a few pulls from the worldwide ink that are just made-up fiction and historical fiction.

She stopped on an article from the archives. The archives had been making things public as long as they do not compromise national security. She opened it

This was the only listing in the entire records with the words silver and eyes.

It was a letter written by a Merope princess, the one killed in the massacre that destroyed the Electra family. She had been married to the Crown Prince of Astrapi, who was the last survivor and the last known Electra.

"I found a reference to it," Tamantha said, looking at the woman still sitting on her bed. Beth crossed her arms on her chest. "A letter."

"Read it to me," Beth requested, humoring the princess for the moment.

"'My darling brother,'. It must be a letter to the King of Sophia, the one that went into a coma later into his reign." Beth moved her head up and down, listening intently. "'I hope everything is well at the palace and Sophia. I will come visit soon. I wanted to let you know that my husband has taken a mistress. This wench is a pretty little thing with brunette hair, but she has the strangest eyes. She has silver eyes.'" The two words were highlighted with yellow.

"Silver eyes like Athan's?" Beth was intrigued. Tamantha nodded.

"Clayton has them too." Tamantha continued. "'The woman has recently enchanted my husband and brought herself into the chamber we share as our marriage bed. I have expressed my dislikes about it to my mother-in-law, but she disregarded me. Even the other royal families are beneath this family. She said her son may take a mistress if he pleases, and I should know my place better.' The Electra family really kept up their reputation, even to a different family of the seven sisters."

"I wonder what they might be like today," Beth hummed.

"'This intruder seems to show signs that she is with child. I have yet to get pregnant by the Crown Prince, and he will not have me while the mistress continues to charm him. I fear he has already taken her as a second wife.'" Tamantha froze.

Here is the piece of history that everyone was looking for. If this mistress survived and indeed had married to the Crown Prince, the child would have been the heir to the throne. Silver eyes had never been heard of, and here is Athan with the same eyes as the mistress. His mother also shares the same eyes. There are no public records of Athanasia's parents.

"What if Athan is a descendant of the mistress? What if he's the missing King of Astrapi?" Tamantha asked out loud. Beth shook her head.

"He would have more obvious Electra Guardians hanging around him. We know the name and picture of our charges once we finish the Academy, even if there's no record of them. It just comes in our head. I don't think the President of Astrapi and the Electra Guardians would hide a hidden heir from the world," Beth remarked.

"Unless they choose not to follow them around and to protect them by not revealing who they are. Wouldn't the leaders of the seven families know who the Electras are? Is that what my father hid this information about Athanasia?" Tamantha put her telecrystal down and laid back. "I can't marry the heir to a throne, so he can't be that. Not unless his brother is the older one."

"I think you should just let it go for now, Tammy." Beth returned to her own bed and her homework, no longer interested in listening to the blonde hair girl's thought process.

Tamantha relented. She wanted to know more about this mistress. The woman might be the key to the mystery of the silver eyed boy.

Someone out there had the pieces of the puzzle in a file. The person had a dangerous piece of kindle in their lap, ready to set a fire with the records of Athanasia. Tamantha didn't notice when she had fallen asleep.

Chapter Ten

Lady Rosaleen Asterope was still absent, and the government of Polemos notified the Merope family that they demand that she be found and returned to her home country. The Sophian royal family had no idea where the missing daughter-in-law had gone off to, or at least Tamantha did not.

Polemos wanted to name Lady Rosaleen as the Crown Princess until Luvina had children of her own, but the Lady had not been seen since the funeral of Nolan Merope. Tamantha remembered the smell of roses emitted in the air when Rosaleen entered the Karavi that would take her from the funeral to wherever she went after. Tamantha watched from a distance as she flew off. The former Crown Princess did not look back at her in-laws.

The General of the Asterope Guardians had relayed to the General of the Merope Guardians that he had lost all contact with the Guardians of Rosaleen. They had completely disappeared off of the face of Atlantis.

Polemos had had enough of the lack of investigation into Rosaleen's whereabouts and blackmailed that they would publicize the Merope family's disregard for the deceased crown prince's wife. This was the advisors of the new Queen's doing.

Today would be Rosaleen's twenty-fifth birthday where she may be taken by the Lost One. If Rosaleen dies, Luvina has no heirs.

Tamantha expected her mother to know something. She set herself to visit her mother unexpectedly with no announcement of her arrival. Tamantha exited the karavi with three of her Guardians, and another karavi followed behind them with the rest of the Guardians.

She slammed her mother's lounge door open. The Guardians of the Queen were almost about to attack the intruder. "Take care of it," Clarisa muttered to her Guardian, not phased at all by the noise. He nodded and left the room. Tamantha wondered what that was about.

"Mother, if you know where Nolan's wife is, you need to tell someone because if you don't, Polemos might just start a war," Tamantha reminded. Clarisa sipped her tea and ignored her daughter. "Mom!" Tamantha approached her dearly beloved mother.

"Please escort my daughter to another room. She seems to think I don't know how to handle foreign affairs," Clarisa ordered. One of her four Guardians approached the princess. Siberius and Beth gladly put their hands on their swords. Clarisa's Guardians were not loyal to the General of Merope Guardians. They came from the Celaeno family and continued that after she wedded the King of Sophia.

"I would like to remind you, Your Majesty, but within the nation of Sophia, your Guardians do not have legislature over removing the Crown Princess elsewhere," Siberius chided, glancing at the foreign Guardians.

"Stand down," Clarisa sighed, standing up from the couch.

"Mother! Answer me! You know where Rosaleen Asterope is," Tamantha pleaded. She realized how dire the situation was with Polemos missing their stand in crown princess. If she even lived past twenty-five, anyways. Rosaleen was an Asterope after all. "The world wants to know where she is. Please, mama." Tamantha had never really cared about her sister-in-law, but she did worry for her.

"Alright," Clarisa relented, putting down her tea. Tamantha sat down on the couch next to her. "Nolan's wife is in a humble abode that she and Nolan purchased. They kept it hidden. It was their own little private getaway. She would go there whenever she had a miscarriage."

"Well, why hasn't she come out and talked to anyone? She didn't even attend her cousin's funeral!" Tamantha argued. She felt like something was very wrong, and her mother was probably the center of it.

"Lower your tone of voice, Tamantha Alexandria Merope! You need to treat your mother with respect. I don't care if you're the future Queen. I am the current Queen Consort," the blonde Queen scolded, refusing to speak anymore more till Tamantha calms down.

"I'm sorry, mother," Tamantha said through clinched teeth.

Beth was having a staring contest with one of the Queen's Guardians. She was winning.

"I was not going to tell you until it was sure or not," Clarisa began, watching her daughter's face. Tamantha stared at the teacup on the table. "Are you going to be reasonable now?"

Tamantha nodded. "Yes, mama."

Clarisa took Tamantha's hands into hers. "Rosaleen Asterope went into hiding because she is pregnant." Tamantha's eyes almost bulged out. "She is seven months pregnant. If this child is born, then you will be second in line for the throne, and Nolan's child would be the Crown Prince or Princess."

"Why would you hide this? Why would she hide this?" Tamantha questioned, squeezing her mother's hands.

"She doesn't know if she will pass the Test of the Lost One. She doesn't want the world to mourn the loss of a child that might not even be born."

"Isn't there procedures for this? If a woman reaches twenty-five, there's usually a team of doctors to rescue the baby if the mother doesn't live through the Test. As long as the baby is still alive and late enough into the pregnancy, there's a chance for the baby to make it," Tamantha reasoned.

"There are people who wouldn't want that baby to be born to protect your crown. We've employed a team to make sure the baby can be rescued if Rosaleen passes away," Clarisa explained. She was harboring something else, but Tamantha doubted she could get more out of her mother. Her mother was one of those people who wouldn't want someone to steal her daughter's crown. Her Celaeno pride was too much to let her stepson's child have it.

"You're not one of those people, are you, mom?" Tamantha looked at her with worried eyes. Clarisa smiled with a mask in place.

"As much as I want you to be the Queen, I would never harm a baby," Clarisa reassured her. Tamantha didn't believe her, but she could only trust her.

Tamantha calculated a plan in her head. She needed to find this getaway home and have her Guardians protect Rosaleen Asterope. She only had six hours to find her sister-in-law before the Test of the Lost One begins.

Tamantha left the lounge with a kiss to her mother's cheek,

knowing her mother could read Tamantha's ulterior motives. "Good luck, darling." Tamantha flinched, slamming the door. She stopped by her bedroom with her Guardians.

"Siberius, I think she's going to kill Rosaleen and probably the child as well. We need to find them," Tamantha requested, knowing it was a very dire situation.

"I could call my older sister. She was Nolan's Captain of the Guardians. She would know where it is," Siberius suggested, fetching out his telecrystal.

"You really think your mother would do something like that?" Beth questioned, brushing her blue hair back, intrigued by what the queen was really like.

Tamantha bit her lip, looking at the door and waiting for her mother's Guardian to interfere. No, her mother was giving her a challenge. Find Rosaleen Asterope and stop the murder that is likely to happen. Her mother would wage war if it would keep the crown on her daughter's head. Surely, she was not that evil? "I'm not sure, but we have to find Rosaleen," Tamantha whispered.

The princess felt like she was going to fall to the ground, never having to maneuver like this on her own. She was acting on her own, and her father would likely not know anything at all about Rosaleen. Perhaps he did, but not to the extent that he would want to interfere.

Siberius ended his call, sighing with despair. "My sister doesn't know. It was bought, but Nolan had never been to the house. She said to ask our mother," Siberius relayed.

"I'm going to speak with my father while you do that," Tamantha announced. Siberius and Tamantha separated to their own goals with the remaining Guardians staying with their charge. Beth's eyes shifted to her brother who went around a different corner.

"I hope he's able to get answers from the General." Beth wished her brother good luck in dealing with their strange mother. Beth stuck to the heels of Tamantha, unsure of what to believe.

The King's Guardians opened the doors for her, surprised to see her in the palace and not at the university. Tamantha's Guardians did not wait outside. They were going to stay close by her in case one of the Celaeno Guardians decide to "kidnap" her for the next six hours.

"Father, do you know where Rosaleen is?" Tamantha questioned. The king looked up from his piles of paperwork, his assistant sitting on the other couch to help sort through all of it. Alvyn dismissed him to leave for a few minutes.

"I do," he admitted, once those who should not hear were out of range.

"Do you know of Rosaleen's situation?"

"Yes, I know about it. I hope the pregnancy is successful. If it is, then I welcome the child to become the Crown Prince or Princess," he explained, not caring if his daughter or grandchild becomes the king or queen.

"So why aren't you protecting her? Why haven't you told Polemos?" Tamantha persisted, crossing her arms on her chest.

"I am letting your mother handle these foreign affairs. She will notify Polemos about Rosaleen once today is over. She will not cause a war to start, and you shouldn't meddle in it either," the king ordered.

"I don't think my mother will be taking care of it in the way you want."

"Your mother is not the kind of woman to harm a pregnant woman or the baby. You just have to trust her," the king continued. "Now, please go home, sweetie. I have work to do."

Tamantha groaned, leaving the king's private lounge.

Siberius was waiting outside. He raised an eyebrow when he saw the other Guardians still by her side. "You know protocol says that only the King's Guardians can be in the private lounge, even if Her Royal Highness goes in there," Siberius scolded his soldiers.

"We don't trust the Queen's Guardians right now, Siberius," Beth told her big brother. He understood that it was the wiser decision.

"Did you get the address, Siberius?" Tamantha asked, desperate to protect her brother's child.

Siberius nodded, holding a piece of paper with it written down. "The General was very reluctant to give it to me. She was worried the wrong hands could get it. I told her of your intent to protect Rosaleen. She said she couldn't dispense any guards to help as she does not want to go against the Queen's wishes. We are also not allowed to contact her Asterope Guardians as they are not under our jurisdiction."

"Let's go then."

The Guardians and Tamantha piled into the two karavi they came in. Tamantha stared off the side the whole flight there, fidgeting with her hands.

Nolan had promised her that she would never have to become the queen. He was going to allow her a normal life. She would be able to marry whomever she wanted. Was Nolan keeping his promise to her through this child? If the baby is born and lives, she would only be the spare and not the heir for the rest of her life.

Tamantha wasn't doing this for her own selfish gains. This was Nolan's child. He had his half-blood daughter, but this was also another piece of her brother that would roam the world with Nolan's features in their face. She reminded herself to go meet her niece soon. She had been sending letters and birthday cards, but she never saw the girl. She knew her father was still doing the same thing Nolan had done, providing for his only grandchild and making sure they're safe.

Tamantha didn't realize her hands were shaking until Beth grabbed them. Beth gave her a sweet smile to reassure the princess's nerves. The flight took almost six hours. They were wasting time. It was dark already.

The silver blonde haired girl hopped out of the karavi quickly, ignoring her troop of Guardians that were panicking because she was breaking protocol. Siberius grabbed her wrist to make her slow down.

Tamantha stared up at the house. It was a larger log cabin in the middle of nowhere. It was the perfect hiding place for a woman who wanted to protect her unborn child. It was raised up ten feet from the ground by large wooden beams. Siberius walked in front of her as they went up the stairs.

Siberius knocked, but there was no answer. He made the princess move a few feet back, kicking the door open. He walked in, searching the place for attackers. There were none.

Tamantha entered her brother's getaway home, noticing the unmade bed in one of the rooms. There was a piece of toast with jam left on a plate at least a few hours old. Someone had moved Rosaleen, and her Guardians were with her, surely.

"Where is she?! Damn it!" Tamantha cried out, kicking a bottle left on the floor. "My mother must have sent her somewhere else, where the baby could be delivered safely, or at least, somewhere it is all a ruse."

Siberius was already on the telecrystal, demanding his mother to tell him where Rosaleen was moved to.

Beth walked around the cabin, looking through the room. She saw one decorated as a nursery. Tamantha saw it too. Rosaleen was planning to raise the child out here, where she could keep him or her safe, but if that was true, then did she want to reveal the child's parentage to Sophia? Did she want the child to become the Crown Prince or Crown Princess? Rosaleen probably wanted to protect the baby from the enemies who would gladly keep the Silver Oath ring on Tamantha's finger.

The princess began to turn that ring around constantly on her finger. She had only had minutes left until Rosaleen's Test. She had failed to find the woman and protect her. Tamantha screamed out in frustration.

"My mother doesn't know where Rosaleen is. The Queen kept it a secret from the General, even though the baby is to be under Merope protection. Tamantha, I'm sorry," Siberius relayed, watching the princess fall apart in front of him.

"Nolan's baby! My mother will do anything to keep me as the future queen! Anything! Everyone keeps telling me that she would never harm a pregnant woman and the unborn baby, but this is my mother we're talking about! That Celaeno pride is enough to murder anyone who stands in her way!" Tamantha ranted. She picked up the plate of toast and threw it at the wall. Siberius grabbed her and put his arms around her to make her calm down. The other Guardians just watched, unsure what to do about the maniacal princess.

A grandfather clock in the corner of the room struck ten in the evening. The Test had begun. Tamantha couldn't do anything to save Rosaleen. She could only hope the Asterope Guardians would wise up and protect their charge in case her mother sent an assassin.

Siberius let Tamantha go, allowing her to be free. She slid down next to the grandfather clock, listening to the constant clicking of the second hand movement. She didn't know what to do. She put her hands in her face.

"The General tried to contact Rosaleen's Guardians as well as the General of the Asterope Guardians. Rosaleen's Guardians hushed up about where she was, and they apparently have not been reporting to their General all this time," Siberius explained. Tamantha didn't know what to say. The clicking of the clock was thrumming against her head. She wanted to break it.

"Perhaps we should try to locate her telecrystal," an older Guardian stated. His name was Isaac, and he had been connected to Tamantha since she was two years old. He held a slight grudge against Siberius for taking the title of Captain, but he knew it was futile. Parentage meant a lot when a person was in this field of work.

"The General said if she did so, it would break treaty with the Asterope Guardians of Rosaleen. They had a contract when she married Nolan that the Merope Guardians are not allowed to track her. They determined they would handle her on their own. Asterope Guardians are stubborn after all. They're just as prideful as a Celaeno. They are too proud of their military skills."

"Well, wouldn't they be cautious when dealing with the Queen of Sophia? They can't be too trusting of her," Beth questioned.

"I'm sure they're being extra careful with anything Her Majesty has been doing about Rosaleen, but no one knows the true nature of the Queen unless you are close to her," Siberius mulled over. Tamantha stood up and put her fingers behind the grandfather clock, tired of its annoying ticks. "Tamantha, what are you doing?"

"Shut up," the princess hissed. She pushed it down on the ground, cracking the glass of it. Siberius pulled her by her wrist, so she doesn't get hit by it on accident. She yanked her arm away from him. She kneeled down next to it, still hearing the clicks. She found the source of the ticking behind the face of the clock. She ripped it out, feeling it vibrate every second in her hands. Tamantha calmly walked over to the window, opening it and throwing it out.

"Have you lost your mind?" Beth wondered, standing next to her charge.

"A little bit. My brother's heir is probably dead, and even though I'm the Crown Princess, I couldn't do anything to stop it," Tamantha muttered, staring out into the darkness that surrounded Nolan and Rosaleen's cabin.

Tamantha's telecrystal began to glow after thirty minutes. She had remained quiet while the other Guardians conversed with themselves. There were no extra guards here, just six of her seven Guardians. One was off for the day.

Tamantha fished the telecrystal out of her jacket, muttering curses under her breath. Her heart skipped a beat when she saw it was her mother. She was hesitant to answer it, secretly hoping it would be good news and not bad news.

"Yes, mother?" Tamantha answered, feeling the watching eyes of the people who were always with her. She could see her mother taking a deep breath. The Queen had joint power with the King, unless the King dies, more than Tamantha does. Then the Celaeno woman would lose all power and just become the Queen Mother.

"I'm sorry, Tamantha. Rosaleen has fallen to the Test of the Lost One," Clarisa stated, not mentioning the child standing in her way of having a queen for a daughter. Clarisa was the youngest of her siblings and never thought she would have power beyond her small role as a princess of Thalassa. Then her marriage was arranged, and she became her oldest sister's equal.

"What about Nolan's baby?" Tamantha calmly asked, trying not to get hysterical over the first piece of information.

"They did the surgery to save the child. It was a boy. He did not make it," Clarisa replied. Tamantha could hear her taking a Queenly tone, straightening up and being formal.

"Did you kill him?"

Clarisa blatantly ignored her like she never heard the question. "I am sorry for the loss of this little one. I must inform Polemos about the whereabouts and death of Lady Rosaleen Asterope. For the record, this baby never existed, since it was stillborn."

"Mother! Did you plan for this? Answer me!" The Queen ended the call between them.

Chapter Eleven

Cole Baldwin dragged Tamantha to his parents, using her as a scapegoat. Tamantha noticed the odd looks she was getting from Cole's younger siblings. Cole has a younger brother who is only ten years old, and his sister is sixteen years old. The two were well tutored by their mother, who took pride in being married into the Baldwin family. The Baldwins used to have reign over a larger province within Sophia, but they have instead passed it on and took turns taking over the Symvoulio. The Baldwins made it their career to be elected to the Symvoulio.

"Are you going to marry my brother, Your Royal Highness?" Cole's little brother questioned, receiving giggles from their teenage sister. Tamantha raised an eyebrow. She looked over her shoulder at her best friend who was innocently pretending he had no idea what the little man was talking about.

"Your brother is icky! No way," Tamantha whispered, grinning at the young boy. Cole pursed his lips in frustration.

If Cole Baldwin married Tamantha Merope in the coming future, one of his siblings would have the task of becoming elected to the Symvoulio instead. There was never not a Symvoulio in the

Baldwin family, even if they weren't the head. It would be a long while before Leoline Baldwin retired from his political career.

If Cole is betrothed to the Crown Princess, the head of the Baldwin family would pass to his sister instead as Cole would become Cole Merope upon marriage into the royal family. The Merope family name was automatically assigned to whoever entered into the family, and they were stripped of their last name they were born with, man or woman.

Cole Baldwin was receiving a huge amount of pressure from his own family to accept the invitation to court the Crown Princess of Sophia. He, however, is not so happy about this particular situation as was Tamantha.

Tamantha was brought to the Baldwin mansion to appease his parents' wishes and to make it seem like he might go through with it.

Cole was still heavily wounded by Alessandra's death, and he didn't even want to consider a serious relationship with anyone. His flirting at the coronation ball with various women was an escape to get his mind off the woman he loved.

"Your Royal Highness, how lovely to see you. I'm off to a meeting with your father about transporting Lady Rosaleen's body back to Polemos to be buried in their family graveyard," Leoline announced. "I'm sorry about your sister-in-law's death. We did consider burying her with your family as she can be considered a Merope by marriage, but there was no fruit born from their relationship." Tamantha winced. Not even the Head of the Symvoulio knew about the son of Nolan that was lost.

Tamantha's mother had been sending little presents to Tamantha, such as dresses and dinners, the little things that she might like. Clarisa was trying to convince her only daughter that she had nothing to do with Rosaleen's death, and everything that happened was of natural causes. Tamantha would have to accept that until she finds answers of her own.

"I hope the meeting comes to a successful conclusion. I agree that the Lady Rosaleen should be buried in the Asterope graveyard in Polemos. The relationship between my brother and his wife never had any real love between them," Tamantha suggested, knowing her sister-in-law would probably want to be far away in her own homeland if she hadn't passed on to the next life yet.

"I'll let the King know about your opinion, Your Royal Highness. I hope to see you soon, my dear," Leoline regarded, bowing in respect to the royalty in his house. Tamantha bowed her head back at him, watching him leave out the front door.

Cole grabbed Tamantha's hand and took her upstairs. Tamantha had only brought four of her Guardians with her today, the Gagnon siblings, her oldest Guardian, and a female Guardian who had been around for a little longer than Siberius. Beth was by her side, while the others stayed downstairs and outside. The Baldwin mansion was well protected as Leoline did have power in Sophia as the Head of the Symvoulio.

Beth decided to stay outside of Cole's bedroom in the Baldwin mansion, leaving them to have a private conversation. Tamantha's Guardians were warned by the General to give any possible courtship some space to make their intentions known.

Cole's mother tried to follow the pair up to his bedroom, offering some tea and snacks, which Tamantha kindly refused. The woman had a sly smile on her face, hoping something would come of this meeting. She left them alone to their own devices.

Cole shut the door and locked it, laying back on his bed.

"How are you doing, Cole?" Tamantha wondered, sitting down next to him. Cole was staring up at the ceiling.

His mother had invited them both to lunch to con them into starting the courtship. She had probably been contacted several times by Clarisa Celaeno Merope to help initiate it.

"Alessandra? Okay, I guess. It hurts a lot. It's only been three months, you know," Cole answered, unknowingly letting out a sigh.

"Yes, Alessandra. I'm here for you, Cole," Tamantha comforted. Cole gave a fake grin, feeling uncomfortable about the missing piece. He didn't know how to feel about Elsabeth. She had replaced the job that Alessandra had of being her roommate in disguise. He would begrudgingly accept her new presence in their circle of friends.

"I wonder how Sara's date went." Cole sat up, looking for some juicy gossip.

"They apparently already are having their third date this weekend. It must be going well. Sara usually drops them after the first or second date. She must really like this guy," Tamantha answered, remembering the brunette's fondness for this new boy. She had giggled and told the princess every detail. "Davin hasn't found any girls yet. He said he cares about his studies more than stupid dating. I'm quoting that."

"Davin was never into any girls in the Academy either," Cole remarked, smirking reluctantly.

"Oh, he was. Back in those days, he was heavily in love with some girl he met when he went home for vacation one year. It was some girl in Astrapi. I don't think he ever tried to make contact with her though."

"I remember that," Cole snorted, probably having met the girl once. Tamantha never had that chance.

"We should find her and introduce them," Tamantha hummed, trying to pretend she wasn't looking at a picture of Cole and Alessandra.

"Sounds like fun. Let's not tell him and do it." Cole picked up his telecrystal to look for the face of the poor girl.

"I'm kidding! Sort of."

"I'm not," Cole replied, chuckling to himself as he whispered a message to the floating face on his telecrystal.

Tamantha shook her head, reminding herself to tell Sara to warn her twin brother of the coming storm.

"Hey, Tam," Cole called, not in a joking mood anymore.

"Yeah, Cole?"

"This courting thing, it wasn't your idea, right?" Cole questioned, sitting up and raising an eyebrow at her.

"No, it was my mother's. If you have any complaints, take it to the Queen," Tamantha retorted, shuffling her feet to browse around his room. She hadn't been in his room in the mansion very often. It was usually him coming to her in the palace when they were younger.

"I want to be your last resort, Tammy. If it comes to it, I will do it," Cole said. His face was serious.

"What? Cole, what? No, you're my best friend and like a brother. I will most likely find someone in this pack of suitors my mother laid out for me," Tamantha stated, fiddling with her fingers from worry.

"I know that, but if you don't pick anyone else, I'll be okay with becoming your fiancé and husband. I would rather you marry me than someone you barely even know."

Tamantha averted her eyes. "Thank you, Cole, but let's change the topic. I hate the idea of being forced into marrying just so there is more heirs and spares."

Cole happily agreed, moving on to things going on at the University.

Tamantha left the Baldwin mansion with a full stomach. Cole would hitch a ride in Tamantha's karavis back to the University. Cole's mother and his siblings were very vocal about the courtship and how much they looked forward to a wedding between them. Tamantha humbly agreed, not hoping to impede on their wishful thinking.

Cole slouched back, used to karavis like these to transport them. He had his own karavi, but he had left it back at the University to oblige with the Guardian's protective detail. They were on high alert until the murderer of his girlfriend was caught.

Tamantha had not seen or spoken to Athan, since Beth requested her to do so. It was in their best interest. She had been too occupied anyways with finding her sister-in-law safely, but that was over and done with. Tamantha would not attend the funeral for her as it was labeled a Polemos only affair. Rosaleen's role as former crown princess and widow of the late Prince Nolan made her less of a priority for nobles of Tamantha's stature to attend events for, even if it was Tamantha's brother's wife. Her mother had specifically declined any chance for her to pay respects to Rosaleen Asterope, making Tamantha more suspicious of Clarisa's involvement in the Lady's death.

"Your Royal Highness, Her Grace, Lady Christine wishes to have dinner with you and Lord Cole," Siberius announced, looking at the schedule for the princess's day. Her schedule was usually unoccupied since she was focused on being a student.

"Alright," Tamantha agreed, looking at her best friend for approval. He shrugged. He would go whether he likes it or not. His mother would be unhappy if he refused an invitation to dinner with the second in line to the throne. "It will have to be a light dinner. Lady Baldwin was too eager to show off her chef's cooking skills." Cole smirked while staring at his telecrystal. He knew how pushy his own mother was and how much she tried to please the royal family.

Cole's mother was not of noble blood. She came from a normal Eklektos family, but she was well taught in the formalities and rules needed to be the wife of the Head of the Symvoulio. Her mother-in-law had made sure of that.

"Siberius, I would like it if you took a day off soon. You've been working too hard and have not taken a vacation for months now," Tamantha commented. Siberius blushed. It wasn't really a request. The Guardians would work specific times of the day, morning, afternoon, or night and would have at least a day or two off every week. Beth happily went to the library on her own day off. She would be off again once they got to Christine's place, and a karavi would pick her up to bring her back to the university. Siberius, however, was working twelve hours a day every day.

"Yes, Your Royal Highness. I will arrange it for next weekend, alright?" Siberius relayed, knowing he was losing his mind over the stress of being Captain. He never realized his best friend would die, and the person he was charged with protecting would become the second most important person in Sophia. He was already being tutored in the hours when he wasn't working on what will be expected of him to become the future General of the Guardians.

The General didn't just handle protection of the royal family. He or she also leads the command of the military. Beth had expressed her wishes to not take this role, making Siberius the automatic chosen General. She would take the job if in the unlikely event, something happened to Siberius.

"Will we be having dinner at Christine's apartment?" Tamantha questioned. Siberius nodded.

"She said it will just be a small dinner between the three of you," Siberius answered, keeping his attention focused on his charge. The Guardian controlling the karavi was too focused on the path ahead, and Beth chose to daydream off the side of the karavi.

"Can't invite Sara and Davin, can we? Christine is one strange Merope. She must have been influenced by the dear queen," Cole said, receiving a one shoulder shrug from Tamantha.

"Christine has always been like that. They come from money, but it's the old money she prefers more," Tamantha replied, checking her telecrystal for what homework she needs to do later today. She needed to visit her dear cousin more often. She had the most in common with her cousin, sharing the title of Princess. According to Clarisa, Christine's father will be retiring his title of Duke to his daughter, making Christine the Duchess of Rosebury. Christine would be referred to as Her Grace instead of Her Highness when the title is passed onto her.

"She's too stiff. Why am I friends with her again?" Cole wondered out loud, earning a smack on the arm from his best friend.

"Because she has been your friend since you were in the Academy, and you know her better than that," Tamantha scolded. Cole raised his hands up in defense.

"Yes, Your Royal Highness," Cole sarcastically muttered. Siberius rolled his eyes. Cole's high priority clearance allowed him to speak to Tamantha however he wished.

Tamantha exited the karavi directly into the front door. The Guardians on duty made a barrier on both sides of the path in. Cole had his hands in pockets as he walked alongside her. Beth waved goodbye as she entered the karavi sent to pick her up. Tamantha winced when she saw the flash of a telecrystal and then another. The paparazzi had been able to locate her, probably hearing a whisper from a friend of Christine.

"Your Royal Highness, are you going to marry Lord Cole?" one of the reporters informally interviewed. The Guardians blocked them from passing into the path that they made.

Tamantha shyly waved to them, ignoring the incessant questions about her relationship with Cole. She was so glad once she made it to Christine's penthouse, being openly greeted by her dear cousin. Cole also participated in the hug, uninvited.

"You have some nosy people outside your building, Chris," Cole remarked, looking around the apartment. He hadn't been here yet and was interested to see what it was like to live by herself with only the occasional Guardians.

"Yes, I haven't seen so many in front of my building. It must be this lovely lady who brought them here," Christine commented, motioning to her darling cousin. Tamantha shook her head and walked over to the kitchen to see what the chef was cooking. "Did you ever contact your partner's husband, Tamantha? It must be so horrible for that family to find out their wife and mother was targeted and used in such a plot."

"I did meet with the family. I paid my respects to them in private. The husband apologized for what he said in the news, but nothing can replace her though. I feel terrible about what happened to her. I have no idea why all of this is happening."

Tamantha picked up the literature book on the counter that Christine was reading for one of her classes. It was a children's book about the origins of Prota.

Tamantha had read this book many times as a child, and she always tried to imagine what the ancient place once was like. She remembered the fear she felt when she heard that the Creator ripped the world apart and made the countries stand far apart.

Tamantha imagined the giant earthquake that must have happened as a result of the major calamity. The Creator was more powerful than any single person in all of existence. There are witches who can exercise a power similar, but none can achieve it. That was why She was treated as a God and worshipped. There were statues that imagined what she looked like. Any real artwork of her was on Prota, and the Creator had not made an appearance to allow people to draw from her image.

"Are you taking a children's literature class?" Tamantha asked, glossing through its contents.

"No, it's for my religious studies class. We're analyzing the stories passed down about how the Creator found Prota and what led to Her moving the lands and having oceans separate the countries."

Tamantha flicked to the back of the book. It was a before and after map of Atlantis. The before map showed one giant continent forming a circle around a central island. There were thousands of miles of ocean that separated Prota from the circular continent. The after map showed the six continents, or seven countries, that the seven families rule over, and Prota has disappeared into nothingness. Sophia was still merged with Astrapi, leading to many wars over the territorial boundaries of the two countries.

Prota was missing from the after map. It was just water where it once stood. There were many explorers and scientists who tried to locate it once again. There were stories of people who would venture out on a karavi to that very spot, only finding more ocean to travel through. Submarines were used to explore the ocean floor, looking for evidence of it. There were conspiracy theories that it vanished, or it was moved somewhere else, maybe the sky. Some people claimed to find it, but they were only making it up, disappointing the people who thought it might be real.

"So, are you courting yet?" Christine interrogated, looking back and forth at the red head and the blonde.

"No. I want to explore my options, but Cole has agreed to it," Tamantha remarked, putting down the children's book. Cole groaned about it, almost tired of hearing about it. "Aren't you supposed to be courting someone also, Chris?"

Christine blushed, not wanting the topic to be on her own possible men to choose from. Cole was not on her list of eligible bachelors. Tamantha's mother choosing Cole to be put into the pool made him intangible for anyone who wants him, unless Tamantha refuses to pursue him. The Queen was also orchestrating Christine's future betrothal. "Is there anyone else that you're interested in?"

"Yes, there is, but I haven't been able to see him lately," Tamantha replied, thinking about the silver eyes.

"Oh, is he cute? What's he like?"

"He is definitely very attractive. He's a graduate student at the university, and luckily, my mother is giving him a chance, although I was only half-joking about it. He's such a mystery to me, and it draws me in for some reason. I don't think Cole likes him." Tamantha raised her eyebrows at the red head.

Cole feigned a look of offense. "He seems nice. It's your relationship, Tamantha, and I will watch him like a hawk," Cole said, taking the stance of a big brother.

"Are you jealous, Cole?" Christine proposed, teasing him. Tamantha smirked.

"Why would I be jealous? I am too wonderful to compare to other men," Cole bragged, trying to show off. Tamantha snorted. She knew all the good and bad about Cole Baldwin. He was no better than anyone else in the pending courtships.

Tamantha sighed. She didn't want to be defined by her

relationships. She didn't want to be known as just a wife or a mother. She wanted to be her own person, and she was tired of being considered as a woman who needs to breed and continue the bloodline. She felt too young to really be even diving into these sorts of things. Her life wasn't going to be a love story. Her life was going to be a girl who went from princess to queen and how she will handle the role she was given.

"Let's move on to other things," Tamantha pleaded, sitting down at the dining table. The chef had finished making dinner. She knew she wasn't going to eat it all.

"Fine, fine. Are you going to spend the summer in Polemos? I heard you were invited to attend Queen Luvina's lessons to also learn about what it means to be a ruler." The group of young adults patiently waited for the Guardians to taste test the food for them. Christine trusted her employees, but precautions are always set in place. Siberius tasted Tamantha's plate first and then Cole's. Christine only had two Guardians on duty, and one of them did the poison check.

Luckily, Christine was rarely followed around by the Guardians assigned to her. Her rank was not high enough to constitute major funding into the guard detail. Half of the Guardians' pay was supplied by the royal family, while the rest is funded by Christine's father, the Duke of Rosebury. She was less likely to be the target of assassinations and kidnappings. There was a Guardian team prepared for situations that might happen, in order to rescue the one being attacked even though it is not their own charge. They are all part of the King's Guardians.

Guardians lose their powers when their charge dies, and they do not receive them till the charge is born. This fact makes the Wright twins very odd. She wondered if Athan had the quick speed like his brother. Clayton Wright had clearly been in touch with what the Guardians can do. She wondered if Athan was telling the truth.

"Tammy? Are you going to answer my question?" Christine spoke up, noticing the princess's mind was elsewhere.

"Yes, sorry, cousin. I will most likely spend the summer in Polemos. My father is insisting on it. He said it would be good for me and Sophia, and it can improve relations with Polemos after what happened recently," Tamantha answered, biting her lip of the true circumstances.

"Yes, it is such a tragedy. The poor Lady Rosaleen, her Asterope blood made it impossible for her to outlive the curse." Christine had no idea what happened and neither did Cole. The three nobles were alone in the dining room. The chef was in the kitchen, waiting for more orders.

"I think my mother killed her, or at least killed Rosaleen's unborn child," Tamantha conveyed, watching as Christine almost dropped her wine glass.

"What in the world do you mean?" Cole was shocked by this bit of news.

"Rosaleen was seven months pregnant with my brother's baby, his pureblooded heir, but with her chances of dying to the Test of the Lost One, the pregnancy was kept a secret. I didn't even find out till the day of Rosaleen's death." Tamantha dunked back one of the glasses of wine. "You know there's procedures for moments like that when an Eklektos woman is pregnant at the time of her twenty-fifth birthday, and the surgery almost never fails if the baby is far enough long. Those doctors would have been prepared. They would have had the equipment to keep the child alive. I think my mother sent her own Guardian to make sure he never drew his first breath."

"You think your mother killed the king's grandchild? Why

would she ever do that?" Christine gasped, aghast that the graceful queen had such an ugly side to her. She didn't have the pleasure of getting to know the real Clarisa.

"To keep my crown," Tamantha whispered, looking down at the half-finished dinner plate in front of her.

"We have to tell someone," Cole spoke, worried what other harm the queen can do.

"We can't. It's done. It could start a war if they found out what my mother did. It will be kept our little secret," Tamantha requested, giving pleading eyes to her two confidantes. Christine and Cole agreed with her, promising to keep it to themselves. She trusted these two the most with the royal secrets, and she knew they would never betray her.

"I am thinking about courting your friend, Davin," Christine announced. Tamantha almost spit out drink, while Cole was grinning wildly.

"Oh, I would love to see that. He's not of noble blood, you know? Did the queen approve of that?" Cole asked, laughing out loud.

"Yes, actually. She knows that he comes from money, and it would help bring more money to my family province of Rosebury. He seems to be educated in rules of the aristocracy at least," Christine commented, hiding her blushing.

"Well, I will have to let him know and give him some incentive to try to court you. Did he get a letter yet?" Tamantha clasped her hands together happily at the thought of Davin becoming a Duke.

"Your mother would be sending them out next week. He's rather handsome, isn't he?" Davin was definitely that. Davin, however, had an opinion about Lady Christine, believing her to be snobby. She was just a very proper lady with the title of Princess of Rosebury.

"If you say so," Cole coughed, getting tired after a long day of being out.

"We'll have to do this again sometime soon." The trio stood up from the table.

"Yes, I miss spending time with you like this. Let me know how it goes with Davin," Tamantha responded, hugging her cousin.

"Let me know how it goes with your mystery boy, Tammy. I hope you might be on his arm at your birthday ball in a couple months," Christine wished. Cole kissed the lady's hand goodbye, leaving with the princess to go back to the university.

Tamantha had forgotten that it would soon be her twentieth birthday, and it would be the religious ceremony that would give her a tattoo that she shared with all of her past lives. She wondered who she might have been before she came into this life as a princess.

Chapter Twelve

Tamantha Merope sighed out loud, trying to get the attention of her blue haired roommate. Siberius was off today, leaving Beth with the task of leading the Guardians and guards. She wanted to see her new friend again. She was tired of being forced to keep her distance away from him. She missed her conversations with the silver eyed boy.

"Captain, I would like to go to our favorite restaurant today! You either go with me, or I go alone," Tamantha announced, watching Beth's eyes almost bulge out.

"We told you it's best for you to keep distance from Athan Wright. I respectfully decline your request," Beth responded, hoping the princess would give up on the idea.

Tamantha put her coat on. It was cold outside, since it was wintertime. The month of Skirophorion was the end of the semester, and many students would go home to enjoy the break before the new year begins. She had already finished her finals and would go home today to her evil mother and her loving father. Her friends had already gone home for the break.

The queen filled Tamantha's schedule with princess duties of attending charities and aristocratic parties. She knew there was also planning for her own birthday ball to do. Her birthday was at the end of Hekatombaion, the first month of the year.

Tamantha wanted to take this small chance to see the boy she had been neglecting before she had to consume her mind in work.

"Tamantha, please. Listen to us," Beth scolded, noticing the princess had every intention to leave.

"Either you go with me, or I'm going alone," Tamantha hummed, sticking her tongue out as she opened the door of her dorm room. Beth gasped, unsure what to do. This was her first time actually running the show without Siberius hovering over her shoulder. Beth grabbed her own jacket. She called two other Guardians to join the princess's protection detail and also a guard or two, such as the weirdo Thomas. The rest of the Guardians were busy with security on campus.

"Why do you do this to me?" Beth begged, stuffing her hands in her pocket. Her sword belt was on the outside of her jacket. She wore a grey beanie over her blue hair. The princess was comfortably walking in sweats.

"It's the last day. I haven't spoken with him in a long time now," Tamantha said, plastering a frown on her face to coax Beth into believing it was okay.

The Blue Moon was almost empty when she went in. She had been avoiding this place, having her meals in her dorm or in other restaurants on campus. If she ever went to the Blue Moon, it would be arranged so Athan wasn't there at the same time.

Tamantha sat down in her usual booth, grinning happily to be back here. She felt her heart skip a beat when the tall and mysterious boy came out from the kitchen.

"Tamantha, I haven't seen you in a while. I was afraid I was never going to see you again," Athan commented, taking out his pen and paper to get her order.

"Don't tell Siberius we came here," Beth ordered the other two Guardians. Athan raised an eyebrow at Beth's words.

"They've been keeping me hostage and making me eat noodles for every meal," Tamantha joked. "How have you been? Are you doing anything this vacation?"

"No, I'm just going to spend my days here just working with what little customers we get. I have no family to go home to, and my uncle is too busy helping the new General of Polemos learn the ropes," Athan explained, obviously adjusted to his status of having no family.

"That's too bad. I'm going home and being forced to be busy, since my studies prevent me from actually doing princess business. My mother made sure that I will have appearances to stay relevant in society news."

"I hope it doesn't get too boring. I'm looking forward to the break. Even though I'm just staying here working, there will be barely anyone around, giving me plenty of time to work on my thesis for my graduate degree," Athan prided, happy to be almost done with college for the rest of his life.

"What are you going to do when you finish?"

"I'm going to either become a historian, an archivist, or a history teacher. I haven't completely decided yet," Athan stated, thinking deeply. Tamantha almost blushed at the image of Athan standing behind the desk in the archives, except she was imagining him in the work suit female archivist's wear. She waved that thought away. "Did you decide on your major yet?"

"I'm leaning towards history, political science, or Sophian literature. My mother is probably going to pick it for me anyways," Tamantha sighed. Athan smiled at the possibility of her joining the history major.

"History can be a fun one. It's amazing to watch how people handled things back in the old days and what we can learn from our ancestors," Athan commented. "You can never truly change the world unless you learn from history itself."

"Sounds like it would be perfect for someone who has to rule an entire country." Athan nodded quickly, understanding how much pressure she is under.

"Now what would you like to eat?"

"I'll just have my usual coffee and also a grilled cheese sandwich," Tamantha ordered, glancing at her Captain of the day. Beth ordered some soup and tea. Athan left to go submit the order.

Beth was staring at her charge. "Please tell me you don't intend to pursue a courtship with him, at least not till the hunt for Clayton Wright is done."

"I won't. Not yet anyways. I'm considering it though, but it's up to him," Tamantha admitted, glancing at the kitchen to catch a glimpse of him. Beth rolled her eyes.

The substitute captain was taking down notes for the karavi ride back home, organizing how they would do transportation home safely. She thought about recruiting the police force in the city to block off some roads, but it would cost a good sum of money to do so. They almost never interfere with city traffic to drive through the city, but Beth was young. It was her first time doing it.

Cole had sent her a picture of the beach in Thalassa. His family was spending the winter break in the summers of the lower hemisphere. He was probably bragging to Davin about all the girls he gets to see. He did just lose Alessandra just three months ago, but he needed those small moments to enjoy life.

Tamantha was going to happily stay away from the cold in the warm confines of the palace. The palace was sitting up higher on the mountains surrounding the capital, so snow did fall on the palace.

Athan returned with the food. Tamantha looked up from her telecrystal and thanked him. Beth took it and checked it for poison like usual.

"Don't you ever just feel that fear that you might die in the next second?" Athan wondered. Beth shook her head.

"If you had a charge too, you will feel this need to jump in front of a karavi for them if they need you to. The connection makes us feel good about protecting our charge, kind of like a drug," Beth explained, eating her own food. Athan understood. They had taught this to him when he was in the Guardian Academy. He just didn't know what it actually felt like to have that.

"Do you have your Guardian powers too, Athan?" Tamantha questioned. Beth was shocked. She hadn't been there when Alessandra died, so she didn't know what really happened outside of the reports.

"What do you mean, Tamantha?" Athan was confused by what she was saying.

"Clayton had his power. How else was he able to move so fast and beat the speed of a trained Guardian?" Tamantha asked, watching as Athan's face turned red with embarrassment.

"It's just like how I told you we never have had to feed. We have no charge, but somehow we inherited the powers of a Guardian. Guardians whose charge dies and Guardians whose charge isn't born yet don't have them, but Clayton and I do. I really don't know why," Athan confessed.

"So, you could duel with Beth right now and be on an equal level?" Tamantha challenged.

"Yes." Beth was shaking with anger at this fact. She had no idea someone so dangerous was so close to the princess.

"You don't use it, do you?"

"Rarely, unless it is an emergency," Athan told her, watching the blue haired Guardian almost about to burst. "Clayton and I made a promise to each other to never use it unless we needed to, but we both know how that ended."

"So why did you need my help?" Tamantha wondered, remembering Athan's panic when people started going after him because he has the same face as the picture put on the news.

"Well, I don't want to use those powers as they can do a lot of damage. I thought it would have been better to protect myself with the illusion of quantity. However, I got these powers, I only want to use it if I need to protect someone important to me. Like you," Athan whispered at the end. He smirked when he saw Tamantha blush.

Tamantha averted her eyes to the grilled cheese sandwich in front of her. "And I would gladly protect you with my own powers. You're a friend to me, and maybe someday that might be more. I want to settle the courtship once the situation is done and over with."

Athan's cheeks turned a little red with a shy smile. He raised his hand and scratched the back of his head. "So I hear your twentieth birthday is coming up? Who wouldn't hear about it?" It was true. The tabloids were speculating who was attending the birthday ball and what was being done to celebrate such a milestone in the Crown Princess of Sophia's life.

"Yes, my birthday is next month on the Seventeenth." Tamantha felt herself fidgeting. "I was actually wondering if you would be my escort at the party," Tamantha hummed, feeling her heart beating even faster, rushing blood to her face.

"Oh? I would have to let you know. It's a big job, you know. The princess's date? The paparazzi would go crazy," Athan mentioned, winking at her.

"That's great. I would advise you to say no," Beth sarcastically announced. Tamantha glared at her new best friend/roommate.

"Ignore my Guardian. She gets a little protective. Take all the time you want, Athan," Tamantha allowed, prepared to throw her sandwich at Beth. A little orange would look great with blue.

"I will let you know soon. When are you leaving for home?" Athan was genuinely interested, almost like he would miss her.

"Probably after I leave here. I can telecrystal you during the break. I probably won't have time due to my crazy mother."

Beth was scrawling madly on her notepad. She was messaging the other Guardians on the telecrystal about bringing the karavis to the front of the Blue Moon. The bags were already packed and ready to go.

"The karavis will be here in a few moments. Please finish up, Tamantha," Beth requested, making eye contact with the other two Guardians and the extra guards.

"Okay, Captain." Beth scoffed, tempted to leave the princess with no guards at all. "I hope I hear from you soon. I think it will be worth your time and would be fun," Tamantha tried to persuade. She paid for the food, leaving a tip for the conversation.

"I look forward to seeing you again when the winter break is over. I hope things might be solved by then," Athan replied, his silver eyes shining.

When Tamantha rose from the booth, he took her hand, receiving a harsh look from the Guardians. He bent down and raised it to his lips, kissing the knuckles of her small hand.

"Until next time," Athan whispered, letting go of her hand.

Tamantha looked over her shoulder as she left out the door

of the Blue Moon. He had already faded into the kitchen.

The other two Guardians had finally made their appearance, standing outside of the karavis that had been brought there. Anyone still left on the campus huddled around, staring at the protective detail. They hoped to get a closer glance at the princess who would someday rule over them. Tamantha waved to them and gave them a smile that mirrored her mother's.

Tamantha stepped onto the back karavi with two of the Guardians and the extra guards in the front karavi. Beth joined her in the back karavi, looking at her notes. The blue haired girl's telecrystal buzzed in her lap.

"He doesn't know how to take a vacation," Beth muttered, looking at the message.

"Siberius?" Tamantha suggested, knowing it was probably him.

"Yes, big brother is sending a bunch of reminders about transportation. He says no sirens," Beth read, scratching something out on her notebook. "Let's make this cavalry a little more discrete. Just two black karavis following each other. Most people will think it's just a government official." She relayed the details into her telecrystal to the other Guardians.

"Your Royal Highness, please put your seatbelt on," Tamantha's oldest Guardian reminded. She listened, grumbling about being ordered around.

"Tell Siberius the Crown Princess orders him to throw his telecrystal in the drawer and go relax," Tamantha said, looking over at the substitute Captain's telecrystal. Beth bobbled her head back and forth, probably already telling him to back off. Both of the karavis started up, heading on the road towards the palace.

"What is so intriguing about Athan Wright, Tammy?" Beth questioned, not sure if she could support the courtship. "He hid such a huge secret. He could easily kill you before we could even stop him."

"I know, but sometimes there are things you just can't help. I can't help having to feed since I was only four years old. I can't help that I have to rule Sophia someday. He can't help whatever is happening to him, but at least he uses self-control and doesn't use it to dangerous advantages," Tamantha explained, glancing out the window to the trees passing by the windows.

"He can, but his brother didn't. I wish we could find him already. The man disappeared in thin air. His money hasn't been used. There are no telecrystals connected to him. He just fell off the face of the earth," Beth summarized, having received information from her mother about the case. "Athan is a little attractive, isn't he? I'm kind of starting to see it."

Tamantha grinned. "It's not just his looks, you know. I really don't even know. The more I see him, the more I want to get know him." Tamantha stuck her tongue out as she thought about it. Beth patted Tamantha on the back.

"I get it." Beth began to giggle. Tamantha shrugged her off. "Really, I do. There was a girl in my Academy. I couldn't ever forget her. She was so wonderful, and one day she was gone."

"What do you mean?"

"We dated a little, and one day, she gave up on everything. She didn't want to be a Guardian anymore, and she asked me to come with her. I would have, but my mom would forever hound me if I did. She gave me one last kiss, and I never saw her again."

"I'm sorry, Beth," Tamantha offered.

Beth shook her blue hair. "No, it's fine. I'm sure she's happy where she went, and I'm happy for her."

Tamantha side hugged Beth as best as she could in the back of the karavi. "Are you taking a vacation at all this winter break?

You don't have to be my roommate in disguise till we get back to school."

"I was thinking about it. I might go to my family's cabin for a week," Beth thought out loud. Tamantha agreed.

"I'll arrange for you to take it before the new year. I'm sure Siberius can handle his little sister being gone for a week. He won't even take a real vacation himself," Tamantha remarked, snorting when she sees Beth telecrystal glow again.

"I would stop whispering him, but he's my brother and Captain. He has to be kept informed about every little thing," Beth noted.

"He will make a lovely General." Beth nodded. Siberius would be too busy worrying about his charge instead of taking care of his office work. "We should tell your mother. She would gladly scold Siberius," Tamantha laughed, almost serious about it.

"Mom, Sibie is doing it again! Make him stop!" Beth fake whined. The two girls heard a grunt from the oldest Guardian in the front, disappointed in their mocking.

"Have more respect for the Captain. He is just doing his job," the Guardian chided. They both hushed up.

Tamantha wondered what her darling mother was planning for her when she gets home. She hadn't seen the woman since Rosaleen's death. Tamantha had decided to stop mentioning it. There was no way of getting anything out of the queen. The queen would probably go over the invitations that might have been accepted by the pool of eligible bachelors, and she would be forced to make more decisions to narrow it down. She thought about Christine asking Davin about the courtship. Tamantha's dear cousin hadn't made any noise on her part of whether not he said yes.

Tamantha looked down at her telecrystal, swiping through

the faces for someone to annoy. She swallowed down the lump in her throat when she passed by her brother's face. He had no idea how much had happened. He probably has moved on to the next life with no care anymore about this life. He wouldn't have any memory of being Crown Prince Nolan, and he would be the person he was born to be.

Beth mumbled a curse when part of the road was being constructed on, forcing a detour around it. She gave orders to the other Guardian. Tamantha looked up from her private thoughts outside of the window. The Guardians veered right down a lesser known path, finding a way around the troublesome road block.

"Shit!" Beth screamed. Tamantha peeked to look at Beth, seeing another karavi making an impact on Beth's side. Tamantha watched the world spin around her outside of the karavi. She could hear the other two Guardians yelling in the front. She felt herself being held back by her seatbelt, seeing the sky at her feet, the ground at her feet, the sky at her feet. Tamantha's head slammed into the window on her side.

A young Nolan climbed up a tree in the courtyard, trying to reach for a kite that flew away. A little Tamantha was on the ground crying, pointing at the tree. The little boy grinned at his little sister, ready to impress her. He went too far and slipped from the tree, crashing to the ground. The little girl screamed as she watched his head fling forward, a loud snap heard. "Nolan!"

Tamantha cringed as she opened her eyes, looking through blood-soaked hair. She could smell smoke. She squirmed a little, trying to peel herself away from her seat. She could see the blue skies and trees at her feet. Her head was racking with pain.

Tamantha looked at her companion and Guardian. Beth was

completely unconscious. She was hunched over on the ceiling.

Tamantha made a soft whimper as she reached for her own belt buckle, groaning as she fell forward onto the ceiling.

The other two Guardians were still in the front seat. One was crushed in by the karavi that had crashed into them. Her oldest Guardians was half outside of the karavi. He apparently didn't put his seatbelt on. What a hypocrite.

She listened for anyone else outside of the karavi. The front karavi surely should have been here and rescued them all. She listened for sound, hearing the distinct sound of metal clashing together.

"What the hell do you think you're doing?!" her one other female Guardian yelled. Tamantha moaned in pain as she crawled to pull herself towards the window. She pulled herself enough not to be seen.

A weak scream escaped the princess's mouth as she watched the Guardian fall down to the ground, out cold. Her breath hitched as she tried to control herself and not make another sound. She searched around with her eyes, looking for the other extra guards. They were slumped up against a tree.

She turned around to nudge Beth with her foot. Beth wouldn't wake up. Tamantha bit her lip, looking back out the window. Her eyes met with silver.

"Athan?" she whispered.

The man with silver eyes grabbed her, dragging her out of the karavi. She winced as she felt broken glass drag against her skin. "Hello, princess."

Tamantha lost consciousness again, succumbing to the stabbing pain in her head.

Chapter Thirteen

Tamantha woke up from her deep sleep, watching things come together around her. She didn't know where she was, remembering the last moments before she came here. She remembered the silver eyes she had grown so fond of, but something seemed different about them. They were darker somehow.

She felt a wave of nausea, feeling dizzy from the throbbing in her head. She was on a chair with her hand tied behind her back. She wanted to slump forward to make it go away.

She could hear a telecrystal vibrating in the background. It was probably the Guardians trying to track her by locating the telecrystal. Guardians may know when their charge is in trouble, but they don't have a built-in locating system in their body.

The said kidnapper grabbed the telecrystal, smashing it on the ground and shattering it to pieces.

Tamantha looked at him through her platinum blonde hair, noticing how red it had turned. It wasn't Athan.

"You're awake. Oh, good," the twin of Athan announced, sitting down in front of her.

"What the," Tamantha hissed, but he grabbed her cheeks with one hand.

"Quiet. Be a good little princess," he ordered, letting go. The pain sunk in some more. Tamantha tried to keep her eyes open.

Tamantha felt a giant hand clash with her cheek. Her chair fell to the side, bringing her with it. The same hand stopped her from hitting the ground, bringing her back up right.

"I don't need you falling asleep. I have a lot of work to do before everything is ruined. I did kidnap the Crown Princess of Sophia after all. How has life been for you?"

"Why?" Tamantha muttered, feeling groggy again.

"Hey. Hey. Wake up." Clayton snapped his fingers at her.

Tamantha glared at him in her dazedness. "What do you want?"

"Revenge," Clayton responded. Tamantha raised an eyebrow.

"What do you need revenge for?" Tamantha moved her head to get her hair out of her face. It jolted her awake slightly.

"I will tell you in a moment I swear, but first, I would like to know how the months have been? How has my brother been? I called him once, but that was when I stole my captor's telecrystal."

Tamantha was confused. "Captor? What?" Wasn't she the one who got captured?

"I have been in some deep, dark basement, you know? Some kind man has been keeping me hostage in the basement. He said it was to protect me. Apparently, I did something," Clayton explained.

"Apparently? You killed my best friend, and you poisoned my partner!" Tamantha gritted through her teeth. She was trying not to yell. If she did, the head wound would probably cause her to fall into darkness again.

"See, the last thing I remember is serving drinks at that fancy welcome ball they had going on, and then, I woke up in that room. I never left it since, so even if I did kill your best friend, I definitely didn't poison anyone."

Tamantha shook her head. "No, you did all of it. I watched as you plunged a knife into her heart, and they found evidence that you were there in that woman's house."

"Well, I'm so sorry, but I don't remember any of that," Clayton denied. "Now how is my brother? Have you seen him lately?"

Tamantha was baffled by his audacity. "Your brother? I've seen him a lot. He's going to be the love of my life," she noted sarcastically.

"What a shame then when he finds out you're dead," Clayton retorted, making Tamantha's heart sink.

Clayton stood up from his seat, tracing an object on the table. He picked it up. It glinted in the moonlight, revealing it to be a knife.

"What did I ever do to you?" Tamantha argued.

"It's really a long story, and I'm not sure how much time I have to tell you." He sat back down on the chair, playing with the pointy end. The eyes he shared with his brother stared back into hers. He could see the fear. "You know I really never cared about you. I wouldn't have really given you the time of day, but I found myself in that basement. The man was very nice, really. Gave me something I've always wanted."

"Sounds lovely," Tamantha half-laughed, unsure of what he was looking for from her. Clayton gave a devious smile. She couldn't believe this was the brother of Athan Wright.

"I wish it was that simple," Athan's twin hummed, getting up again. He reached in the back pocket of his jeans. She just noticed his shirt was covered in blood.

"Did you kill any of them?" Tamantha wondered, worried her Guardians and friends were dead.

"No, I didn't have time for that. I was only after you anyways. Some blue haired girl did get up though. I had to slam her into the top of that overturned karavi. She put up a real fight," Clayton stated, watching Tamantha's face turn from worried to shocked. He sat back down with a piece of paper in his hands. "This is the proof I need. It's my reason for revenge."

"What?" Tamantha recognized it from the light that was shown through. It was a record. She had seen so many like them in the archive. "Where did you get that?"

"Again, it was the very nice man," Clayton casually blurted, tracing the words on the page with the knife. "He told me he stole it. He knocked some old broad out and found it. I had been looking everywhere for something like it."

"Who is this, um, very nice man?" Tamantha asked, hoping to find out in case she gets out of here.

"I'm not really sure. He wore a mask the whole time," Clayton answered honestly. Tamantha believed him. She didn't understand this whole plot, losing her mind over who assisted Clayton in escaping and helped him get to this moment.

"You should find out, so I can send him a thank you card." Tamantha gave a fake grin. The effort made her head hurt more. She leaned her head down to get the pain to stop. Clayton grabbed her shoulder and slammed back up right. "Ow."

"I'm not sorry." Clayton let go of her shoulder, putting the paper back in the hand. He shifted the knife back and forth. "Story time, okay? Stay awake, or I'll be using the knife on you."

Clayton was laughing maniacally. The time in the dark hole he was stored in must have driven him mad, causing him to lose all sanity if he had any.

"Alright. I had a mother once. Well, we all do in one way or another. Anyways, her name was Athanasia, and I had a dad. He died, as you may know," Clayton was rambling on. "Are you listening?"

Tamantha nodded in response to keep herself from getting hurt.

"I barely remember her really. I just remember she had the same eyes as me and Athan. She died one day mysteriously. I really had no idea why she did, and my uncle never could tell me why. Her death left Athan and me orphans. We were only eight years old, but with age, your memory fades."

Tamantha felt her eyes closing. She screamed when he plunged the knife into her leg. "You asshole!"

"That should wake you up a little bit." He left the knife in her leg until he would use it again.

"When my mother died, you were there," Clayton paused. Tamantha was barely listening because of a sharp object in her knee, but she heard that last part.

"No," she stammered.

"Yes," Clayton replied. "You and your father visited my mother that day, and when you left, she was gone forever. It says right here."

Clayton grabbed a lock of Tamantha's blonde hair, strumming his fingers through it. Tamantha grunted in response, trying to pull away.

"Would you like me to read it to you? It was written by your father," Clayton offered, wrapping his other hand around the handle of the knife. He was using force to push it down a little more. Tamantha could feel the tears running down her face. She didn't even notice she was crying. "Answer me!" Clayton got up in her face and yelled it.

"Fine! Yes!" Tamantha responded, wishing all of it would go away. She wished she could escape from the pain.

"Great! Let's start then." Clayton straightened up like an excited boy getting to hear his favorite story. "Ahem. 'Today, I brought Tamantha to Athanasia as she requested. She said it was very important that I do so, and I must comply to her wishes. She told me that she heard about Nolan's fall. She said what happened after had to do with my little girl. She promised to explain everything to me when I see her. Tamantha is only four years old. What could Athanasia want with my beloved Tammy?'"

Tamantha took a deep breath, ignoring the aches she felt from the knife wound and her head injury. "I don't even know, Clayton. Why does it matter if I was there? I was a little girl!"

"I know," Clayton muttered, putting his head on both of his hands with a moment, the paper still in the left one. "Let me continue. 'Athanasia spoke with Tamantha in private, saying that not even I could be there. I would have to trust Athanasia. Athanasia's little boy was also in there, the one who shared his name with her. I wish I knew what they were talking about. When Tamantha and Athan were led out of the room, I found Athanasia dead. There was no injuries or illness. She was just gone. I didn't even know it was possible.

"'Whatever happened in that room died with her memories. The boy came out with amnesia, and my baby fell right to sleep in my arms. My Guardians handled Athanasia's body, and I alerted the other families of her death. Whatever happened in that room led to her dying, and no one else was in there with them. I'm certain Athanasia has left a note somewhere of why it happened.'"

"It doesn't say I killed her," Tamantha hissed, trying to rip her hands from the rope tied tightly around her wrists.

"No, it doesn't, but you being there caused her to die.

Whatever you and my brother did caused my poor mother to leave Atlantis forever."

"We were four and eight years old! What in the love of Prota could we do!" Tamantha was trying to talk him out of this.

"Enough to get her killed. 'Athanasia spoke of a gift for Tamantha, and she was also giving a gift to her son as well. There was another boy, but he was not part of it as she said he was not needed for it. Athanasia must have used some special ritual on them as far as I can tell.' I can forgive my brother for it. He didn't know, and he still doesn't know."

"It still doesn't say I was the one who killed her!" Clayton slapped her across the face, and everything faded to black.

She awoke once again with him still sitting there, watching her.

"I should have used a little less Guardian power in that last one. Good morning, sweetheart," Clayton confessed. Tamantha could feel the blood trickle down the side of her mouth from the impact of his hand.

"Piss off," Tamantha groaned. She wanted to wake up from this nightmare.

"I know it doesn't make any sense at all to you. It doesn't say it was you, but I know it was you. You might have been four years old, but I still want to punish you. I, at least, want to punish your father for allowing that situation to happen. Tamantha, I'm so sorry you have to be here, but I have to do it," Clayton suggested, putting his hand around the handle of the knife again. He ripped it out of her knee. She screamed some more, feeling the warm sticky liquid spread all over her leg and down her foot, dripping to the floor.

"Please stop," Tamantha begged. The sobs escaped her. She was about to pass out from the agony again.

"It'll stop very soon, I swear." Tamantha knew what he meant by that. She begged the Creator to save her. She didn't want her life to be over like this. Nolan's image popped into her view.

"Big brother," Tamantha called, watching the figure through blurry eyes. She felt herself drifting off into sleep again.

Clayton placed his hand on her head, pressing his fingers into the head wound she got from the karavi accident. Tamantha shrieked some more, almost too far gone to even feel it anymore. "No, you can't die yet. You'll die when I say you can die." She gasped for air. "Are those Guardians ever going to find you? What worthless Guardians. They deserve for their charge to die."

"Don't," Tamantha pleaded, losing a grip on the world around her.

"Too late," Clayton whispered into her ear, blowing a little air into it. He took the knife he had been treasuring so dearly and thrust it into her stomach.

A squeaky gasp escaped from her. She looked down at the knife. She was going to die here.

Clayton brushed his hands along her cheek. "It's a shame you have to die."

A door slammed open, and Clayton was thrown against a wall. Tamantha looked at the savior with tired eyes. It had happened so fast that she couldn't even register it.

Tamantha felt her breath hitching, grasping for dear life, so the rescue hadn't been for nothing.

Blue eyes met with silver. It was the silver she had come to know for the last couple of months.

"Oh, my Creator! Tammy!" Athan cried out, approaching her.

"Welcome to the party, brother. I was just getting revenge for our dear mother. If you would please, I would like to finish the job," Clayton giggled, getting closer to the princess.

Athan slammed his hand into Clayton's throat, making Clayton's head collide with brick wall. It was enough to knock him out. Athan would deal with him later.

Athan untied Tamantha's wrists. He caught her as she fell forward. He gently picked her up in his arms. He could hear gasps for dear life. Her hands instinctively grasped for the knife in her stomach. "No, don't pull it out yet," he sweetly whispered. He carried her out of the room to the outside.

There was no one outside as he kneeled down onto the front yard with her body. He reached into his pocket, whispering to his telecrystal. Whoever it was answered, but he didn't say anything to them.

"Tammy, don't die. Don't die. You're going to be fine." She had lost so much blood already. She weakly squeezed his hands, feeling the life fade out of her. She had no words left in her.

All she saw was the night sky above her, the stars shimmering. There were no sky beings tonight.

She could hear Athan calling out her name, his voice was disappearing into the background. She wondered where she would go after this. She wondered what her name would be. She wondered if she met her soul mate in this life, if she will meet them in the next.

She could see Nolan above her, smiling.

The person on the telecrystal ordered Athan to do something. Tamantha didn't hear what. Her eyes closed for a second or two or three. She opened them again, wondering how long it was when the world went dark.

Tamantha's eyes bulged when she felt the blade be slowly pulled out of her. Her mind drifted to the boy whose lap she was laying on. She watched as he sliced his own hand open. He put the knife down on the ground, covering her stomach with the hand he didn't cut.

Athan put his hand to her lips. Instinct took over as she reached out for the hand. She grasped it weakly, putting it to her mouth, feeling his blood trickle into her mouth. She had never drunken from another Eklektos. It had only been Anaxios as they were the better choice of food.

The warmth of the blood gave life to her parched throat. She greedily sucked on the hand. "That's it, Tammy. Drink it. Beth and Siberius will be here soon," Athan mentioned, scanning her body for wounds. He felt disappointed in his brother. He wanted to do so much more to Clayton, but she needed him here.

Tamantha moaned in delight at the delicious liquid. She could feel her own body reacting to the source of replenishment, slowly healing the wounds she had received under the care of his twin.

Eklektos have always been the slowest healers, slower than Anaxios even, but with blood, they can heal almost as fast as a Guardian. Tamantha would need a little more than just this to recover from these injuries, however. It would take more time than anything.

Tamantha stopped drinking when she couldn't take in anymore, gasping for air as she let go of his hand.

"Athan?" she sluggishly whispered.

"It's okay. Don't talk," Athan responded, still holding onto the gaping wound she had in her stomach.

"Thank you," she muttered, drifting off into sleep. She could hear Athan calling her name, afraid she wouldn't wake up from it.

Chapter Fourteen

Tamantha opened her eyes to the familiar ceilings of her bedroom. She squinted her eyes at the bright light, feeling her head throb. She looked around the room, recognizing her furniture from the palace. She took a deep sigh of relief.

She was safe and alive, somehow. She lifted her hands to look at them, seeing little pieces of bandaging along her arms from the scratches she received from being violently taken from the karavi. An IV was in her arm, keeping her hydrated.

It wasn't just a dream. She had been kidnapped and tortured for one man's intent on revenge for something she can't even remember. She wondered if they caught Clayton. She wondered what happened to Athan afterwards. She wondered if Beth and her Guardians were okay.

Tamantha closed her ice blue eyes, trying to fight back the burning fear that he would be there in her room. Is he watching her and ready to strike again? She flinched when she felt someone grab her hand, snatching it back.

"Tammy? It's okay," Siberius whispered. She felt herself breathe deeply, feeling panic. She opened her eyes to make sure it was really him. She couldn't hold back the tears when she realized it was her faithful Guardian that had been with her for so many years. She let out a weak cry, unable to lift herself up, so she can hug him and express her happiness to not be there in that room. "Shh, it's okay, Tamantha. It's just me." He brushed his fingers on the back of her hand and started holding it.

She wanted to ask if Beth was okay, if everyone was okay, what happened, but she couldn't open her mouth to say anything. She bit her lip and looked up at the ceiling, studying the designs of it. She stared at the ornate trim etched onto the beams to make the room more royal and formal.

"Would you like me to get your mother and father?" Siberius asked politely, not sure if she wants company. He knew the real princess. He knew how she liked to grieve in private and hide her pain away. He knew how careful she was with showing when she was scared or sick.

"No," she whispered in a raspy voice, swallowing back saliva because she didn't know how dry her throat was. "How long has it been?" She searched the face of her gentle Guardian. He was scared he would break her. She looked so fragile in that bed. She had sunk into the bed.

"A couple of days. You were out for a long time. They fixed you up, but you didn't wake up. The shock put you out for a little while," Siberius suggested. She could tell he was struggling not to go kill the one who did this to her. He felt like it was his fault because he couldn't be there to protect her.

"It's okay, Siberius. It's not your fault," Tamantha told him, trying to make him feel a little bit better. Siberius closed his mouth and sealed it shut. He didn't want her to know how much he wanted to change that he wasn't there to keep her from being in this situation. He should never have taken that vacation, and she would have been fine.

The Guardian and his charge stayed in silence for a while. She took deep breaths, thinking about every moment before she had fallen into this short coma. She thought about the laughter and gossip with Beth. She remembered the karavi turning, the karavi flipping, and her Guardians so vulnerable. She remembered being dragged away. She remembered waking up to see that face that resembled Athan so much. She remembered the pain and fear that she might never wake up. She remembered each stab wound.

Tamantha began to panic from the memories, whimpering and squeezing Siberius's hand tightly. "He's not here, Tamantha. He can't hurt you," Siberius calmed, letting her hold his hand as hard as she needed to.

Tamantha wanted to sit up and hide in her Guardian's arms. She wasn't sure if she could ever feel truly safe. "Why did he do that?"

"Bad people do bad things. There's no reason to ever hurt anyone, no matter what they think has been done," Siberius explained. Tamantha nodded, relaxing a little bit.

"I want to sleep, Siberius. I'll let you know when I want to see them. Don't tell them I woke up yet, okay?" Tamantha requested, falling back into the lull of the high dosage of pain killers. She didn't feel the pain now from everything, but she knew it would hurt later.

Siberius kept holding her hand till she fell back to sleep. He didn't leave her side once, resuming the role of her main protector and Guardian. He didn't tell her that he had been here since they found her in Athan's arms.

A little Tamantha nudged her brother on the ground. She began to shake his body, screaming his name. She cried and held him to herself. Her small body could barely hold him up. Her tears soaked the little boy's shirt. She didn't care about that stupid kite anymore. She just wanted Nolan to be okay.

Tamantha took a deep breath as she came back into the living world, grasping that she was here and not there in her dreams. It was dark now in her room, save for the lights on the IV and the cardiac monitor. She turned to the right to see Siberius sitting there, snoring away as he took a nap. She sat up as best as she could, grunting from the cramping feeling in the pit of her stomach. She was quiet as possible, so she wouldn't wake up her Guardian. It wouldn't take long for him to realize she was awake.

Tamantha was in her pajamas and not some hospital gown, probably at the request of her mother. They had to make the Crown Princess as comfortable as possible and not treat her like some commoner patient. She would be in a hospital room and not at home if she wasn't who she was.

She stared at the IV tube in her arm, tracing the wire down to the clamp on her finger, making sure she was still alive. She thought about ripping both off, but if she did, Siberius would know she was awake. The whole palace would know that she wasn't sleeping anymore.

The princess's fingers wrapped around the bottom of the hem of her shirt, pulling it up slightly. She bit back the gasp that was lurking in the throat, seeing the bandages wrapped around her stomach. She wanted to see the damage done. She wanted to see what might become a forever scar, a story of what she went through. She pushed the comforter down and pulled up her pant leg, seeing more white paper covering where he dug a knife into her leg. She scooted up the bed a little more, trying to figure out how to turn the heart monitor off that would tell the world that

Tamantha Merope was here to stay.

Siberius cleared his throat. Tamantha put a finger up to her mouth to tell him to hush. He gently nudged her to get back under the comforter, not letting her mess with the medical equipment.

"What happened, Siberius?" She would finally ask the questions she had been holding back. "Is Beth okay? The other Guardians?" Siberius smiled, happy to see she was letting down one of her barriers.

"Before I talk to you, I have to notify their majesties that you are awake, so I don't get scolded for withholding your status from them," Siberius reminded. He turned to his telecrystal, and he relayed the message to whoever would let her parents know.

Siberius put away the telecrystal when he was done, noticing how blue the princess's eyes were. He tried not to get lost in them. "Siberius?"

"Yes. My sister is okay. She broke her arm and a couple ribs, but other than that, she's okay. The rest of the Guardians are all alright, except for Jodie. She's still in the hospital, recovering from the beating she got. Those hired guards are fine also," Siberius explained. Tamantha nodded at the information.

"I'm glad Beth's okay. I was so worried that something might have happened to her, and let the Guardians know I hope they will be okay. Also, I want to send Jodie a get-well card and thank her," Tamantha replied, acting the role of the grateful princess, but Siberius could see the walls she was putting up. "What happened after I, um, you know?" She glanced down to her stomach for a moment, wondering how much it was going to hurt once the painkillers wore off.

"Well, Athan Wright found you. I'm trying to get the details out of him on how he found you, but he's been keeping silent. We can't really push him about it because he did save you. He called us because he knew there was a search team looking for you. It had been three hours since you were taken. We told him to give you blood when we heard him telling you not to die. We were there within a matter of minutes after he rescued you. The General sent a number of the king's Guardians with us, and those Guardians arrested Clayton. We took you back to the palace by ambulance, and the crown doctor was already there to treat you. Athan requested to go with you, but we could not allow him to do so. He got treatment for where he gave you blood after some of us escorted him to a hospital to get it stitched up."

Tamantha listened intently and did not interrupt at all, taking in all the details. She didn't want to ask questions about where Clayton was, and she didn't want to resolve why he said the things he said until she felt she was ready for that. As much as she wanted to know the truth from her father, she couldn't help but feel the panic rising up again whenever she thought about it.

"Your mother is in high hysterics right now because you were kidnapped and hurt. She has penalized a number of your Guardians and is settling punishments out for not properly protecting you. She won't even let any of them near you, right now. She let me because I wasn't there. However, the Queen has requested to suspend Beth's Guardianship without pay for as long as she sees fit. She deemed my sister unfit to protect you after her plans for transporting you back to the palace went awry. My mother is currently in a heated discussion with your mother about how to properly punish Beth for you getting kidnapped under her watch."

Tamantha bit her lip and tried to protest. She and Siberius both knew the blame would be put on Beth for the entirety of the situation. Somehow Clayton found them and successfully created the karavi accident that led to most of the Guardians being unconscious. Elsabeth was the designated captain while Siberius was on vacation. Her failure compromised Tamantha's safety, and it was going to be a heavy punishment on her for it.

"A handful of the king's Guardians are currently outside your door because your mother wants your Guardians to be dealt with until they can be allowed to resume their duty. She refuses to let any of them do their job."

Tamantha took a deep breath through her nose, waiting for her mother to barge in based on Siberius's description. "Do I have to deal with her?"

"Yes, Her Majesty has every right to care for her daughter," Siberius noted.

"Can I pretend to sleep or something?" Tamantha joked, giving a half-ass grin. He shook his head.

Siberius rose from his seat when he heard the door to Tamantha's bedroom open. Siberius bowed to the tall blonde woman. She waved him to straighten up. Clarisa sat down next to her little girl, brushing her fingers along Tamantha's face. "Are you okay? I was so worried about you, my darling. I wish you didn't have to go through that. Nobody gets to hurt my little girl," Clarisa hummed.

"I'm fine, Mama," Tamantha croaked, not realizing how much she wanted to feel loved. She couldn't hold it back, clinging onto her mother and crying onto her mother's shoulder. Clarisa just brushed the back of Tamantha's hair, letting the princess finally need her mother. Everything that happened to cause a rift between Tamantha and Clarisa was gone for this small moment. The princess's wails could be heard in the hallway.

Clarisa had never been needed by her daughter, not till now. "It's okay, darling. You're okay," Clarisa soothed, brushing her hand up and down Tamantha's back. Clarisa held Tamantha for as long as she needed to, being the mother that she should in that moment.

Tamantha calmed down, letting go of her mother. Clarisa handed Tamantha a handkerchief, feeling sorry for her daughter. She wished she could take the pain away. "I'm sorry, mama."

"No, it's alright." Clarisa softened because of her daughter being so scared and fragile.

"Please don't punish any of them. It's not their fault. I wish it didn't happen, but it's not their fault. I beg you, mama. Please don't punish my Guardians," Tamantha pleaded, asking her mother to do something for the first time. "Not even Beth." Clarisa took a deep breath as she straightened up her back. She shooed Siberius to another room. He did what he was told.

"Darling," Clarisa began, taking a strand of her daughter's hair. "There are procedures. Whenever a Guardian's charge is put into mortal danger and they are unable to save them, then the Guardian must be punished accordingly, even if it is not their fault." Tamantha stiffened.

"I don't care what procedures are. They are my Guardians. They are Merope Guardians, not the Celaeno's Guardians. I will discuss what will be done on my terms."

Clarisa smiled, and Tamantha wondered if she was hiding her anger over being defied by her daughter. "It's about time you started acting like a princess," Clarisa surprised the princess. "I will say as an advice from a queen, you must give some form of punishment for what happened. It won't be as severe as I was planning, but there must be repercussions. You could have died, Tamantha."

"I know, mama." She felt sleepy again, relaxing back into her pillows.

The doors were opened again to bring in another visitor.

Tamantha had a sloppy grin on her face. The visitor sat down on the other side of the bed, instantly holding her hand. "My baby."

"Hi, dad," Tamantha answered, feeling the pain killers slowly taking over her consciousness.

"I was worried about you, Tam. I was afraid I would lose you too," her father comforted. "I love you so much, Tammy." He kissed her forehead. Tamantha grunted in response, being taken by sleep once again as her parents lovingly watched the child they made together.

It was morning when she finally woke up. She was awoken by the doctor, coming to check on her injuries and see how they are.

"I wonder what was in that blood. These injuries are healing very nicely," the doctor commented. Was he talking about Athan?

"When I can leave the room, doc?" Tamantha asked, tired of the confines of her bedroom.

The doctor paused his inspection, looking up for a moment as if he could see inside his head. "Well, I can permit you to go outside, but I ask you to do so in a wheelchair. I'm not sure of what extent the leg injury might have impaired your ability to walk. I'd rather it would heal a little bit more before we test it out."

Siberius was in the corner reading a book on military strategy. "Siberius, let's go for a walk in the gardens," Tamantha called from across the room. He put down his book and approached the bed.

"I will be back tomorrow to check up on you. Have a lovely day, Your Royal Highness."

Tamantha waved at the doctor as he bowed. Siberius picked Tamantha up in his arms and gently put her down in a wheelchair that had come with all of the medical equipment.

"Thank you, Siberius. I need the breath of fresh air." Siberius wrapped a blanket around Tamantha since it was cold outside.

Her heart dropped a little when Siberius's words were confirmed. None of her Guardians were outside of her room, not even one.

"I want to stop by the General's office before we go back to my prison. I want to deal with this situation before my mother changes her mind," Tamantha requested, thinking about how to properly do it.

"Yes, Your Royal Highness."

Siberius wheeled Tamantha out into the gardens. She felt warm when she saw the white blanket covering the garden. The location allowed winter to truly happen on the grounds of the palace. "It's beautiful."

Tamantha stared at the big tree in the garden. She reflected on the small dream she had been having. It was a memory she had long forgotten. She had been too young to remember it, but the trauma she had been through in the last few days had brought it back to her.

Clayton had mentioned that same moment when he retold her father's accounts of Athanasia. She wondered where the rest of the file went if he only had that small piece. Did he have no idea the implications that Athanasia's folder contained?

The dreading panic raised up in her chest as Clayton's face came into her mind. Siberius placed a hand on her shoulder to calm her. He knew what she was thinking. It might have been his Guardian sense, the call for help when the charge is in trouble. The charge has no control over it.

She returned her thoughts to Nolan on the ground, only ten years old. The branch he fell from was way up high. "Did you know Nolan fell from that tree?"

"Are you serious?" Siberius questioned. The Guardians and

hired guards were outside, watching the fences and making sure no one sneaks over.

"Yeah, he fell down from it trying to get some stupid toy for me. I think he got hurt, but I can't remember. You didn't know about that?"

Siberius shook his head in response.

Her eyes drifted to the sky above them. "It's strange how it came back to me. The rest is a blur though. Something about that fall brought me to Athanasia. I need to ask my father about it. I need to know," Tamantha thought out loud.

"Don't push too far."

"I don't think he will be unable to answer if it's about Nolan," Tamantha commented, knowing her father has a soft spot for his children.

Tamantha stood up from her chair before Siberius realized it. "Your Royal Highness," Siberius warned. She hobbled over to the tree that had almost ended Nolan's life, placing her hand on it. She traced the grooves on it.

"Do you miss him?" Tamantha asked.

"I do. He was my closest friend."

Tamantha gave a half-hearted smile. "I miss him too." Tamantha hugged the blanket more to her body, finally feeling the nip of the icy air against her body. Her toes were sinking into the snow, curling with it. Her feet were freezing. "Let's go inside, Siberius."

Siberius didn't allow her to walk back to the wheelchair. He instead chose to carry her and put her back on it. He wheeled her back into the palace halls. She was relieved when she felt the toasty warm air blowing throughout her home. He took her in the opposite direction of her room, bringing her to the place she previously requested.

The General rose in the presence of Tamantha, kneeling in front of her. "Your Royal Highness. I was expecting you. Your mother told me she is giving the task of punishment to you." She rose after Tamantha greeted her.

"I wonder how much pain my Guardians are in. They're all suffering after I went missing. Siberius, what did you feel?" Tamantha wondered.

"Your Royal Highness, I'm not sure I should discuss that." Siberius looked to his mother for approval. The General nodded. "The call happens when our charge is in trouble, in physical danger. We feel it the entire time you're in distress. It burns in our body. There's an itch we can't scratch, and it gets worse the longer you are in peril. It doesn't stop till you are safe, and it flares up again when you begin to panic."

"So the Guardians can feel it when I think about what happened a couple days ago?"

"Yes. I can tell when you are going to have a panic attack because you put yourself back into that situation."

Tamantha turned back to the General who was watching the conversation. Tamantha wondered for a moment if the General had been friends with her father like this when they were younger. "It's been three or four days now since I was kidnapped?"

"Three days, yes," the General replied.

"I think my Guardians have been on a long enough suspension and should be allowed to return to work. As for Elsabeth, I would request that she be put on a week suspension without pay."

"I agree, Your Royal Highness. If her majesty had anything to say about it, they would have all been suspended for a month. I am glad you have decided to put your input for it. I will arrange for your Guardians to be put on schedule, and I will inform

Elsabeth about this arrangement," the General relayed.

"Also arrange for her to spend the suspension at your cabin please," Tamantha added, watching the General's expression change to confusion.

"It's supposed to be a punishment."

"It is. She has to be up there by herself to reflect on it. It was her first time making a mistake like this."

"You almost died," the General commented.

"I did, but I'm not dead. I'm here. It is what I feel would be the best way to punish Elsabeth for the lack of coordination. Did you ever figure out how Clayton found us? Did he tell you about the basement?" Tamantha questioned.

"He hasn't said a word to us. We will be bringing in someone to give him a truth serum. I honestly think it is someone who had knowledge about the transportation plans. What did he tell you?" the General interrogated informally.

"It was the person who stole the files on Athanasia. Whoever that was took Clayton away in the last couple months. The person deliberately used Clayton's love for his mother to make him go after me and get revenge. Something I really want to know is why I was there when Athanasia died. He seemed to think it was my fault." Tamantha gripped the wheelchair a little bit as she thought about the aftermath. Siberius grabbed her hand and held it.

"I was there that day, but I have no authority to give you information about it. That is up to his majesty."

"Do you know who Athanasia is? Who Athan and Clayton are the sons of?"

"Again, Your Royal Highness, your father is the only one who can tell you. I know every detail about the woman, but my lips are sealed," the General answered, feeling disheartened by the princess's disappointment.

"I understand," Tamantha sighed. "Is my father busy right now?"

"I'm afraid your father left early this morning on business. He is going to a discussion with the seven families about the reinforcement of the world peace treaty. I'm not sure when he will be back," the General stated. Tamantha groaned.

"His daughter gets stabbed a couple times, and he takes off on a business trip," Tamantha snorted. "Siberius, I'm tired again. Thank you, Neda, for having this talk with me. I hope to see my Guardians back on duty."

Tamantha shook the General's hand.

"One more thing, what happened to Nolan when I was four years old?"

The General almost dropped her cup of coffee. She was at a loss for words.

"It is what started all of this."

"Nolan snapped his neck after he fell from a tree. When we found both of you and saw this, we realized the injury was gone when we brought the doctor. That's all I can say, Your Royal Highness."

Chapter Fifteen

Tamantha was a little glad she almost died. It kept her in the palace away from the list of things her mother wanted her to do. The queen had complained enough about the princess shirking her duties at their dinners together. It was usually only the two of them, since her father had not returned. She wasn't sure if the king would even be back before she returned to school.

Discussions about the world peace treaty were long and always happened at the end of the year. They kept countries from initiating a war between them, and it set the standards for exports and imports.

Today was the last day of the year, and the palace was having a special party for the staff members and Guardians. Elsabeth was coming back on duty today, so the rest of the Guardians could enjoy the festivities. Siberius would take the day off as a request from his mother to enjoy himself. He practically never took a break since the incident, only to sleep and eat. The General was about to scold him for taking too many hours. He would still show up with his sword on.

A special caterer was hired. He was one of the finest chefs in

Sophia, well renowned and usually at the parties of aristocrats and celebrities. The royal household had first dibs on using him for tonight, and they rarely didn't use him.

"Your Royal Highness. Your Majesty." The chef kissed each on the back of their hands. "You both look stunning as always."

"Thank you, Kalvin. I hope your food is delicious like usual," Tamantha commented, wearing the same emotional mask as her mother. She is still tired from the injuries she received, and she had little energy for tonight. She would still join in the festivities though. It celebrated and thanked the staff members and protection for their service, and it showed hope for a new year.

Tamantha limped as she walked over to the head table. She had asked her friends to come, but they were all busy. Christine had her own party for her staff members at the mansion of the Duke of Rosebury. Cole's family was doing the same.

Sara and Davin were still at home with their father. Apparently, Sara brought home her new boyfriend and showed him off to her father. She must have taken a great liking to him, and her father seems to approve.

The staff began to pass by her table, bowing directly to her, and they thanked her for the party. It was a long process to get through all of them. Her mother stood at the end of the line, mingling with each one and giving them comments about their attire and well wishes about their families.

Tamantha chose not to wear a tiara. It pissed off the queen. Tamantha butted in that the day wasn't about them. It was about the people who worked for them. The queen huffed and threw her hands in the air over her daughter's stubbornness, muttering something about stupid mortal lovers. It didn't stop the queen from displaying her crown, marking her the ruler when the king is not here.

Siberius passed by the table, glancing at his sister who was in full regalia, standing behind Tamantha. "Your Royal Highness." Siberius bowed. He looked like he was about to start laughing at his sister. Elsabeth stood still, trying not to glare at her brother. She was on edge after what happened to their charge, and she was trying her best to remain professional to get back on the good side of the queen.

"Hello, Siberius. I hope you enjoy yourself tonight," Tamantha hummed, curtsying to him. He grinned, moving on in the line towards her majesty. "Beth, are you alright?"

Beth's arm was no longer in a sling. Guardians had superior healing, and her broken arm had already fixed itself, along with the ribs. "I'm fine, Your Royal Highness."

"Relax please," Tamantha requested, grabbing both of Elsabeth's hands. She squeezed them.

"I will. I'm really sorry," Elsabeth apologized again.

"No more. It's done, and you and I are both okay."

Tamantha continued greeting the maids and butlers, along with the gardeners and whatever else was necessary to maintain the main palace of the Merope family.

Sophia's royal family did not make money from taxes. They instead ventured into the business world, buying shares and running small companies. Taxes went to whatever was needed for Sophia to function as a world-renowned power, such as education, military, health care, and other government programs. It was important for the Merope family to be self-sustaining. It gains more respect from the citizens of Sophia for putting the country before themselves.

Tamantha would be taking a business class next semester as per the request from her father, so she can continue to sustain the family's companies.

The queen was not used to this aspect. Her own family had lived solely on taxes. When she first arrived as the bride of King Alvyn, she was aghast that none of the taxes went towards the royal family. She almost demanded it begin with the marriage, but she eventually quieted down, realizing how profitable their own companies were.

Tamantha had not told her mother that she also invited Athan Wright. He did not deny or accept it. He would have been spending this holiday alone as his uncle was all the way in Polemos, and his own brother is in jail. The General had not let Tamantha know about the progress they have made with interrogating Clayton. She suspected if Neda got wind of Athan's possible presence, the Gagnon mother would be asking him to assist in getting answers out of his brother.

Clarisa sat down at the head table in her seat as queen. Tamantha sat next to her in the king's chair, representing him. Clarisa nudged Tamantha to make a speech. Tamantha begrudgingly obliged and stood up.

Tamantha raised her glass for a toast, making the audience rise. "I'm so glad that you have all gathered here today, and I hope you all will enjoy this, the last day of the year. Tomorrow will bring a new year with new joys and new adventures to each and every one of you. We, the royal family, thank you all for your service and hope that life has been well for you in the old year. I, Crown Princess Tamantha Merope, know that this has been a hard year for all of us with the loss of my brother, the Crown Prince, Nolan Merope, and I wish that wherever he is, he is enjoying his new life to the fullest."

"May the Prince find a wonderful life," the audience chimed in, drinking to that. Tamantha also did so.

"Drink and feast. This day is yours as our thanks for all that you do," Tamantha ended, receiving cheers from the crowd. Everyone finished their glass and received the ordered meals in front of them. Tamantha sat down.

"Thank you for that lovely speech, Tamantha," Clarisa complimented, putting a comforting hand on her daughter's hand. Tamantha knew it was genuine. It had been Nolan making the same speech every year as the king was always away for the conference for the peace treaty, and her mother also did it when Nolan was too young.

The door opened, causing some heads to turn in the noisy dining hall. Tamantha grinned at the intrusion, leaving the table to greet him. "Athan," she called sweetly.

"Your Royal Highness," Athan kissed the back of her hand after bowing.

Tamantha guided him towards the table of the royal family. "Mother, this is Athan Wright, the man who saved me. I would like it if he could join us." Athan bowed before the queen. It was his first time meeting her formally.

Clarisa looked Athan up and down, noticing his less than fit attire for a visit to the palace. "Very well. Athan Wright, I would like to extend my gratitude for rescuing the crown princess from the clutches of the one who wished to harm her. I would like to award you for those efforts. Please sit."

"Your Majesty, thank you for granting me the chance to sit with you for dinner," Athan replied, sitting down on Tamantha's right-hand side. One of the caterer's waiters poured him a glass of wine and asked him what he would like to eat.

"It must be nice to be on the other side of the ordering. It's always me giving you my order," Tamantha joked, taking a bite of the food the chef is well known for.

Athan smiled, taking a sip of the red nectar. "It is nice to be served instead of the server. How are you, Your Royal Highness? Are you okay now?"

"I am thanks to you. My leg still hurts, but it's better now. I would probably be dead right now if you hadn't come to save me in time. I wish I had been able to thank you earlier," Tamantha stated, putting her hand on top of his and squeezing it lightly. She removed it quickly before her mother disapproved.

"I couldn't let him do that to you. They asked me if I knew where my brother was, and I asked them why they were bothering to ask me again after all this time. They told me he had kidnapped you. I was thinking about it, and I realized he took you to our mother's home," Athan explained, mulling over his glorious rescue of the princess of Sophia. "I couldn't bear to see you like that. I was scared you would die, and I'm glad to see you here alive."

"I'm sorry your brother did that. It must be hard for you to imagine he might be facing execution," Tamantha apologized, watching Athan's face fall.

"I know he will likely be judged harshly for his crimes. I wish I knew why he did it. I wish I could talk to him," Athan expressed, looking at the princess. The servants were not completely ignoring the presence of the man who saved their future queen, and some wondered what his role might be in the princess's future.

"I might be able to help with that, but we will have to discuss it after. It's a party. Let's enjoy it," Tamantha remarked, clinking her glass with his.

Clarisa chimed in, "Athan, I heard my daughter has given you an invitation to be her date to her birthday ball. It's such a large role. Have you decided?"

"I think I have, Your Majesty. I will accept," Athan

announced, peering over at Tamantha's shocked face. It caused him to smirk. "I'm not completely sure of the customs of a princess's twentieth birthday ceremony and ball, but I'm sure I can learn."

"Thank you, Athan," Tamantha whispered softly, glancing down at her plate of food. "I would be glad to have you as my escort for my twentieth birthday." Tamantha smiled gently, averting her eyes with shyness.

"Athan, I was wondering what your thoughts are on courting my daughter. Of course, there are better choices, such as Cole Baldwin," Clarisa suggested, hoping the princess will choose the red head as her life partner.

"I think her royal highness is a lovely young woman, and any man would be lucky to have her, including me," Athan replied, studying the girl he was speaking of. Her ice blue eyes met his silver ones, holding his gaze for a small moment.

The dinner came to an end, and Tamantha was forced to mingle with the palace servants and guards. Athan stood in the corner quietly. He was watching her travel all over the room. She could feel it.

"Is that the young man who saved you, Your Royal Highness?" Neda Gagnon questioned, locking her eyes on him. "He is Clayton's brother, correct?" Tamantha knew it would come to this moment.

"Yes, he is the man who saved my life. If he doesn't want to do anything, don't force him. He does wish to speak with Clayton though, so he might take you up on your offer," Tamantha mentioned. The General nodded, taking it into consideration.

"We are still unable to get information out of him, and we are on our last ends. We will most likely give him the truth serum if nothing works anymore. The truth serum however has bad side effects as you may know," the General explained. She looked at her daughter for a moment, trying to hide her grin from seeing Elsabeth in the formal uniform. She had a lot of pride in her children. "How are you, darling?"

"I'm fine, mother. Thank you for asking," Elsabeth calmly spoke, trying to maintain a professional tone.

"I hope your little suspension at our cabin has been relaxing for you. I hope it taught you a valuable lesson about protecting the crown princess."

Elsabeth swallowed the lump in your throat. "I will always protect her life with my own and will never fail her royal highness again."

Tamantha called over Athan to distract the General from her child. He obliged to avoid the people glancing at him. They all spoke of his resemblance to Clayton Wright. He kissed the back of her hand. "Finally, it's my turn?"

"Athan, the General would like to speak with you about Clayton. I think she will give you a chance to talk to your brother, but probably for something in return." Tamantha turned her attention to the General of the Guardians who was eager to get this chance.

"Athan Wright, I would like to thank you for protecting Her Royal Highness, and I hope we can thank you in some way. Don't be afraid to ask," Neda began. "If you would be obliged to do so, it would be much appreciated if you could join us in the interrogation process of your brother. I know you went to the Academy, so you would be familiar with it. I know it must be very hard to be in this position."

Athan was not surprised that he was the target of information. It was expected the twin would know more and would find out more. "I would actually like to see my brother if I can. I haven't seen him since the incident that put the princess in harm's way. I will agree if I can help the country of Sophia in any way." Athan bowed to the General and guided Tamantha away, so he could enjoy her company more privately. He could see something was wrong with her. "Are you alright? Your leg?"

"I'm fine, Athan. It's a dull ache, but we royals can afford some pretty fun pain killers," Tamantha joked, giving a sly smirk. Athan didn't smile back.

"You have no idea how hard it was to watch you fade away in my arms. I was so afraid you would be gone from this life and onto the next one, and I wouldn't see you anymore," Athan admitted. Tamantha tried not to show her shock. She looked down at the ground at her and Athan's feet.

"I'm sorry," she whispered. She rested her head on Athan's shoulder for a moment, ignoring the stares from servants chatting amongst themselves. She didn't know why she did, but she felt safe with him here, burying the anxiety over the trauma she endured in the darkness.

Tamantha heard someone clear their throat from behind her. She turned to see her gracious and loving mother watching them. "Athan, mind your distance from the crown princess. Don't want anyone to get the wrong idea," the queen warned.

"Yes, Your Majesty." Athan maintained a proper distance for Tamantha's sake. Tamantha rolled her eyes at her mother's intervention. She allowed Athan to pursue a courtship with the princess and forcing a gap between them doesn't help. Athan bowed as the queen went back to greeting the party guests. Tamantha didn't understand why her mother even bothered to speak up if she wasn't going to stay.

Athan escorted Tamantha through the rest of the greeting and talking. He quietly listened and observed, absorbing what

Tamantha was like in this setting. He had seen her before in a formal setting at the welcoming party at the college and the Asterope queen's coronation ball, but he never personally experienced for almost the whole duration. He had never been in this position as her guest. Tamantha glanced back at him for a brief moment, her eyes shining and a genuine smile coming out from behind the mask. It was a look was only reserved for him.

Chapter Sixteen

Tamantha eyed the new couple from behind her menu, watching them flirt and tenderly holding hands underneath the table. She couldn't hold back her grin to see her friend so much in love. She had invited them to join her for lunch today, so she could give her approval of Sara's new beau.

"Peterson, how did you like visiting with Sara's father?" Tamantha began, putting the menu down on the table. She was at a much fancier restaurant than usual, so Athan wasn't here to distract her. School did start again this week however, and she was not looking forward to the new semester.

"It was very nice. Sara's father is great. He didn't even bring out the sword and threats. He seems to approve of me. I had met him before at Astrapi events as he is a very influential businessman within our society, and I guess he likes my rank as the nephew of President Chauncey," Peterson explained, rubbing his hand up and down Sara's back and looking at her with such fondness. Sara blushed, giving a minor glare to remain proper in front of her best friend and the future queen of Sophia. She grabbed the hand back and made him remain holding hands.

"I'm very surprised Davin hasn't tackled Peterson and told him to go away," Sara commented.

"I wouldn't say he hasn't," Peterson coughed, obviously having experienced some kind of protective brotherly cornering. Sara raised an eyebrow.

"What do you plan to do when you finish college?" Tamantha asked, wanting to know what future prospects Peterson offers to having the chance to date Sara Fletcher.

"I am going to major in international affairs, and I hope to get a position on the Symvoulio of Astrapi after an extensive political career," Peterson remarked, knowing this whole charade was an interrogation. He was not fazed by the higher rank she held over him. He had been around nobility and political leaders enough to feel comfortable around them.

"You have the Guardian blood, right? Have you been to the Guardian Academy?" Tamantha surprised him. He wasn't expecting the question.

"I have been to the Guardian Academy. We, the Electra Guardians, prepare ourselves for the possibility that the Electra family comes back into power," Peterson mentioned, gritting his teeth a little bit. Tamantha knew the Guardians will know their charge based on a name that whispers into their ear. He had probably been able to identify the Electra heir, but he would not reveal it to another soul, not even to the royal families, that is if the Electra family is still alive today.

"Enough interrogation please, Tammy," Sara pleaded, gripping Peterson's hand.

"Fine." Tamantha sighed and relented, wishing to crack the surface of the mystery of the Electra family. She would figure it out someday.

"If the Electra family does come back, your family will be

trembling at the might of the Astrapi army," Peterson threatened. Tamantha watched as Siberius came out of nowhere and gripped the back of his neck.

"Do not threaten the Merope family with your unfounded ideas," Siberius growled, letting go. Peterson rubbed his neck, biting back the retort.

The Electra and Merope families were in a long-standing feud for centuries. Astrapi and Sophia were on the same continent, and there had been many wars over the location of the border. A treaty three hundred years ago put an end to the feud, solidifying the wall between Astrapi and Sophia. It was done through the marriage of the Merope princess to the Crown Prince of Astrapi, but with the letter Tamantha found in the archive, it apparently was not a truly happy marriage.

The Guardians of Electra who came into power in the government of Astrapi were not afraid to hold onto the ideals that the Electra family was supreme. There were rumors that the Electra family was plotting to war with the entire world to become the top leadership above their ancestral relations. Peterson was no stranger to these ideals and would gladly uphold them based on his Astrapi pride. Sara and Davin, however, were raised in Sophia and have grown to respect all of the families as equals.

The general population of Astrapi worship the lost family and pray for the return of their beloved rulers. The Electra are indoctrinated into some religious teachings as the saviors who ended the Eklektos slavery to Prota and put a stop to the Creator's tyranny. The Creator has been known to never like the Electra family and is well known to keep her distance from the descendants of the man who took her family. This ideology is not highly believed in Astrapi and is regarded more by the radicals who want to put the Electra family back into power. There are even radical groups who want to find Prota, retrieve the Lost One, and place her on the throne if no other Electra exist.

Siberius resumed his position of standing nearby. Tamantha's Guardians were scattered all over the restaurant. Elsabeth was standing in a military pose next to her brother. Peterson sniffles at the idea of a Guardian sitting next to him, even if he himself has the Guardian roots as well. He believes his relations to the President of Astrapi puts him above the lowly Guardians, even if the Gagnon siblings are the children of the General of the Guardians and are potential contenders for that position. Tamantha begins to wonder why Sara likes him, but she truly seems happy.

Sara was glaring at her new boyfriend, but she softened and turned back to look at her best friend with an apologetic look. "So, Tammy, your birthday is in a couple weeks. You ready for the birthday ball?"

Tamantha grinned. "I am more than ready. I want to hear who I was in my past lives. The recorded ones at least," Tamantha said, almost gleeful over the prospect.

"I have my dress already for it. It's purple and just a long, straight gown. I made Peterson get a matching tuxedo. It's being held at the palace, right?"

"Yes, in the grand ball room. The identification of past lives will be in the Hall of the Creator. Of course, that part is open to only the people close to me. My mother has been extremely overwhelming with who is getting an invitation to the birthday ball. She's been flinging them left and right at anyone who is worthy enough to witness my twentieth birthday."

"You're going back to school though," Sara remarked. "Are you still planning the details, or is it on the queen's lap to choose everything?"

"I am going back to school and letting her do it all. As much as I should use this as a learning experience, my mother is planning to turn this into a grand Celaeno type of ball, and I know I can't fight with her on it. The Merope family is more modest, and my mother still won't grasp this concept and probably never will," Tamantha explained.

Sara smirked. She didn't completely know the true face of the queen behind the mask, but Sara had heard enough about how the woman really is from the mouth of her daughter. "Let's hope she doesn't spend the entire Merope fortune on it. I remember Nolan's ball. The King didn't let Queen Clarisa do the planning and handed the whole thing over to Nolan. Nolan went the Merope way and invited his closest friends and family and enjoyed a private party. Your mother did have a hand in making sure you stood out as her child and the princess by putting you in that extremely expensive ball gown."

Tamantha smiled and scowled at the memory. Her brother had so much fun making fun of her for weeks on end. His party was supposed to just be casual wear as that was what he chose, but her mother had other ideas for the princess. "I'm going to burn it if I ever find it," Tamantha muttered. "I won't be moving back into the dorm." Tamantha let out a solemn sigh.

"What? Is it because of the attack?" Sara wondered, perplexed why Tamantha must give up on her planned year of residing in the Pleione dorms.

"Yes. My mother says there have been too many attacks, and she would like me to come back to the palace. However, she agreed to allow me to stay at my cousin's apartment since it is closer to school," Tamantha answered. "My mother's thoughts are there is more security at Christine's home, and Christine's Guardians, although connected to her, would be more obligated to protect the heir over their charge. It is true though. Even if Guardians are the Guardians of the lowest ranking Meropes, they are obligated to protect those who are to inherit the crown despite what their Guardian connections tell them to do." Tamantha glanced at her two favorite Guardians. They were lucky enough to not have to make that choice, but if her brother were still alive, they would readily protect him if they needed to no matter how much it hurt them.

The Queen was adamant that her safety was more important above all else concerning education. Royal families technically do not have to get a degree to be a leader, but royalty and the general public believe it allows them to become a fairer ruler. The Queen would fight tooth and nail to lock Tamantha up in a tower if she had to, anything to protect her only child. The tower would have to be a shining pedestal though to keep the limelight on the crown princess. The King would never allow his wife to go so far, and he has stepped in many times to protest her motherly protectiveness.

Tamantha processed the amount of packing in her dorm room that had to be done, although it would all be moved by a servant. Her mother had arranged for new furniture specifically for Tamantha's new bedroom and only personal items would need to be delivered to Christine's apartment. Christine had cleared one of her many bedrooms, relenting the second best to her superior. Christine was happy to have her as much as anyone was when giving up the privacy of their own home. Tamantha would be heading straight there after her meal with Sara and Peterson. Siberius was going to be arranging the new Guardian rotation schedule with Christine's Guardians.

"I hope you are comfortable in your new home, Your Royal Highness. I'm sure it will be quite lovely with regards to the Merope fortune," Peterson noted, probably meaning it as a compliment. Tamantha nodded.

"It's true the Merope family has a lot of fortune, but this money is not extended to Christine as she only received her inheritance from her mother's standing as my father's sister. The rest of the money she has is from her father's position as Duke of Rosebury. But thank you, Peterson, Christine has a very lovely home," Tamantha explained.

It was not widely taught in economics class in how royal money is processed. Royal money is almost always limited to the immediate royal family with trusts set up for those who had come from the immediate family but has been displaced by the rising of a new King or Queen. When Tamantha's father became King, Christine was displaced out of the immediate family as she was not a child or grandchild of the new king. She still received all titles and money that came with being the daughter of a princess of Merope, but she did not receive an allowance from the royal family just for being descended from them.

People who are so far distantly related from the King or Queen and have little royal blood left within them have likely not seen any money that was inherited by their direct ancestors, unless that ancestor was wise with their investments. It was decided by Symvoulio law almost towards the beginning of the rule of Sophia.

This was just how it was done here in Sophia and might be decided differently in the other countries. Even though the money the Merope family has is not from the government, it is still decided by the Symvoulio to prevent lawsuits and arguments resulting in battles and civil wars.

"That's very interesting to know," Peterson genuinely admired. "The Electra family would rarely take care of those who were no longer in the immediate family. Astrapi does have some very lovely palaces due to the Electra extravagance."

"I will agree with you there. The architecture is gorgeous in Astrapi. The Electra spared no expense when it came to their own castles," Tamantha commented. Sara looked at the both of them. She had not personally ever been in the walls of the famous Electra palace in the Astrapi capital. It was being used as the government building for the president and his government. It would be easily cleared out if the Electra heir is known.

"You should show me around the palace sometime," Sara told Peterson, giving him pleading eyes. He just smirked and kissed her cheek. "Oh, Tamantha, how is the courtship with Athan going, or is that not official yet?" Tamantha felt her cheeks glowing with warmth.

"He will be escorting me to the ball, and we shall see if anything official will be on the record by the end of the night. My mother is making sure of it." Sara was biting back the urge to giggle.

"If he asks you, or if you ask him rather, will either of you accept? I don't know what it is between you two, but I think there's something there," Sara analyzed. Tamantha was a little taken aback that her best friend had noticed.

"I will. I think I want to try out a real courtship with him. I haven't dated anyone as you remember," Tamantha revealed. Peterson raised an eyebrow.

"A beauty like you has never dated before?" Peterson questioned.

"It's best for avoiding scandals and any possible chance encounters with Anaxios. The Merope family is famous for their Anaxios loving, and it will likely happen in my own future."

"I hope you find love with whomever you choose to marry. Do you think the King loves the Queen?" Sara wondered, never catching a glimpse of the royal couple in the same place unless it's an official event.

"I don't know really. My mother and father rarely display any affection towards each other in front of me. It's likely the both of them have some kind of lover on the side that is kept behind closed doors," Tamantha said. She pondered on it. Her mother never held hands with the King or even kissed him in front of her. The Queen and King had their own bedrooms separate from each other, allowing them to be free to choose someone to fulfil their needs. Clarisa had finished her purpose with the one child she produced, and she was free to do whatever she wanted to do. The King and Queen chose not to be together romantically. "I hope my own marriage is never like that."

Sara reached across the table and squeezed Tamantha's hand. "It won't be."

Elsabeth approached the table with a bow. "It's time to leave, Your Royal Highness. Excuse me, Sara and Sir Peterson," Elsabeth stated. Elsabeth was moving into the room next door to Tamantha. She would be on twenty-four/seven duty as a live-in Guardian. It was much like the arrangement at the dormitories.

Tamantha rose from her seat and said her good-byes to Sara and Peterson. She paid the entire bill, a gift for the couple.

The trip to the apartment was short, since the location was close to the university. It was also in the middle of downtown near the much fancier restaurants and stores.

Christine greeted them as graciously as she could, but Tamantha could see the future Duchess feeling a little annoyed about the intrusion. She no doubt hosted many parties here with her aristocratic friends, and the new tenant would limit the amount of guests she can have.

The apartment is almost the tower her mother wanted, but

Tamantha was not afraid to let down her hair.

Chapter Seventeen

Tamantha fiddled with her fingers as she patiently watched the priestess drink a memory spell specially sent by the General. She had requested directly to the General to see what occurred during the interrogation of Clayton Wright, performed by Siberius and Clayton's own brother, Athan Wright. The memory would be immediately destroyed after she finished viewing it.

Tamantha called Elsabeth over into her room. Tamantha felt like Elsabeth needed to watch this too for her own benefit. Elsabeth sat down next to Tamantha on her bed, her face as calm as possible. Elsabeth was settling more and more into her role as a Guardian, and the Elsabeth who once was rebelling against her mother and looking to a different future was slowly fading away. It saddened Tamantha a little bit to see the bright blue haired girl darkening just as her own hair was doing as time passes by.

"Your Royal Highness, are you ready?" the priestess asked. Tamantha didn't notice her own hand grabbing for Beth's. Beth didn't pull away.

"Begin." The priestess put her hands on both Beth's and Tamantha's foreheads. Her hands glowed as she gave them Neda

Gagnon's memory. Tamantha and Beth could see the interrogation beginning through Neda's eyes.

The familiar etches of Athan's face graced Clayton's features. He seemed uninterested in the crime that he committed. Did he feel any remorse? Tamantha held onto Elsabeth, almost about to collapse. Tamantha remembered the knife making contact with her skin. She remembered the devious smile that took over his face as he proclaimed he would kill her.

She watched his façade fall as Athan entered the room. This was the first meeting in a long time, besides when Athan knocked him out. Their mystical silver eyes locked onto each other. Clayton's jaw almost dropped. The General was watching the small communication, flicking a pen back and forth as she measured Clayton's reaction. It was what she wanted. It was her way into the mind that had been untouchable.

Clayton tried to get up from his chair, but he found himself unable to do so. The metal table gently rocked as he pulled at the chains on his wrist.

"Athan," Clayton called. He adored his brother. That much was apparent.

"Hello, brother," Athan acknowledged, but his face remained stoic, taking a seat next to the General. He kept his gaze on his mirror image.

Clayton gave up his small attempt at escape. Did he wish for the familial touch that was his only solace in his doom?

Tamantha let out a breath that she didn't know she was holding.

"Let us start," the General announced, glancing at the piece of paper in front of her. She had likely tried a series of questions over and over, but nothing had worked on the Guardian trained Clayton. "Where have you been in the last few months?"

"Go see the Creator," Clayton growled. Tamantha let out a small squeak as Athan slammed Clayton's head into the table.

"General, may I ask the questions?" Athan asked calmly, already back in his seat.

"Why did you do that?"

"I'm trying to save your life," Athan answered. Clayton released the brick wall. Clayton could be put to death.

"You may give the questions, Athan, but I will end the interrogation if I feel like the interview is being twisted by one of you." The General slid the paper over to him. This is what she wanted.

"Where were you, Clay? You disappeared after what you did in the first incident," Athan said, reading it with his own words.

"I really don't know," Clayton responded.

"I need a clear answer, Clay. You were taught about national level interrogations, and you need to cooperate. This is your last chance to redeem yourself." The General watched the exchange. Athan was desperate to save his brother no matter what had been done. His loyalties are with the Crown and his family.

"I was underground. It was dark save for a desk lamp. I don't know the location."

"Why did you kill Guardian Alessandra Aki?"

"I don't remember doing that. Honestly. I remember being at that stupid school event. Then I was in that underground place."

"How do you know it was underground?" the General joined in.

"It smelled like mold and dirt. I never saw the light of the day creeping in. The only light was the desk lamp, and the light pouring in from upstairs."

"Upstairs?"

"Yes." Clayton would likely not go further unless the

questions are appropriate.

"Was there anyone with you?"

"Yes." The General cleared her throat, annoyance crossing her face.

"Could you be clearer, Clay? These aren't only yes or no answers," Athan reminded. Clayton stared at his brother. Tamantha wondered what was going on in his head. She remembered the man accusing his brother of being part of their mother's death.

"I only saw one person the entire time I was down there, but he, or she, was wearing a mask. They were also disguising their voice somehow," Clay admitted.

"Can you describe the mask?" Neda questioned. Clay was going to draw this out as long as he could, but what was there to hide? The only option besides answering their questions honestly with cooperation with the sentence of death. Forking over all the answers would keep him alive.

"It was in the shape of an owl. It had a long nose with orange paint, and it had gigantic dark eyes, black as the darkness that surrounded me. I swear I still have nightmares about those eyes." Clayton's handcuffs clinked as he violently shuddered.

"Tam-," Athan paused, "Her Royal Highness is going to have just as many nightmares about you stabbing her over and over." Tamantha felt a wave of what felt like joy when he almost said her name, but her hands began to clench as she remembered the knife going in her leg. A phantom pain spiked up in her knee, and she whimpered a little bit. Elsabeth placed a hand on top of Tamantha's.

"He's not here, Tamantha. It's just us, and it's just my mother's memory," Elsabeth calmed the princess. Tamantha nodded, pushing away the feeling in her knee.

"Athan, please do not mention Her Royal Highness like that. Only refer to her in an investigational way," Neda reminded. She tapped her pen on the table. She was carefully watching Clayton Wright's demeanor.

"She deserved it!" Clayton slammed his fist on the table. Athan lunged at him and wrapped his hands around his neck, pulling both of them down to the ground. It painfully yanked on Clayton's wrist as the cuffs would not allow to go any further.

Tamantha watched through the eyes of the veteran Guardian as she moved quickly, pulling both of them apart by throwing Athan towards the wall and somehow positioning Clayton back in his chair. "Sibling rivalry is not to be used here. This is a formal interview about the events that occurred over the last few months. Now sit down, Athan. Any more of that, and I will end the interview along with sentencing Clayton's last days."

Athan stood up and straightened himself. "Understood, General," he muttered, relaxing back into his own chair. "Did you ever get a hint of who he or she was? Was there anything that stood out to you?"

Clayton shook his head. "I only saw the darkness. He turned me away from the upstairs door, so I could not see up there. It's very likely he lives there and that he lives alone."

Clayton was not Tamantha's only enemy, she realized.

"Clay, do you remember anything odd before the event that occurred on the night of the Welcoming Ball at Sophia University?" Athan was reaching for something concrete, but he was only finding the rough gravel.

Clayton stayed silent for a moment as he remembered that night. "I remember passing out drinks at the party, and someone touched me on the shoulder. Then, nothing." Neda wrote that last bit down. She would check the memories of Guardians of that night for possible suspects to see if what he said was true.

"That's all you remember?" Athan wasn't sure if it was the true answer.

"Athan, I would like your permission as his family member if we could give him a dose of truth serum," Neda asked, looking directly into Clayton's eyes. Athan slumped back in his chair.

"What are the side effects of truth serum, Beth?" Tamantha wondered, pulling away from the priestess's hand for a moment. Beth shook her head. Tamantha wasn't sure if her young Guardian did not know or would not say. "Please, Beth." Beth urged to Tamantha to go back into the memory. She returned to Neda's memory.

"Yes," Athan answered. Clayton's mouth opened wide in shock.

"Athan, please don't let them do that! You know what will happen!" Clayton begged for once in his life. Clayton was tugging on his cuffs.

"You knew there would be consequences for kidnapping and attempting to murder a royal official. We have to know the whole truth if we are going to gain any ground on this case for her sake," Athan explained. Neda called in another Guardian who was holding the syringe. Neda held Clayton down as he struggled to put space between himself and the needle. Athan looked away, a bit of sorrow he was the one to do this to his own brother. The Guardian injected directly in his arm, leaving quietly as if he was a ghost. Neda let go of Clayton when the door shut. She returned to her place next to Athan.

Clayton put his head on the desk. His chest began to move quickly. He was looking at his arm. He screamed. "Symptoms include burning at the site of injection," Elsabeth whispered. Tamantha looked at her in disbelief.

"I need water! Ice! Please! It's on fire!" Clayton was shouting at his brother. "You bastard!" Clayton's breathing quickened. "Help me. I can't breathe."

"Panic attacks."

Clayton's breathing calmed for a brief moment, and then he let out all his breakfast on the floor.

"Vomiting."

"I need water!" Clayton licked his lips.

"Minor dehydration."

"All this in just a few short moments?" Tamantha was unsure what to think of this.

"There will be more."

Neda pushed over a glass of water, which Clayton hurriedly gulped down as if he had been stranded in a desert for days. "Are we ready to resume questioning?" Neda asked the person who was suffering. Athan wiped away any remorse he was feeling about putting his brother through this.

"Yes, please," Clayton answered. Tamantha was confused about why Clayton would be ready to proceed.

"On the night of the Welcoming Ball, do you remember anything strange before the murder of Alessandra Aki?" Athan proceeded with the rest of the interrogation.

"I was tapped on the shoulder by a woman. She looked at me directly in the eyes, saying 'I need you'. Then, everything went black. I felt like I lost all control of my body."

"Why didn't they give him the truth serum sooner?" Tamantha wondered aloud.

"Because of it's long term effects, Tammy."

"Can you describe the woman?" Neda asked.

"She was wearing a black strapless gown. She had a straight nose, and she had curly brown hair. Her eyes were brown. That is all I remember, I'm sorry." Neda nodded, writing it all down.

"Do you have any details about the person in the basement with you?"

"They wore a cloak and an owl mask. They had gloved hands. They brought me a letter written by King Alvyn, but they didn't say where they got it. I do not have any physical details pertaining the man or woman as they carefully shrouded themselves in the darkness."

"Did you kill the blood partner of Crown Princess Tamantha?"

"I never left that basement until the night I kidnapped her." Neda leaned forward at this detail. Tamantha and Elsabeth did too.

"You don't remember killing the blood partner?"

"No, I never left the basement. I never blacked out again after the night of the Welcoming Ball as far as I know."

"How were you able to call me when you were down there?" Athan wanted to know.

"The person who kept me against my will left the telecrystal on the desk. They said I could call you," Clayton explained.

"They let you?" Athan was confused by this. If they were holding Clayton against his will, why would he allow the hostage release information?

"Yes, they said I could have one telecrystal call." Clayton was beginning to speak in monotone.

"Athan, we're going to lose him soon," Neda announced, obviously knowing the effects of the truth serum. The monotone voice a sign of the nearing end of this interview.

"Lose him soon?" Tamantha stared at the clone of Athan Wright. Elsabeth did not answer.

"Do you remember any details about the telecrystal itself?"

Athan had little time to ask these questions. Now, it was a matter of picking what was important.

"It was a brand new telecrystal. There was nothing out of the ordinary." Neda tapped her pen at the dead end.

"On the day of the kidnapping of her royal highness, how did you escape your prison?" Athan was watching Clayton for signs of the end. Tamantha could see the sadness becoming etched on his face. She wanted to soothe his worried silver eyes. She wanted to hold his hand and tell him it would be okay.

"The kidnapper read the letter out to me. They detailed the murder of our mother. Our mother," Clayton began to sob.

"It's okay, Clay. She already moved onto the next life. How did you escape?" Athan wanted to reach out and comfort his brother, even if he was a violent individual. He was the only family he has left.

"Why not ask him about the letter?" the princess asked, wanting to know every little detail about it.

"We already have the letter as part of evidence," Elsabeth said, pointing out the obvious.

"Can I read it?" she wondered.

"If the General allows it, then yes."

"The kidnapper injected me with something, and then I woke up in the karavi. He put the letter in the car, and he also put the telecrystal in the karavi. The karavi had the keys in the ignition."

"Can they track the karavi? Did they find the telecrystal?" Tamantha pulled away again.

"The karavi was stolen, but we're trying to trace its path before the time of the accident. The telecrystal was missing from the site of the accident, and it was not on Clayton's person when we arrested him," the blue haired Guardian explained. Tamantha suddenly remembered the time of the impact. Elsabeth motioned to the priestess to continue the memory. Tamantha decided she would not interrupt anymore and save her questions for the end.

"I felt so angry about how our mother died and who killed her. The kidnapper whispered on the telecrystal to me saying that the karavi containing her killer would be passing by the intersection in front of me and exactly what time. I watched the clock, and I started the karavi and pressed so hard on the accelerator the other karavi flipped over. It was great. She didn't die so easily though." Tamantha watched Athan twitch and almost lunged across the table again, but he seated himself when Neda glared at him. He cares that much about her? "I fought those Guardians, beat one to an inch of their lives, and I tore down the little blue haired brat without much effort. I could hear her bones snap." Tamantha felt Elsabeth shake next to her. This time Tamantha would be the one to comfort her friend.

This time Neda was the one who reacted. Her pen smashed through the table. "The little blue haired brat was my daughter, you monster," Neda hissed, almost ready to kill him herself. Tamantha watched Neda remember who she was and regain composure. Elsabeth felt a smile spread on her face, letting go of the trauma that held her for a brief moment.

"Continue, Clay," Athan ordered. How much time was left?

"I took the princess to our mother's home. I took her to the place where you and that woman murdered our mother. I was hoping she would remember and tell me what happened in that room, but I eventually realized it was futile. I don't care if she had nothing to do with it. She was there. She caused our mother to die by being there, and you did too. I stabbed her so many times, and I would do it again." He started banging his fist on the table in a stabbing motion. "Stab. Stab. Stab." Every stab resonated within the wounds on Tamantha's body, a dull ache flaring up in each one.

Clayton began to laugh out of nowhere. "The next symptom is temporary insanity."

"I stabbed a princess! I stabbed the princess! I win!" Clayton exclaimed, grinning violently at his brother. "I would stab you too, but you're my brother. You're cool with me for now."

Athan slammed his hands on the desk and stood up. "We've lost him, General." Clayton kept making stabbing motions on the table.

"The long-term symptom is permanent mental damage. Clayton lost a piece of himself by receiving the serum. We are only supposed to use it in extreme circumstances. Letting them do it was the hardest decision Athan could ever make." Clayton creepily looked directly into the camera above. He continued the stabbing motion for the final moments of the memory. Tamantha could feel those menacing silver eyes staring into her own soul.

The memory ended, and the priestess put her hands to her side and bowed. As a gesture of destroying the memory, the priestess poured the rest of the memory potion down the sink. "Thank you," Tamantha said, grateful for the chance to figure out why all of this happened to her.

Did she really think it was going to be so easy? The real menace was hiding behind a mask, carefully planning out each move. They wanted her dead specifically. He would make a mistake somewhere, right? Tamantha felt like this whole interview led to a dead end with more questions than answers. She hoped the Guardians would be able to gain something from this.

Tamantha left her bedroom to join her cousin in the living room.

Christine preferred being alone, and she pretended her more

important cousin was not taking up space in the place that was her own. Tamantha did appreciate, however, that Christine came into her room when Tamantha began screaming in her sleep. Christine just rubbed Tamantha's back and reassured Tamantha that no harm would come.

"Is it over?" Christine asked.

"It's far from over," Tamantha revealed, picking up the coffee pot and pouring herself a cup. She peered up from her cup while she was sipping her coffee. She observed each member of her staff. The guards were conversing with the Guardians. The maids were cleaning the house. The cooks were preparing tonight's dinner. It could be anyone.

Chapter Eighteen

"Your Royal Highness, thank you for allowing me to perform your ceremony," the tall high priestess said, clasping her hands around Tamantha's. The Guardians were on edge, taking extra care to watch the priestess for even touching the princess. Tamantha glared back at them with a silent order to stand down. She had been waiting her entire life for this moment.

Tamantha's twentieth birthday would reveal answers about who she was in the past. It was a pivotal moment to mark where her soul stands in this lifetime. Being royalty in your past life accorded some respect in society, even if it did not grant those privileges again. If you were royalty in a past life, employers and teachers would expect you to have some of the same traits in your past life. The religion believed to be royal in a lifetime is to be chosen for greatness, important enough to hold such responsibilities. Most people in the highest standing had been royalty in past lives as well.

It was rare for the crown to be of only commoner past lives, but it was entirely possible Tamantha had just been ordinary.

Tamantha stood in the hall where her ceremony would be

performed in a couple days. Athan was off in the corner, being briefed by another high priestess. He would play a role in the ceremony by leading her in, but that was as far as the queen would allow him. This was going to be Tamantha's special day.

"Now, Your Royal Highness, before we begin the practice, I need to get a feel for your soul, so I can accurately determine the link to your past lives," the high priestess explained. She glanced over at the Guardians with a question in her eyes. Siberius relented, ordering the Guardians to relax for the moment.

"Alright," Tamantha granted, wondering what steps would be necessary. She had never observed this process as it was always private.

"Close your eyes and breathe deeply. You may feel the past lives while I am doing this. Don't be alarmed. They are not your memories. They are the glimpses belonging to you in a different lifetime." Tamantha nodded. She shut her eyes, feeling the warmth from the priestess's magic.

A child ran through a regal kitchen with an older woman scolding her. The older woman scooped her up and took her back through giant doors.

A man sat on a bed, putting on clothes of silk. He looked back at another man on the bed. He kissed the other man's palm.

A woman stood on a boat with her husband. Another woman tapped on her shoulder. The two women looked the same.

A woman stood on the ocean, decorated in an ornate gown. She was alone. She peered out into the sea, waiting for someone. Someone called her name. Seven women approached her, adoration in their eyes.

"Thank you, Your Royal Highness." Tamantha opened her eyes, looking around at the familiar scenery. She felt like she had just been in another world.

"How many lives do you usually see, and do you see your soul mate at all?" Tamantha asked. She was fascinated by all the lives that rushed through her in just a moment. She didn't know them, but she knew she was once them.

"The glimpses are suspected to be times when you were with your soul mate as it is the time when your soul is at its most powerful. Many people I have done this on before have always mentioned another person being there. I myself saw one of my lives. It is common to only see one life because you might not always meet your soul mate," the high priestess explained. Tamantha took it all in. "The Creator blessed all to at least meet our soul mates somehow in our lives, but it will not always be romantic. They can be your family, your friend, your lover, or even a stranger. Your soul does not need your soul mate to live your life."

"Could you determine my soul mate for me at least?" The high priestess shook her head.

"Only your soul knows when its other half is close by, and you yourself might not even feel it." The high priestess could only give her the symbol she shared with her other past lives and record this life in it.

The tattoo used in the ceremonies has been used for everyone's past lives and has always been the same for each soul. Tamantha's own tattoo will allow her to appear in the Book of Souls and mark who she was in this lifetime. She can go to the archives after the ceremony and see who she once was. The book could not give details of their entire lives, but it can give a name, what they may have done in that life, how long they lived, what they died of. As long as someone reached the age of the ceremony, their life has been recorded.

Family details are unimportant as those are blood

connections and not spiritual connections. Those details can be found in ancestry archives, but they have very little benefits to understanding your own soul.

Athan approached the two women, bowing to the princess. The high priestess, while highly regarded in society, was beneath the crown. The king was seen as the head of the church in Sophia, but even with that, the Merope family has very little involvement with how the Creationist religion is taught. It takes a special soul to sit on the throne.

"We shall begin," the sister dictated, directing the couple to the entrance of the ceremonial hall. Athan and Tamantha stood in front of the door. Tamantha took a deep breath, linking her arm with Athan's. Athan stood still and proper, not letting out the nervousness creeping in. The whole world was watching.

Most twenty-year-olds walk into the ceremony by themselves, but the queen wanted it as formal as possible, including an escort.

Athan lifted his arm, and Tamantha took it. She felt a shudder as her skin touched his, tingling with warmth. She peered up at him, thinking he wasn't looking. He smirked when they met eyes, causing the princess to quickly avert her eyes towards the priestess. The high priestess also had her own smirk on her face, having witnessed this intimate moment.

"Please stand!" Siberius called. Anyone who may have been sitting quickly rose. "Her royal highness, Tamantha Alexandria Merope, Crown Princess of Sophia!" All the women curtsied, and the men bowed. Siberius would not say Athan's name. He was not the center of this ceremony. It only belonged to Tamantha.

"Now approach the ceremonial circle," Sister Ophelia directed, pointing towards drawn chalk. Tamantha traced the lines with her eyes. Tamantha and Athan walked around the circle, a symbol of the cycle of rebirth.

Tamantha and Athan reached the edge, and Athan let go of her arm, backing away. The priestess and Tamantha bowed to each other.

"Please grace me with the Creator's gift of reincarnation and show me what She has given to me with Her eternal promise," Tamantha recited the words. She had heard this line enough times. She would not get a sneak peek of the Priestess calling upon the spirit of the Creator. It would wait. Tamantha kneeled in the middle of the circle.

Claps echoed from a corner of the ceremony hall. Athan bowed to the presence. "Absolutely beautiful," Tamantha's mother said. The couple had been tirelessly practicing the routine back and forth for hours now. Her mother wanted it absolutely perfect. It would be a show of the princess's pure-blooded nature and worthiness to accept a role that was not hers to begin with.

"Thank you, Sister Ophelia, for your guidance in the ceremonial rites. Please connect this life with the others, and may the Creator bless you," Tamantha thanked the priestess for her tireless work. The Sister bowed to the princess and then to the Queen. Siberius escorted her out of the hall.

"How do you feel, my lovely daughter?" Clarisa clasped her hands around Tamantha's cheeks. Clarisa was glowing with pride.

"Strange, but excited. I think I saw my own lives. They were so vibrant and whole. Did you experience the same thing, Mom?" Tamantha was curious about who her mother could have been in the past. Was she the same kind of person, or was she much kinder in those lives?

"I had a dream of war and standing on the battlefield with a General. I must have been dying, but the man was trying to keep me alive," Clarisa explained, briefly losing herself in the dream as she was not clearly looking at her daughter.

Athan stood awkwardly to the side, but the Queen was quick to notice. "What dreams did you have, Athan?" She peeked at the etchings on his wrist. Tamantha did too. There was nothing there.

"I never did the ceremony," Athan confessed. The Queen curled back in disgust.

"Do you not believe in the Creator?" Clarisa interrogated. It was blasphemy to the royal families as they were proof of Her existence.

"I do, but it was just me and my brother. We never discussed actually having it done. I'm not as curious about what I might have been as what I can become in this life. I might have it done in a year or two, but for now, I can wait," Athan dutifully explained. Clarisa could only encroach so much.

"Adina! Please hang that ribbon elsewhere. It does not flow well with the others!" Clarisa was quickly distracted, running off to control the staff with the same mask as always.

Tamantha sheepishly smiled as she watched her mother barking more orders. Tamantha just wanted her ceremony done and could care less about the decorations. She peered again at Athan's wrist. She wondered if this man could be her soul mate, but how could she truly ever know? "Thank you for your help. My mother was losing her mind over whether or not a suitable candidate would be available for the escort, not that I need one," Tamantha admitted. Athan stared down at her, a smirk curling on his lips.

"It is my pleasure, Your Royal Highness. I would never have turned it down because I would not want anyone else to be in my place." A blush rose up on Tamantha's cheeks, averting her eyes but quickly meeting his gaze again. "I wonder though if I should really be doing this. Does a crown princess really need the likes of me to be her escort when she could have a prince or duke to actually shine?"

"Athan, you are definitely worthy of performing this task. You would never have been in this hall if I didn't think you required the respect deserved for my daughter. She will be Queen someday. Your role as King Basset's friend, but also just being the son of your mother proves you can do this," Clarisa explained, butting into their conversation.

"Thank you, Your Majesty. I hope I live up to it." Tamantha was surprised her mother actually has a heart. Athan straightened up, prepared to do more for the princess. Tamantha shook her head. When someone much higher up the ladder gives you a real compliment meant for only you, it instills confidence and pride into oneself. Athan intertwined his fingers with Tamantha while her mother wasn't looking. Tamantha stood on her tippy toes and met his lips. He was her savior, her light in the dark, and her grip on reality.

Chapter Nineteen

Tamantha kneeled in the circle, her white gown pooling around her. Gold trim decorated the lace, and the bodice had lace flowers with diamonds. Her hair was up in a decorative bun, but she lacked a tiara. Here, she was a humble servant to the Creator. The crown would come later.

The Priestess brought out a scepter with a golden ball decorated with sapphire jewels on the end of it. Instead of chalk, this time there was a powder molded to fit the ceremonial circle. Tamantha was careful when she stepped into it.

"A child of the Creator has decided to seek out what gifts the Creator has blessed upon her. The child is willing to find the light that will guide her through this life and on to the next," the priestess recited.

"Blessed be the Creator!" the crowd responded. The crowd included select important sons and daughters of dukes, duchesses, baron, baronesses, and even some had their own title. Athan stood dutifully at the front of the pack to act as the princess's escort into the light. His status as someone who has not received the light in this sacred ceremony matters little here. It is

Tamantha's own soul that takes priority because it was her tribal rite to seek out the past and shape the future.

Cole was also here. Sara and Davin were also here for the ceremony at Tamantha's wishes. If her mother had her way, the only guests would be those with an official royal title and not those who made their way through society with money.

The priestess twirled with the scepter, chanting sacred words from the ancient tongue of Prota. It is said these words even trace all the way back to the Creator's birth years, molded by users of magic for many years. A spell book was created as an ultimate guideline for how the Creationist religion should be worshipped. There were no specific books labeled as the one and only rule book to follow. If the Creator wished Her story to be told in full, She would write the book Herself.

The powder began to glow a bright silver as the priestess chanted louder. "Show the child her path!" Tamantha felt warm as something resonated in her.

"Show her the power of eternity!" the audience called.

"Let this child have a taste of the immortality that our souls hold," the priestess finished. "Give me your hand, sister."

Tamantha presented her hand with her inner wrist facing the priestess. The priestess traced her fingers along Tamantha's wrist.

"This child's own soul reaches back to the times of Prota. The Creator has personally touched her soul in one of her lifetimes. She is eternally blessed," the priestess announced. Tamantha was unsure what it meant, but it holds great power if the Creator has appeared to her in one of her many lives.

"Blessed be!" The audience began to hum and stomp their feet.

"I call upon the Creator to show this child her mark!" The priestess began singing in the ancient tongue, dancing around

Tamantha. "Show yourself, child!" The ceremonial circle began to enclose Tamantha and wrap around her body, reaching up onto her wrist. The silver lines began to take shape, announcing the mark that matched all her other past lives. It was glistening under the warm glow of the silver candles around the hall. "And it is as it always was," the priestess finished, kneeling on the ground and bowing to Tamantha.

"Thank the Creator," the audience announced together, bowing just as the priestess was. Most ceremonies do not include bowing, but a sign of the Creator's blessing warrants special significance to the person being performed on. Some theorize it meant all your lives would be blessed, and some believed it just meant you would see your soul mate in each lifetime from then on. It could also mean nothing at all, or that your soul has a one-track ticket to whatever might be the final resting place.

Tamantha stood up from her circle. "Thank you all for witnessing my mark, and thank you, priestess, for showing me the light," Tamantha spoke. She raised her right hand in the air, showing off the mark. The silver light on her wrist glowed even more, sending a burning sensation through her arm. The shining beam broke, dissipating into fine glistening powder dissolving in the air.

Athan linked with Tamantha's arm. They stood outside the grand door, waiting for the ball to begin. He peeked down at the new tattoo. "It's beautiful, Your Royal Highness." Tamantha glanced down at her own wrist.

"Yes, I guess it is," the princess replied.

The mark was in the shape of a straight line. Two lines spiraled around the center line. A circle stood at the top of it all. It was in the same glistening silver that resonated from the powder.

The priestess said the shimmering could fade, but she also said it was unlikely since it is known Tamantha has met the Creator in one of her lives. Tamantha has only seen a couple of people with wrists that resemble the same color as her own. Most people have black marks. It was perfectly normal and nothing to be ashamed of.

The archivist had already taken the liberty of drawing it and mentioning she would soon have a list for Tamantha to read through. She was in no rush though. A photo shoot was lined up for tomorrow to reveal to the world her mark. No doubt the newspaper would have all the details about Tamantha's past lives before Tamantha even looks into it.

"I see your mother has spared no expense for the crown princess's birthday," Athan admired, peering around at the lavish decorations in the palace halls. The queen hired the most esteemed party planner in Sophia to put on the event of the century. She will have to top this when Tamantha marries.

"The Celaeno always believes royalty must display the respect it deserves. Royalty must be seen as perfection in the eyes of the common folk. This is all a show to those who were invited today to showcase her daughter's worth. It is my mother's pride," Tamantha answered.

The keeper of the crown jewels presented himself to Tamantha with a formal bow. He turned to his side and picked up the crown princess's tiara from a blue silk pillow. The tiara was tall, a size usually meant for a queen. Tamantha bent over for a second, allowing him to place it on her head. Her hairdresser was by her side, fixing each strand that may have come out of place.

When Tamantha fully stood, she was no longer a child of the Creator, but instead, she is now a crown princess to one of the great nations of Atlantis. Tamantha looked into the eyes of her chosen escort. She could see the change in his eyes. She was no ordinary woman. She carried the weight of a country on her shoulders.

Tamantha wished the only look in his eyes would be seeing her just as Tamantha and not as a future queen. She wanted him to love her as a woman.

"Are you ready, Your Royal Highness?" Siberius asked, dressed in full Guardian uniform. Tamantha took a deep breath, letting the mask fall on her face.

"Yes, we're ready, Siberius. Open the doors," Tamantha announced. Athan linked his arm again. Tamantha could feel him shaking a little bit. "I believe in you, Athan." He straightened up at her words. She glanced at him as the door began to open, releasing the mask for a second to give him a cheesy grin. Once the doors were fully open. She wore the same placid face her own mother carries.

"Her Royal Highness, Tamantha Alexandria Merope, Crown Princess of Sophia!" Siberius called out. Tamantha watched as a sea of colors made waves at the announcement.

Tamantha wished she had insisted as much as her own brother did to make the twentieth birthday party as private as possible, but then again, he never took his role as Crown Prince seriously.

Tamantha could see her friends off in the background, hiding behind the esteemed guests. They were full of pride for their little Tamantha all grown up, but they were also smirking at her embarrassment.

Athan led Tamantha to the middle of the ballroom and let go, allowing her to be by herself in the middle of the crowds. He bowed to her, and she curtsied back.

"Ladies and gentlemen, thank you for coming to my birthday celebration. I welcome you all to enjoy the festivities and dancing and eat to all your heart's content. It is my twentieth year in this life, and I hope the years to come will be full of happiness and love. I wish the same for all of you. Let us begin the ball to celebrate my twentieth birthday," Tamantha spoke, earning applause from the entire room.

Athan approached her once again, holding out a hand to her. She curtsied as she took at it. Music began to play in the background. It was classic Sophian. Athan placed a hand on her back, and Tamantha also put a hand behind her back, linking with Athan.

This type of dancing was part of her education in her childhood. She would do the appropriate dances accustomed to each country. She took a step back, and Athan followed. They twirled on the dance floor.

While still linking their arms, Tamantha turned and faced the other way. The couple walked in a circle and returned to their original position. Tamantha took her unused hand and grabbed on to his arm on her back. She guided her fingertips on his arms and pulled the arm away, placing her left hand in his right hand. Athan's unused hand went around her back and grabbed her other hand. He extended that arm outward, and they began to waltz. He released the hand she had grabbed, and he lifted their arms and spun her in place.

The dance ended with him gently leaning her whole body backwards. The people clapped in awe. Guests began to move onto the dance floor and start their own dancing. Athan bowed to her and helped lead her off the dance floor.

"Thank you, Athan," Tamantha whispered, looking into his strange eyes.

Athan smiled sheepishly, kissing the back of her hand. "I am only so lucky that I have the best dancer on the floor."

"That was lovely, my dear," the princess's mother piped in, clasping her hands together. The King was by her side as a formality.

"Your Majesties!" Athan bowed to the both of them.

"I was wondering if we may have a discussion with our daughter," Alvyn commanded. It was not a question. The King would always have his way. Athan nodded, bowing as he left the three of them to their conversation.

Tamantha watched the boy make his way over to her friends. Cole patted him on the back rather hard. Sara held onto the arm of her boyfriend, marking her territory. Davin jokingly asked Athan for a dance. Tamantha listened to the burst of laughter coming from them all. She wished she could be over there, rather than in the gaze of both of her parents. They never spoke to her together unless it was serious.

"My darling daughter," her mother mused, "a soul touched by the Creator. It's an honor to have the heir to the throne as my child, but a blessed soul as well? I could never be any prouder. My oldest sister will be jealous of how good my life is, despite being the youngest child of the Caleano royal family."

"Let us save this for another time, wife," the king chided. He didn't want Clarissa to get too full of herself before the night is over. Tamantha raised an eyebrow.

"What do you need, Papa? Mama?" She was growing tired of the attention already. One of them was bad enough, but two of them meant Tamantha felt enormous pressure by being in front of the most powerful couple in Sophia, despite them being her parents.

"Right," Alvyn cleared his throat. The king, the queen, and

the princess hovered near the wall. A wall of Guardians formed, barely hiding the fact there is a secret discussion going on. "Before this night is over, I would like it if you chose the man who will be your husband. As the heir and one of the only direct Merope descendants, it is time you perform your royal duty to continue the bloodline." Tamantha could barely hold her surprise that her own father was just as much behind the plan as her mother is. He had barely uttered a word about it until this moment.

"I invited as many of your suitors as I could to your ball, but I suspect you already have chosen whom will have your hand. I would like to add that even though I would rather you marry the son of the Head of the Symvoulio. He would bring about the most beautiful red headed princes and princesses." Her mother peeked at Tamantha's best friend and Tamantha's last resort.

"Yes, I think I have decided. I am aware of the importance of producing more heirs for the throne," Tamantha admitted.

"It is not only about producing more heirs. It is also about sharing the throne with someone who will support you in every way. The one you marry will be there for you every step of the way, He will be your rock and your shoulder," the King reiterated, following Tamantha's gaze towards the silver eyed boy. "He is just as worthy to be your husband. Maybe even more."

"I know," Tamantha whispered, feeling the warmth rise in her cheeks.

"There is one other thing, my daughter." The princess turned to look at her father, sensing his next words would carry the true purpose of this talk. "There must always be a blood heir to each of the Seven sisters. It is what the Creator commanded. To not have an heir will have dire consequences for the Eklektos, for the world. She put a spell in place to ensure the seven families must always exist."

Her mind played the last sentence over and over in her head. "But that would mean," Tamantha pondered.

"Yes, even the Electra family must have an heir," Alvyn answered her silent question. "That heir is unknown to us, but their existence is real. The Guardians of the Electra family do their part to make sure the Electra heir exists. All talks with those Guardians end with little to go on about whether this heir will rise up to take the throne of Astrapi or who they even are. We can only trust them."

"Let's move on to the topic at hand, dear. Tamantha, you must make your intentions known tonight. Please turn this birthday celebration into an engagement party as well," Clarissa beckoned, placing her hands on Tamantha's bare shoulders.

"Okay, I will. Let me enjoy my party as much as I can for now, please? I will make the announcement as soon as I hear his answer," Tamantha responded. She hugged the queen and king, being one of the only people in the world who could get so close. She curtsied to her parents, leaving them to themselves. The king would go off to enjoy a bit of drink, and the queen would go on to entertain the guest and ensuring that the night is perfect. This was the only rare moment where the king and queen could be witnessed together.

Tamantha strolled over to her group of friends. "There she is!" Cole called, leading the bow. Tamantha smiled gently, eyeing her escort.

"What a gorgeous dress, Tammy," Sara hummed. Sara twirled around with her beau, letting her own sparkly lavender dress shine.

"Thank you, Sara. You are just as stunning. Peterson, you are a lucky man. Don't ever let her go," Tamantha commented. Sara squealed in delight, clinging herself closer to the man who had captured her heart.

Davin disappeared into the crowd before Tamantha came. He was already on a quest to find a woman who would spend the rest of the evening with him. She caught a glimpse of her cousin with her ladies. Lady Christine was watching him flirt with other girls, but she tried to hide it amongst the high-born women. Tamantha wondered if Christine would ever go through with a marriage proposal to a man with no status. Davin only had money at his disposal and the blood of the Eklektos. Her cousin was always about titles, so it was a wonder why she would choose someone who was much lower than her.

Cole was currently entertaining a princess of the Maia. She had been asked to come as a representative of the Seven families. She likely had no idea she would capture the attention of the guest of honor's best friend. Cole met eyes with Tamantha, asking her for permission in silence. She flashed him a grin, turning her sights on the man who had garnished most of her focus.

Cole escaped the mini party with the Maia princess on his arm. The two would dance most of the night away.

"Excuse us, Your Royal Highness. Peterson and I are going to go enjoy this song," Sara announced, leaving Athan and Tamantha by themselves.

Tamantha took Athan's hand in hers. "Let's step outside for a moment, shall we?" Tamantha asked. Athan followed her obediently, ignoring the two Gagnon siblings who chose to accompany them. She and Athan went out onto the balcony overlooking the Palace gardens.

"How old is this palace by the way?" Athan wondered, studying the details of the towering walls.

"It's as old as Sophia herself. You've read about the wars that went on to decide where the seven families would each go. When the country borders were finally settled, the Merope made this their home. That must have been seven hundred years ago. Most of the palace has its original stones, save for expansion. My ancestors spared no expense when choosing to create their throne to look upon their newfound kingdom." Athan marveled at her words. He was a historian, and the castle grounds were a focal point in Sophian history.

"You know the losers of that war had to split a continent," Athan remarked, a sly smirk painting on his face.

"Yes, I suppose so. All the other families got their own islands to themselves. The Electra and Merope were in a battle for the last few hundred years over where that split would occur. Don't ever tell anyone I said this, but I think with the Electra family gone, us Merope should just take over the whole continent."

"I will leak that to the press," Athan chided.

"Don't you dare. I will just deny it anyways. Rumors like that happen all the time. It's just a matter if anyone acts on them." Athan chuckled, stroking a thumb on the back of her hand. She let go and ushered him to sit next to her on the concrete bench. He paused a moment, knowing if he chooses to sit there, it will be very hard to turn back. Tamantha smoothed the creases of her dress, trying to focus on something else. She peered into his silver eyes, searching for an answer to her question before she asked.

Tamantha felt the weight of the crown pressing down on her. She was so tied to it. Even if love came of a marriage with him, this was always going to be about duty.

Chapter Twenty

"Athan Wright, as you may know, the princes and princesses of the royal families marry early on in life. We have a mission to always have an heir ready to sit upon the throne. Not all of us have a chance to marry for love," Tamantha began. Athan mulled the weight of her words.

"Are you trying to say something, Tammy, or rather, ask something?" Athan teased. Tamantha straightened her posture. She wanted him to see how serious this situation is.

"You are my first choice, and you are the only one I would want to be with. You have done so much for me, and you have shown me what love might really be like. However, I will understand if you decide to say no. I will be okay if you refuse. Although, I might be a little heart broken." He placed his lips on hers, causing her to freeze up.

"Ask me the question, Your Royal Highness," Athan beckoned

"Would you like to do me the honor of marrying me?" Tamantha would admit her heart was beating so wildly, but it was also slowly dropping off of the pedestal in fear.

"I will, always and forevermore. There is nothing that would ever get in the way of becoming your husband," he stated, kissing the back of both her hands. He locked his lips with hers.

Tamantha erupted in a smile, overwhelmed with joy. She felt so strange, but she also felt free. She wrapped her arms around him, nuzzling her head in his chest, wishing it would always just be the two of them in this quiet world.

This small happy moment would only last for so long.

"Hello, everyone. Thank you for coming to my celebration. I have an announcement to make. With the King's blessing, of course," Tamantha paused, peaking at her dear old father. He was smiling sheepishly. He had gotten into the wine, but he was also drunk on his happiness.

Tamantha hovered closer to her fiancé, relying on his closeness to calm her nerves. He snuck a hand behind her and pinched her back.

She cleared her throat. "I have decided to make Athan Wright my future husband, and he has agreed to marry me." The crowd gasped and awed, erupting in claps throughout the room. "Athan, despite all that has happened between us, I am happy to choose you to be with me every step of the way, through thick and thin. Thank you for allowing me to be your wife someday. I believe this will be a marriage of true happiness and love, and it will be beneficial to our great country of Sophia."

"To the Crown Princess of Sophia and her fiancé!" Cole called out. People raised their glasses and sipped the wine.

Tamantha grinned, happy to receive so much support from those closest to her. "Back to dancing, shall we?" Tamantha said, earning a loud cheer.

The people in the ballroom resumed what they were doing

while Tamantha turned to look up into those familiar silver eyes. Athan tilted his head, sneaking a kiss as Tamantha kept staring at him. She weakly squeaked in surprise. He smirked at her.

"Tammy, I'm so happy for you!" Sara cried, embracing her best friend. "I think he's the right choice for you. It's like you and him have already been together over thousands of years." Tamantha squeezed her best friend's hands.

"Thank you, Sara." Tamantha never dreamed she would find someone she truly cared for. She never understood why people were gushing over true love when she was expected to just settle and assume her role. It probably would have been easier if she wasn't the one wearing the crown. It would have been easier if it was Nolan.

She wondered what Nolan would say about his little sister getting married. He was never excited about his own marriage, but he accepted his duties. He always told her she had to marry someone for love if he couldn't.

"Congratulations, Your Royal Highness, and congratulations to you, Athan. You make a fine couple," Sara's boyfriend said, shaking Athan's hand and bowing to Tamantha. "Honey, shall we step outside to explore the gardens for a little while?"

Sara giggled sweetly in response with a nod. "Sorry, Tammy. We'll be back soon. Peterson really wants to see the grounds. He's always had a soft spot for architecture. He never dreamed he would be inside the Sophian palace."

"Be safe, okay?" Tamantha chided, almost ready to push the two out the door herself.

"Of course, we will." Sara and Peterson snuck past the guards in front of the garden doors. Sara didn't really have to try hard to be let outside, since they recognized her as one of the princess's beloved friends.

"Your Royal Highness, may I have this next dance?" Athan asked, offering his hand to her. She nodded politely and curtsied to his bow. They twirled their way onto the ballroom floor.

Tamantha never understood what it meant to be in love, but now, she never wanted to let go of this feeling. She never wanted to let him go for as long as she lived.

Her eyes glossed over, letting time escape from her fingertips. She could be here forever if need be.

People gawked and eyed the new couple. If anyone had any objections, it was not up to them. This would be their future prince.

Tamantha's father interrupted the shared dance between them. "May I speak with the two of you for a moment?"

"Sure, father," Tamantha replied, wondering what was troubling her dear father.

The three of them went to a small room behind the thrones, shutting the doors behind them. The Guardians of the King and Princess huddled closely on the outside, a face of grave importance decorated on them. If anyone came even ten feet close to the door, the death stares would surely scare them off.

"First off, allow me to say congratulations to you, my darling daughter and my future son-in-law. I've been waiting for this day to come since the day I found out you were going to be my child." Tamantha blushed.

"Thanks, father," Tamantha whispered, feeling him stroke his hand along her cheek. He would have gladly ruffled the top of her head, but the giant crown was in his way. Plus, his wife would not be afraid to start her daughter's reign if any hair was out of place because of the King's recklessness. He was married to her long enough to know better.

"Thank you, Your Majesty. I promise to treat her right and be there by her side through the many years to come," Athan offered, glancing at his beautiful fiancé.

"I know you will, Athan. We expect nothing else of you, not me, the queen, or your mother." Tamantha raised an eyebrow at that last word.

"My mother?" The king had mouth was etched in a straight line. His eyes focused hard on Athan and Tamantha.

"I believe it's time I told you the truth about Athanasia Wright. It is just as vital to your impending wedding. Now that I know you two will be together, it does not feel right to keep it as the King's secret anymore."

Tamantha felt warmth rise inside her. She had longed to give Athan his mother all this time, and she never knew their love would be the key to unlocking the mystery surrounding Athanasia.

"Before I tell you, you must make an oath of silence about everything said from this moment on while we are in this room. If it is ever leaked, the world will change, and the marriage between you can never happen. Swear it, Tamantha. Swear it, Athan."

"I solemnly swear to never speak these words to anyone else," Tamantha said. Athan repeated her words. He began to grip hard on her hand, and she squeezed back, letting him know she was here.

"Good."

The King glanced at the door in case it would swing open in the next few seconds. The barrier was sealed shut, and the Guardians outside were already sworn to never divulge the secret innings of their charges. Not a single normal guard would be anywhere close to those doors.

"Athan Wright, are you ready to hear about who your mother really is?"

Athan nodded, eager for any information about the woman who gave birth to him and his brother.

"Athanasia Wright has always been known as Athanasia only. The last name was only tacked on after the marriage to her last husband. It identifies her place in this timeline, but she is Athanasia. She is the immortal."

"She is the Creator," Athan continued, letting go of Tamantha's hand in shock.

"Yes, your mother is the Creator, the one who brought about Pleione and Atlas. She is the one who gifted us with the looks of youth forever for whoever descended from Prota."

Tamantha felt her heart drop. Her original theories were incorrect. Athan Wright is not the descendant and heir of the Electra family, but rather, he is the son of the Mother of all Eklektos.

"This is something that would put Athan's life in grave danger. The world would want to use him. By keeping this secret, it protects him, but it also protects the Creator."

"The Creator has existed all this time? For all these years?" Tamantha asked. Athan was busy standing there without a word escaping his gaping mouth.

"Why wouldn't She? She can never die," the King spoke. "What this means for Athan in terms of his life expectancy is questionable, but it is assumed he will be just like the Creator's other child from Prota. He will also die like any other normal Eklektos or Anaxios."

"But what about his Guardian powers?" Tamantha continued, trying to get out answers for her beloved fiancé because he was unable to speak.

"It's assumed that Athan and Clayton cannot truly have a charge because their mother's own blood surpasses the Guardian blood within them. It is also why they do not have the same afflictions as other Eklektos like the drinking of another's blood. Their blood is above even our own, all of the royal family's. They are one of the purest entities of the Creator because they were directly born of her. We are beneath them." Tamantha was shocked at his words. The royal families were always valued as the highest among the entire world and were considered the closest to the Creator herself.

"My mom is the Creator?" Athan croaked, finally finding his voice.

"Yes, and this is why you are worthy of marrying the future Queen of Sophia," Alvyn answered, confirming his blessing on this union.

"Why was I never told about this in the first place? Why keep it a secret? My mother is dead! She died when Clay and I were children," Athan stated. The King had a grim look on his face.

"I know of this incident, but I cannot divulge any further details about the situation for the time being. That is something I am sworn to secrecy on until the Creator's qualifications for release come to pass," Alvyn said. Athan's mouth quivered as he knew he could not press the issue any further. He had no idea what came of his mother.

Athan stepped away from Tamantha and walked towards a portrait on the wall. The portrait was a picture of seven sisters surrounding Atlas and Pleione. The Creator was hovering above in the distance with a golden aura around Her, holding Her arms out to Her children.

"Is this the only thing that protects Clayton from the death penalty?" Athan questioned, thinking of the only family he had left.

"Yes. Any other person who tries to kill a member of the royal family would be executed without hesitation. Clayton's relation to the Creator ensures he will not face it. This incident would have also disqualified you from becoming Tamantha's betrothed, but because of your mother, all doubts are washed." Tamantha reached out to Athan, pulling him towards her. He stared into her ice blue eyes.

"Thank you, Your Majesty, for giving me this information. I was always curious to know who my mother really is. I know plenty about my father, but I knew very little about my mother."

"Not all is known about what it means to be a blood child of the Creator as there are very few of them in the world. The most famous one is your half-sister on Prota, but everyone felt the effects of immortality while there."

Tamantha peeked over at the man she had proposed to. He was a literal child of the Creator. Her crown meant very little in his presence.

"I believe you should get back to your party, Tamantha. I am sure you will keep this information absolutely discreet. I trust you both. I would very much like to see the merging of the Merope family with the Creator's bloodline." The princess and the pauper bowed to the King as they made their way out of the room. As the door shut behind them, the truth was mute.

Athan held out his hand and led Tamantha back to the dance floor. They swung around the ball room, letting the world fade around them. The cheers, the laughter, and the murmurs all drowned away. Tamantha caught his silver eyes with her own ice blue eyes. She was looking into the eyes of the Goddess that all beings of Atlantis worshipped. She could feel something had changed within the man in front of her.

Athan leaned forward and silenced her thoughts with a long kiss, ignoring the stares of those around them. Tamantha closed her eyes. He is the man she is going to marry. He was just Athan Wright, but it was a name broken in half in honor of his mother, the Mother of them all. Should she really be risking his life for her own selfish needs?

The garden doors slammed open, and screams echoed from the nobility as they watched a blood covered man enter the ballroom, carrying a small woman. Dirt mixed with blood covered the woman's face.

The Guardians hurried the King and Queen out of the room, not taking any chances. The Guardians of the Princess quickly huddled around her.

"Your Royal Highness, we must take you to shelter," Siberius called, grabbing her wrist. Tamantha yanked it away as she studied the silhouette. Siberius tried to reach out to her, but Athan stepped in his way. The tall Guardian gave him a death glare, ready to cut down this man. Tamantha slowly tip toed her way over to the bloody man.

The man fell to his knees with a loud cry. "Please help her," he begged, looking towards the Crown Princess. Tamantha reached the couple and knelt down in front of these strange creatures. She put her hand on the woman's face.

"Sara," Tamantha whispered. The world went black.

Tamantha eyes opened wide, studying the people hovering over her.

"Your Royal Highness!"

"Tammy!"

"Tamantha," the last voice called. She met with silver eyes. She rose into a sitting position. She was not in the same spot as before. She was on a velvet couch in the corner. She peeked around the people so concerned around her, looking for the bloodied man and Sara.

They were gone.

She noticed Davin standing in front of a Servant's door that led to the kitchens.

"What happened?" she questioned, staring directly at her Captain of the Guardians.

"Sara was attacked in the gardens. Peterson was with her, but he was unharmed. He brought her in to the ball room to try to save her, and then you passed out." Tamantha tried to stand up, but Elsa nudged her back down.

"Please stay, Your Royal Highness. We don't know why you fainted like that."

Most of the guests had been forced to leave, except for Tamantha's closest friends.

"Where's Sara?" Tamantha asked, hoping for an answer that meant everything would be okay.

Siberius continued, ignoring the princess's questioning for the time being, "Peterson told us that Sara had been attacked by a man in an owl mask. We believe it is the same person connected to the Clayton Wright case. The Guardians are searching the Gardens and the Palace. We have some Guardians checking outside of the gates."

Davin stopped staring at the servant door and walked over to the fallen princess. Tamantha could see the glimmer of his tears. Her heart was breaking as she put the puzzle together.

"Sara Fletcher is dead, Your Royal Highness," Siberius announced. Tamantha shook her head, furiously.

"That's not true. It's going to be okay, Davin. She's going to be fine. Where is she?"

Davin got down on his knees in front of Tamantha. Tamantha got down on the ground with him. She felt his voice vibrate through his whole body as her bare shoulder was glistened with the tears of a broken man.

"She can't be gone, Tammy! She can't be! Not my Sara!" Davin cried out.

Tamantha could not help but feel like this was because of her. She let Davin use her, gently running her fingers up and down his back. Was his sister's death because of Tamantha?

Was Sara the real target, or was she a decoy?

Tamantha knew it was her fault, just like Alessandra's death was her fault. The crown gained even more weight on top of her head as she added another lost soul to its jewels.

"Peterson took Sara's body into the kitchen to shield her away from her loved ones. You can go see her if you would like?" Siberius offered.

Tamantha pulled herself away from Davin and looked into his green eyes, asking, "Do you want to see her, Davin? I will only go if you want to." She didn't want to accept that Sara was dead, but this was the only way to confirm the truth with her own eyes.

Tamantha kept her composure even though she was surrounded by people who knew the woman behind the crown. She decided she would have to be the rock that holds down the people who wished to float away. She held onto those strings tightly. She would not let her loved ones lose their grip on reality.

"Let's go see her, Tammy," Davin answered, rising with Tamantha with the help of Elsabeth.

Tamantha felt the world spin around her again. She heard a sharp ring in her ear. Tamantha did not understand why she felt this way. "Your Royal Highness, please go easily," Elsabeth warned.

Tamantha walked slowly towards the servant door, linking her arm with Davin's. Athan was holding her other arm, holding her steady. The Guardians were carefully trailing behind her in a protective barrier. Elsabeth stood in front of her and paused their pursuit.

"Let me go in first to make sure it is safe. Wait for my signal."

Tamantha agreed with a grimace. She turned to look at Davin's face. He was visibly shaking, staring directly at a random spot on the floor. "She was my only family. She was the only one who ever really understood. I can't lose her too."

"I know. I'm sorry. I wish it didn't happen this way," Tamantha acknowledged, feeling the weight of the crown drop her head even further down.

Elsabeth returned from the kitchen, a deep frown decorating her face. The Gagnon siblings made eye contact, and Elsabeth shook her head at her brother.

"Your Royal Highness, I don't know how to say this, but they are not in there."

"What?!" A loud clang hit the ground, and Tamantha's crown rolled away into a wall.

"What do you mean she's not in there? Where is Sara?" Davin demanded, letting go of Tamantha. Tamantha began to fall forward, but Athan caught her. He leaned her up against him, letting her use his body weight.

"Peterson and Sara are gone," Elsabeth announced.

"Davin, let's not be rash. We will have all of the Guardians looking for them when we get the chance," Siberius soothed, moving between Davin and the princess.

"Don't be rash?!" Davin yelled. "Don't be rash?! That's a lot of bullshit coming from you. You talk about the Guardians doing this and that, but now my sister is dead! You Guardians can't do a damn thing right! Sara would be alive if it wasn't for you guys. If you guys weren't so damn incompetent and caught the killer sooner rather than later, she would be here. She would be with me."

Tamantha watched the exchange in shock. "You don't mean that, Davin," Tamantha whispered. Davin glared at her.

"I do mean it. This is all your fault, Tamantha! You dragged my sister into this. You killed her," Davin cried out, approaching her. Siberius blocked him and forcefully shoved him away. "Back off, man! You think I would hurt her? She's still my best friend."

"Our duty is to the Merope crown, and it will always be that way. Whatever happens to anyone else is not our concern. We are sworn to protect our charge, a member of the Merope family. What little resources we can use to help you out, we will use, but Tamantha is our upmost priority," Siberius chastised. The other Guardians of Tamantha grabbed him by both arms, pulling him even farther away.

Davin began to laugh, looking directly at Tamantha with wild eyes. "I don't need you. I will find Sara on my own. I will bring her home," Davin said, breaking away from the two Guardians. He turned around and walked toward the servant door.

"Davin, don't go! Please!" Tamantha begged, feeling tears well up in her eyes.

"Davin, your sister would not want you hunting down for her body," Cole told him. Davin shook his head.

"I have to go. I'll write to you. I'm going to find her, and I'm going to punch that stupid boyfriend of hers." He stepped closer to the place where his sister and her boyfriend disappeared. He kept his eye on the door.

"Please, Davin," Tamantha squeaked. She didn't know what she was asking him for. "Be safe."

"Stay away from any owls, Tamantha. I hear they got sharp talons," Davin advised. He didn't turn around to look back at her and walked through the door.

Tamantha felt like she would never see Davin Fletcher again.

Chapter Twenty-One

Tamantha rubbed the etching on her wrist, trying to wipe away the silver shimmer. The mark didn't matter to her right now. The little ceremony could not replace the loss and hurt she feels in this lifetime. The Creator may not have even met Tamantha in a past life. Apparently, she had already met the Creator in this lifetime, and that was all that was needed to count. She could have been a nobody in all those lifetimes ago, but in this life, she was cursed.

Silver eyes were watching her closely while also being squished between Siberius and another large Guardian. This man was the child of the Creator of all Eklektos, but the Guardians didn't care. How much did that connection matter in the grand scheme of Tamantha's life now? It could mean very little, but it could also mean her life was destined to be intertwined with the man sitting in front of her.

Tamantha averted her eyes from her betrothed, looking out the window into the great distance beyond. The green forests blurred into grassy plains, and then washed into deep waters. Tamantha wondered what it would be like to live on the bottom of the ocean, unaware of the politics that ruled all lives in the lands of Atlantis.

Tamantha craved a life where the shackles of the monarchism could not hold her down. She wanted to live in peace. It was inevitable in this life. She was destined for greatness. Why else was she born into this world?

"What part of the beach are we going to?" Athan asked, trying to pull himself from the suffocating blockade.

"My family's castle on the ocean. We don't use it much lately," Tamantha answered, noticing the warning stare from Siberius. She rolled her eyes and looked away from him. The castle was reserved as a secondary home for heirs. Her own brother refused to make it his home though. He didn't want to be so far from his family. The castle was a safeguard in case anything happens in the Palace. The heir would be safe. Tamantha's own mother was unwilling to let Tamantha use this as her home after college.

Tamantha was swimming through murky waters, unable to reach the surface. It was a hand from above that kept her from sinking to the bottom. She was grateful for Athan's presence.

It was not a familiar itch. It was a coping. She believed she loved him, but she clung to him for his warmth. She clung to the draw. If that tie was ripped apart, she would not give him a second look. She needed him, and he needed her. It was simple, but it was oh so complicated. Who was he? Who was she? The simple tie between them kept her drawn to him. She could not pinprick it out of a lineup, but she would always latch onto it.

"Tamantha?" She gave a small smile, swerving her eyes to the window. She wanted to love him. Really. She did, but how much?

"Yes, Athan?" she responded, clasping the hand in front of her. She avoided looking into his eyes. What drew him to her, but what divided them?

"I want to be with you for the rest of my life." Her breath hitched. She pretended to hold onto his feelings, clinging to them. She could believe it, wholly, right?

"I do, too."

The karavi stopped.

They arrived at the family beach home. She stepped out. Is this what she really wanted, or is this what so many unreasonably died for?

"Athan!" she called, grabbing his callused hand. It was unfamiliar but comforting. This was Athan Wright. She was going to marry him.

"It's beautiful here. You're beautiful. I love you." Does he really? How long had they known each other? She clung to him, letting go of the inhibitions. She let go of the rationality. This man would be her fate. That is all.

Tamantha Merope is a princess. She will marry. She will have children.

It was unfair.

Her eyes glanced at this man. She was trapped as he was. They were destined, but they were not. They were tied, but reluctant. They had only known each other so for long. They would give into this lie. It was okay.

The two of them walked into the castle. She gave into the call of the walls around her. She was home. This belonged to her. His singular thumb rubbed her cheek. She leaned into it. It was going to be okay.

"Athan?"

His silver eyes met the ice blue eyes, "Nothing."

It would be nothing.

She was born into this life, and she would suffer its doings. Why else was she born here?

Her body clung to another thought, however. What would it be like?

She smashed her lips into his, hushing all of the thoughts that echoed in her mind. She loved him. She would be with him.

They stumbled into what was her brother's old bedroom, escaping the watching eyes of the Guardians. It was just him and her.

She removed her jewel encrusted high heels. She removed the medium pleated denim skirt. She removed the silk buttoned shirt with the royal crest. She removed the shackle of her title looped around her finger.

She stood as a woman and nothing else.

"You're absolutely perfect," Athan whispered. She felt whole in the embrace of those silver eyes.

It was going to be alright. It was going to be her future. She accepted it.

She leaned forward, mashing her body onto his, peeling his clothing off. She wanted him to her absolute desire. She was his, and he was hers.

Her eyes opened, staring up at the ceiling.

"Athan?" She searched the empty bed beside her. It was void of his presence.

She wondered if he was even there.

She grasped onto the sheet next to her. Her cheeks flushed. What?

Tamantha rose up out of the bed. Her face flushed, unable to realize where she was. "Athan, where are you?" She blindly searched the room, ignoring the dark feeling deep inside of her.

She put on a pair of loose pants and a too big tank top from the dresser, searching for rhyme or reason. Her eyes focused on the wooden door.

Tamantha refused to believe it. She refused to give in to the dread. Did he use her? Was it all for nothing? She pushed the door open and peeked out down the long cobblestone hallway.

"Princess?" a voice echoed along the empty hallways.

Her blue perplexing eyes captured on the distant shores past the castle window. She wanted to ignore this feeling. He wouldn't leave her, right?

She searched for the voice.

Why would anyone abandon her?

Who was really there anyways?

The uncertainty crept in.

She hugged the stone walls, looking for any reprieve. Had she spent a night drunk on love with a man who was almost a stranger? She felt robbed. She felt the aching pain so familiar to her these days. Is he okay?

"Your Royal Highness!" A hand placed itself on her shoulder. She turned around to look into the eyes she had known for most of her life.

"Siberius, where is Athan?"

A grim look painted across the Guardian's face. "He left."

Tamantha collapsed to her knees, letting the weight of it all crush her. "I can't lose him."

"I know, Your Royal Highness, I know," Siberius replied, kneeling beside her. He reached inside his breast pocket, pulling out a note. He took her hand and put the letter on it. "I didn't read it, but he said he was very sorry he had to go."

Tamantha shakily opened it, reading it silently.

Dear Tamantha,

I regret we cannot continue our engagement any further. The longer we are together, the more danger you will be in. Through my love for you, something finally awoke within me. My mother is Athanasia, the Immortal, the Creator. I remember that fateful day when she left my brother and I.

You came to our house with your father. You brought a whole entourage of servants and Guardians with you, but my mother was unmoved. She had called you there. "Are you certain?" your father asked. What was she so certain of? She took only you and I into her bedroom, and after we left, she was gone. She was dead.

The Creator was dead? She performed a ritual on both of us. The almighty Creator used her magic on us. I never understood the whys. She gave us her soul, joining us in this life. She had been waiting for us to come into this life, and she wanted to give us her protection. With the protection, no one will find us, and no one will harm us. We will live our lives innocently and freely.

However, with our love for each other, we broke that seal. We unleashed something deep within ourselves, whatever it was that drew her to us. The closer you and I are, we merge the two pieces of Athanasia's soul. She told us we will have her powers when we are close to one another. This is a power too great for anyone in this world to use. I hope you will eventually remember this truth. We must stay far apart, but it's so hard to stay away from you.

Here is why I left. She left me a memory for when the seal is broken. She said we cannot be together. I know you can sense it too. She sent me on a mission for when I awaken. I must find the children who descended from Athanasia's soul: Atlas, Pleione, and Harmonia. They are the souls the Creator had created herself. They are the ones who will bring about the end of the

Eklektos bloodline. They will restore peace to all of Atlantis.

Until I am able to bring about the change the world needs, I cannot be with you. I cannot marry you. I love you with all of my heart, Tamantha. I am sorry it had to be like this. If I had known it would end like this, I would have kept my distance. You will find someone else to marry. You will find someone else to love. You will be a glorious and just Queen someday. The nation of Sophia needs you more than you need me. I will find you when this is all over, and if you are with another, I wish you all the best even if it breaks me. Maybe in the next life, you and I will be together. I'm sorry, Tamantha. I love you.

With all my love,
Athan Wright

Tamantha felt her lip quiver, biting down on it to fight the pain. She leaned her head against the wall.

She understood.

He was following his duty, and she was following hers.

She couldn't help crying into Siberius's shoulder though. Her heart was broken into a million pieces. He sat still, unmoving, letting her use him.

The Creator had so cruelly pushed them together, and then she ripped them apart.

Tamantha rubbed the etching on her wrist, wondering if this life was the first time she ever met Her. She glanced down at the mark. She admired its shimmery gold.

Gold?

She shut her eyes and opened them again. What changed? She glanced at Siberius, but he said nothing. He was eyeing the glittery shimmer on her wrist.

"It is said Gold is the rarest color any sign should take. It has only appeared in history a couple of times. Only the most special souls can obtain this color: a child of the Creator herself," Siberius said, not taking his eyes off of it.

Tamantha hunched over, trying to hide her wrist from anyone's view. "It's bad enough I'll be the Queen of a whole kingdom one day, but this means so much more, doesn't it? Nothing will ever be the same." Siberius nodded.

"Everything will change, Your Royal Highness, but that is what life is. Nothing ever stays in motion. What it means for you, I do not know, but I do know your life is more important than any one of us can ever imagine. You are a child of the Goddess," Siberius responded. "I will always protect you no matter who or what you are." He put an arm around her, letting her lean into him.

This was the only moment where she could be no one. She would revel in it until footsteps echoed on the cobble stone. Siberius was giving her the only gift she ever wanted, even if it was only for a small time.

When she leaves this spot, she returns as Crown Princess Tamantha Alexandria Merope of Sophia. She returns as a blessed soul from the Creator, whatever her name once was. She returns alone.

Chapter Twenty-Two

"You are making a mockery of the Merope crown!" Clarisa Merope screamed at her only child. "You tell society you will marry, but then you turn around and change your mind? It's not allowed!"

"I'm sorry, mother," Tamantha whispered, shrinking under the harsh gaze of the Queen.

Clarisa shook her head furiously. "You bring that boy into our lives, and then you tell me he just walked away?! No more. It is an embarrassment to your father, to you, to the whole country! It's unacceptable. I can't believe you would to this to our family."

Tamantha dropped her head and clenched her fists on her thighs. "I know."

"Your engagement is out of your hands now. You will marry who the Symvoulio and I choose. You lost your chance."

"I understand, Mama." Tears streamed down her face, dropping onto the back of her hands.

She slammed her coffee cup on the table, shattering it into a million pieces. "Maid! Clean this up!" A woman rushed over, pulling a towel out of her skirt pockets.

Clarisa stood up and walked over to her daughter. She grabbed Tamantha's chin and forced her to meet her eyes. "Mama. I'm scared."

"You made a mistake, and you will live with it. How could you possibly give your heart to him?"

A knock came on the door.

"Come in!" A Guardian of her mother bowed after he came in.

"Your Majesty, the results have arrived," he stated, handing an envelope to the Queen.

"Thank you, Jon." She shooed him off, turning back to the situation at hand.

"What is that?" Tamantha questioned, trying to avert her mother away from the crisis at hand.

"It's an ancestry trace," Clarisa calmly stated, opening the envelope. "With your engagement to this Athan, I ordered an ancestry trace into his father's tree. With his mother being pure Eklektos since she created the bloodline to begin with, it's only proper to look into his father's side of the family. It took so ridiculously long to get our hands on it. Since he is the citizen of a different country, plus the Creator Herself put a seal on the records of her husband. It took a lot of persuasion, bribery, and blackmail, but here it is."

"What does it say?" Tamantha knew it didn't matter what the answer is. Any hope for a future with him has dwindled to next to nothing.

Clarisa peered at the paper, a scowl painting on her face. "Why don't you read and find out?" She handed it over to her daughter.

Tamantha took it into her hands, staring at the paper. "He has Anaxios in his bloodline." Tamantha felt all hope leave her body. The results showed his father's side of had an Anaxios marry into the family a few generations back.

"I guess the curse of the Merope family has chosen you. Your brother loved an Anaxios. Your father loved an Anaxios. You love an Anaxios, even if he is the Creator's child. Out of reach just like every Merope's true love." Tamantha's hands started shaking. It was doomed from the start.

"I didn't want this. I didn't want it to hurt so much like this. I want to be with him. I love him," Tamantha cried, letting the tears fall. She let herself become weak in front of her mother.

Although he fit the role perfectly, he was not meant to be. He could not marry her.

Clarisa's mask broke. "I know, darling. You're going to be okay. You'll find a right and proper man to marry. You'll marry a pure Eklektos who will support your throne and hold you when you feel scared. The person you marry will be your shoulder and your rock. They'll be there till the very end. I know because I am doing the same thing for your father." She was a mother at that moment.

Tamantha would cherish this little bit of compassion from her mother, the same mother who was going to grip her control on Tamantha's marriage with an iron fist. She relaxed in the gentle embrace of her mother.

"His Majesty, the King!" one of her mother's Guardian announced. Tamantha stood up with her mother, trying to wipe away the tears. King Alvyn walked in and motioned for the rest of the Guardians to resume positions as normal.

"Tamantha, I heard about Athan. I am so sorry it didn't work out between you both. He would have made a perfect husband and son-in-law." Alvyn wrapped his arms around his daughter, refusing to let her escape.

"I'm sorry for leading you guys down this path. From now on, I will not let my emotions get in the way of my duty," Tamantha offered.

Alvyn shook his head, putting her at arm's length. "I once did the same thing, my darling. I loved an Anaxios."

"Really, Papa?" She was confused that this great king and father of hers could ever have been in a different relationship.

"It was after Nolan's mother died and before I married your mother. I wanted to spend the rest of my days with the Anaxios woman. She was beautiful, kind, funny, and just everything I ever wanted in a woman, but it was not meant to be. Your great-grandmother knocked some sense into me. All of us Merope are doomed to love someone we can't have, and it seems you have fallen into the same trap. You both can never come back from this scandal. He will not be allowed to take your hand again. It's never going to stop hurting," Alvyn admitted, picking up a strand of Tamantha's hair and twirling it in his fingers.

Alvyn had never been this close to his own daughter. He was a king first before he was a father.

"But I'm scared, Papa. I only want to be with him. How can I ever love someone else?" Tamantha questioned, letting the regrets and sorrows seep into her being.

"You might not ever fall in love with the man you marry, but you will love who they are. They might keep their distance from you, but they will be there when you need them. It's true your mother and I do not have such a deep love for each other, but we are comfortable and appreciate the roles we have in each other's lives. Without your mother, I would never have you, my beautiful daughter. Together, we created you."

"Oh, papa," Tamantha whispered, hugging her father close. She didn't know when the tears would stop, but she felt reassured everything might be okay someday.

Tamantha filled out the application for her major.

"Are you sure, Your Royal Highness? You can always change it if you change your mind," the secretary questioned, taking the form and making notes on it.

"Yes. It's near and dear to my heart, and a Queen must learn from the past to give her country a bright future," Tamantha explained. She wondered what he would have thought of it.

It was a lie. She knew it was hopeless to think of him and try to bring him back, but he had made his choice. She wanted to feel close to him somehow, even if it is the most basic form. She wanted to follow in his footsteps. She wanted to be selfish. She wanted to understand his passions. She barely knew him, but he was a whole part of her she never knew.

Tamantha would try to take some control of her own life.

"Good luck, Your Royal Highness. We shall contact you when we have confirmation of an appointment with your guidance counselor. For now, please research the classes necessary and what path you might like to take." Tamantha nodded, taking a pamphlet on the History major from the secretary.

"Thank you," she whispered. She left the office with Elsabeth following close behind. She only had a handful of Guardians today. The rest were in a mandatory annual training session. The Guardians with her had done their training sessions the weekend Athan left.

"I'm sorry about Athan," Elsabeth muttered, shifting her eyes away.

Tamantha stared at her, shaking her head. "I love him, dearly, but we cannot be together. I just have to accept it," Tamantha answered. "He has a different purpose in this life than

I do." Elsabeth frowned.

"I admire your resilience in the face of grief," Elsabeth commented, putting on the mask of a Merope Guardian. The small moment of chit chat is over for now.

Tamantha pulled out her telecrystal and stared at it. A group photo of herself and her best friends floated on it. Tamantha realized how small her circle of friends had shrunk into. Alessandra is dead. Sara is dead. Davin has left the country to find Sara's boyfriend. Now she only has Cole left.

She didn't realize how alone she felt.

Elsabeth and Siberius were her friends as well, but they were paid to always be there by her side. They didn't grow up with her or seek her out because they wanted to be friends with her. They were here because of the call. They see every little moment of the Princess's life, but it wasn't the same.

"Tammy!" The princess turned to look at the voice. Christine approached her with a few of her own friends following close behind. It had been a while since Tamantha had seen Christine. Even though they were housemates, Christine usually spent most of her time outside of the penthouse, and Tamantha did vice versa. They could barely even sit together for one meal.

"Hello, Christine," the blonde hummed, taking one of Christine's hand in her own.

"I am sorry about your engagement," one of Christine's friends chimed in. Tamantha pursed her lips.

"Thank you," Tamantha breathed out.

"Sorry, ladies. I need to spend some time with my beloved cousin," Christine announced, linking an arm with Tamantha.

"Of course!" Her friends bowed respectfully to the two in line to the Sophian throne and departed. Elsabeth rolled her eyes at the show.

"How are you feeling, Tamantha? Let me see that tattoo!" Christine tugged on Tamantha's hand, turning it over to look at the back of the wrist. Tamantha had a bandage covering her wrist. She was worried what people might think of the unusual gold glow. She didn't know why the color had changed, but she wasn't ready for the world to see it.

"Sorry. It's really itchy lately. I'd rather keep the bandage on it till I can see a doctor about it," Tamantha excused herself, tugging her arm back away from Christine. Christine shrugged, taking it as the truth.

"I heard back from one of my suitors, and he proposed!" Christine had a large grin painted across her face. Tamantha was astonished Christine had already taken the necessary steps. "Well, not quite that he proposed, but his father arranged the marriage between us. Soon, I will be married."

"Congratulations, Christine. Who is the lucky fellow?"

"It's Davin Fletcher," Christine answered. Tamantha choked on her own breath.

"My Davin?" Christine nodded. Tamantha didn't understand how a grieving father could decide to just let his only child be left to be forced into marriage. The loss of Sara was still fresh.

"Davin sent word to his father that he would be alright with whatever his father decided. I would have preferred Davin proposed in person, but it's the best I will get. We will get married whenever he gets back. He's off on some a hell-bent mission to find that boyfriend who stole Sara Fletcher's body. Oh, right. I'm sorry for your loss," Christine comforted.

Tamantha sighed, letting the weight fall down on her shoulders again. "Thanks," Tamantha muttered.

"It'll be okay, Cousin. Let's go to lunch at the Blue Moon," Christine offered. Tamantha's breath hitched, remembering the face of the one she loved. He wouldn't be there.

"Okay," Tamantha agreed, letting Christine drag her off to the one place she was dreading. Christine ordered sandwiches for the both of them, chattering on about her pending engagement and the end of the school year.

Tamantha realized how little all of it mattered to her. She was expecting Athan to walk back in from the kitchen. She took a breath and closed her eyes, pushing away those thoughts. She doesn't have the time for a broken heart. She already cried her tears. Now, she must focus on the future.

"Tamantha, are you listening?" Christine hissed, annoyed about how little attention she was receiving from her cousin.

Tamantha took a bite of her sandwich. "Yes, Christine. I'm listening."

The woman in front of her was ready to take the crown that Tamantha was holding the keys to. She would not push Tamantha out of her way, but she would take it if she had the chance.

Tamantha spent very little time with Christine throughout her entire life. They only saw each other at parties and in passing at the Royal Academy. Christine tried to become a part of Tamantha's life, but Tamantha was resistant, keeping her distance from the second in line to the throne. It was out of duty to keep the next heir in line safe, but it was also because Tamantha felt little connection to her blood relative.

The two of them had been raised very differently. It was evident in Christine's tendency to make friends with only Royal blood and in Tamantha's ability to form a group with the most unlikely people for her to be close to.

If Christine left the country or decided to venture off elsewhere, Tamantha would not give her a second glance. The titles they shared and the blood that flowed through them was the only thing keeping them together. Why should Tamantha be obligated to make friends with her dear cousin?

Tamantha had very little friends left.

As different as they were, Tamantha could not push her away. She enjoyed the company of Christine, and she cherished the little moments they had together.

Tamantha knew the indifference coursing through her veins right now was because of tragedy after tragedy that has pushed Tamantha down to the ground. She is trying to push everything else away, so the same thing won't happen.

She does not wish to be alone, but it is a path on the fork of the road she stands on.

"I am going to Polemos for the summer. I will be studying under the same tutor as Queen Luvina. It is also supposed to strengthen the alliance between our two kingdoms, especially after the debacle with my brother's widow," Tamantha announced, sipping some hot tea. Christine nodded.

"Well, I hope the sessions prove useful. Please share any notes you have with me if at all possible. I got to rule a duchy someday," Christine said, grinning at the little kingdom she had control over.

"Of course, Chris," Tamantha hummed, gently smiling at the next runner up to the throne. "Did you pick your major yet?"

Christine nodded, takin a sip of her coffee. "I picked Politics with a concentration in Astrapian government."

"Oh?"

"I want to understand the government, their influences, and the culture. Plus, it would help to understand where my future husband is coming from." Christine peered at the princess. "You just came from the admissions office. Did you pick a major?"

"I did. I picked History."

"Interesting choice, I guess," Christine sighed.

Tamantha raised an eyebrow. She didn't feel like defending her choice. She made up her mind, and she was going to stick to it.

Tamantha stood up, putting down cash to pay for the whole bill. "I need to go study for our finals." She began walking away with Elsabeth following close behind.

"Wait! Tamantha, let's go home to the penthouse. Let's have dinner and talk. Let's make plans for our pending weddings. I know your engagement was cancelled, but it's more than likely your mother will have something for before you know it." Tamantha let out a big breath of air, turning back to Christine. She was really persistent today.

"Fine," Tamantha replied, waiting for Christine to finish up her own lunch. Christine gulped it down quickly in an unladylike manner. Tamantha pursed her lips.

Should she latch onto her cousin, make close friends with Christine? She would be a replacement for the missing holes Alessandra and Sara had created with their deaths, but Tamantha felt so reluctant to do so. She couldn't do that to them, even if they weren't around anymore to care.

"Yay," Christine hummed, linking arms again with Tamantha. Tamantha thought how strange Christine was today, almost a different person, but maybe Tamantha could get used to this.

Elsabeth trailed carefully behind, falling in line with Christine's own Guardians. She didn't seem very amused by this arrangement, but it was what her client chose.

"Where do you think the seven sisters are? Do you think they are living the lives of celebrities, or maybe they are less fortunate in this life, living paycheck to paycheck?"

"What kind of question is that?" Christine wondered, bewildered by her cousin.

"Well, we put so much emphasis on past lives, but we never are able to really trace our identities exactly, especially since the practice of the Mark did not exist until two hundred years after Prota disappeared. No one really knows who might be one of those sisters. No one knows where Atlas and Pleione are. The Creator is supposed to be immortal, but she hasn't appeared in years."

"True, but I don't think we're supposed to know. Their lives on Prota must have been much different. It must have been extravagant and luxurious, descending from the Mother and Father of the royal families," Christine answered.

"Maybe they never even existed."

"Huh?"

"The books could have been written in false pretense to worship a divine being, but what if she was never really divine?" Tamantha herself wondered why she was asking all of this. She knew the Creator existed. It was evident in Athan's blood. He was born to this immortal creator, or was he? Why do the people of Atlantis follow a book blindly without rhyme or reason? "What if it was created just so our ancestors could grasp power?"

"Then what?" Christine asked. Tamantha wasn't sure where she was going with this.

"As the royal family, we are meant to uphold the religion of the Creator. We are evidence to the people of Atlantis of what once existed. The Eklektos is our evidence, but what if our origins are different?"

"Tamantha, we aren't supposed to go looking for the answers. We're supposed to believe in what we know, and we are supposed to show the People that this is the truth path to follow. We are pillars to hold the Creator, the Mother and Father, and the seven Sisters. That's all we are." Christine let go of Tamantha's arm.

Tamantha looked at her, staring into the brown eyes of her family. "To plant a new idea will lead to chaos. You only know what you have seen or heard. I wish there was a way for us to get all the answers since the beginning of Atlantis before Prota even existed. Why is this the path we must follow?" Tamantha sighed, raising her hand to stare at her bandaged wrist.

Christine started to drift away from the conversation, unable to understand the tangent Tamantha was on. "Never mind, Tamantha. Let's do those dinner plans another time. After school starts? I'll see you at home, I guess." Tamantha nodded, letting Christine escape. Tamantha wasn't sure if she wanted to start the conversation about her pending doom due to whatever stranger her mother was going to choose.

Tamantha turned around, staring up at the tree she first saw when she came to the school. It was unchanging, growing ever so slowly. It would look the same to her when she would attend school here, but if she came back many years later, it wouldn't look like the tree she had grown so accustomed to seeing everything at Sophia College.

Tamantha searched the leaves that had finally returned to the tree.

Would the path Tamantha follows lead to destruction or happiness? The uncertainty was what scared her the most.

Chapter Twenty-Three

"Your Royal Highness! Thank you for joining us for your freshman year here at Sophia University. We look forward to seeing you again next year! We hope the major you have chosen will be beneficial to your role as our future Queen, and we hope you enjoy diving into our ancient past," the History major advisor announced, bowing graciously. He gave her a list of all the courses she would need.

Tamantha was unsure if she wanted to concentrate on the government side of history or if she wanted to focus on the religious side of history. Both were intertwined, but they had their own separate purposes.

It was especially indecisive for her at the moment after the strange conversation she had with her cousin.

Tamantha was grateful finals were over, and now, she could go home to her own bed in the palace.

She did dread the other things that were painfully attached to that palace. She would have to see her own mother and be forced to go to social events.

Clarisa was also going to tease Tamantha about all the

choices the Symvoulio and the Queen were making about who she would marry, but she would not fess about who the final pick would be. Tamantha will probably go into her own wedding blindly and hope her future husband will be someone she could get along with.

The bright side of things was that in a couple weeks she would be going overseas to Polemos to stay there for the summer, far away from her own mother.

Tamantha shook the Counselor's hand. "I'll make my decision about any concentrations next year. I promise." Tamantha grinned, showing a little bit of true self to this man.

Siberius escorted Tamantha out of the advisor's office. "Is that all for today, Tamantha?"

"Yes, Sibi. We have no other engagements for today! Let's go home. I think Christine might actually be home today for once," Tamantha confided. She was excited to go back to that penthouse and pack up her bags for the summer. She knows Christine will be going home to Rosebury for the summer, so they would not be seeing each other again until next year.

Tamantha almost skipped her way to the karavi, but she maintained proper pose and walked so gracefully her mother would have been delighted.

Tamantha took out her telecrystal, staring up at the picture of her and all of her friends. She let out an inaudible sigh, clicking open her messages. She whispered Cole, trying to make plans with him for tomorrow before her mother gets her hands on Tamantha. She had not seen him for the last few days, but he had constantly whispered her about his annoyances with his own finals. He kept threatening to drop out of school, but he knew it was not an option.

Once they got back to the penthouse, Tamantha was greeted

by the smell of Christine's chef's gourmet cooking. "What's cooking, good looking?" Tamantha sang, standing behind her cousin.

"What?" Christine raised an eyebrow, wondering if this woman in front of her was really her cousin. Tamantha smiled and shook her head.

"School is over!" Tamantha cried, raising her hands in the air in triumph.

"Yes, it is," Christine answered, slightly worried about her cousin.

Tamantha returned to her own bedroom, looking in her dresser for the carefully wrapped box. She had gotten a thank you gift for Christine. She returned to the dining room and placed it in front of Christine.

"What's this?" Christine hummed, always happy to receive gifts.

"Open it and see. My mother and I decided to pick this out for you. It's a gift from the King, the Queen, and me. We wanted to thank you for opening up your home to me this year after I had to leave the dorms," Tamantha explained, sitting in the stool next to Christine.

Christine carefully tore off the wrapping paper, revealing a jewelry box. She flipped open the box, staring down at the gift. "Thank you! It's so beautiful. Please let your mother and father know how grateful I am!" She slipped out the jewelry, placing the diamond bracelet with sapphires on her wrist. There was a metal disc on the bracelet with the sigil of the Merope family.

"You're welcome, Chris!" Tamantha chimed.

Tamantha's telecrystal began to glow. Tamantha looked down at the telecrystal and saw Cole's face floating on it.

"Oh, I need to answer this. I'll be right back!" Tamantha

excused herself, taking the telecrystal to her room. She felt it would be rude to her housemate if she started talking loudly on the telecrystal when her housemate was trying to wind down from finals being completely done. "Hey, Cole!" Tamantha answered.

"Tamantha," Cole replied. "Are you alone?"

Tamantha raised an eyebrow to no one. "Yes, why?"

"I'm so sorry, Tamantha."

"Cole?"

"Please don't come here!" Cole yelled, his voice drifting off into the background.

"Hello, Tamantha," another voice answered.

"Huh? Who is this?" Tamantha said.

"Don't panic. Pretend you're still talking to Cole. You know, unless you want him to die," the mysterious voice ordered. Tamantha's heart sank. She ignored her shaking hands and legs.

"Okay, Cole. What is it you want?" Tamantha responded, playing the mystery caller's games.

"I have your boyfriend here, Cole Baldwin. If you don't do what I say, he will die. Do you understand? Do not involve the Guardians. I will know if you do."

Tamantha took a deep breath. "Yeah, Cole. That sounds great!" She added fake cheer to her voice. She was unsure where this conversation was going, but she felt this man would go through with his threat if she didn't comply.

"Tamantha, don't do it! Stay away!" Cole demanded, trying to interject in the call. She heard a loud smack on the other line. She gasped, covering her mouth.

"Quiet, boy, or I'll make good on that threat!" the stranger growled.

Distant memories of a not so long ago past flooded into her mind, the torment in a deep unknown place, unable to fight back.

She felt like she was back in the basement with Clayton, but she wasn't. She was safe in Christine's penthouse.

"What do you want do after that, Cole?" Tamantha kept repeating his name. It felt so unreal.

No, no, no.

She couldn't lose him too.

"Anyways, Tamantha. I need you to come alone to the playground at Sophia Academy, and I mean absolutely alone. You must not tell anyone where you are going. You must be rid of all Guardians and guards. I will slit his throat if you don't."

"Why do you want to do that, Cole?" Tamantha asked.

"You will not ask questions. You will come here. You have one hour to get to the playground, or he will be dead," the stranger explained. "It starts now!"

The telecrystal stopped glowing.

Tamantha sat down on her bed, feeling the rising panic. She couldn't control breathing. She felt a single tear slide down her cheek.

What should she do? Let her only best friend left die, or will she help ensure he might live to see another day? She doesn't even know what this man has planned for her.

If it has anything to do with the events of the entire last year, then it did not mean anything good.

Tamantha grabbed a pillow off of her bed and screamed into it, trying to silence her voice as much as possible.

She couldn't let him die. She wouldn't.

He said he would know if she alerted the Guardians. It must be how he knew the route that would ultimately lead to her fated meeting with Clayton Wright. This stranger has always been here, but who is it?

She had to save Cole. She was the only one who could. With

everything that happened, she knew this stranger would make good on the threat. This was the man in the owl mask, the one who had ripped so many of her loved ones away from her.

It was all his fault.

She put the pillow gently back on the bed and put her telecrystal in her back pocket.

She breathed slowly, pushing away all of the dread.

She had to be the one to finish this. It all led back to her.

She stared in the mirror, barely recognizing the woman she now is. Tamantha had avoided the mirrors because she believed it would show the image of her brother, but now she realized she was her own person, making her own choices. She accepted her fate and would become Queen.

She could see the protector in herself. She wanted to protect this country. She wanted to protect her friends. She wanted to protect Cole.

It had to be done.

She sent a whisper to Christine, which was quickly followed by a knock. Tamantha opened it to see her cousin. Elsabeth peered up from the couch, probably sensing the fear and pain in Tamantha.

"Hey, Christine. I'm not feeling so good. I'm having a lot of anxiety right now because of that encounter I had months ago. I think I am just going to go to bed. I'll have breakfast with you in the morning," Tamantha announced within earshot of her Guardians.

"Do you want me to lay with you, or do you want Elsabeth?" Christine offered. Tamantha shook her head.

"No, I will be alright. Please enjoy your dinner. I'll see you in the morning." Christine shrugged and returned to the dining room. Tamantha met eyes with her blue haired Guardian.

Tamantha offered a fake grin and waved to Elsabeth, trying to reassure her everything is fine. Everything is going to be okay, right?

"Goodnight, Elsabeth!" Tamantha called, shutting the door. She slid down on the back of it, clutching her head, madly pulling at her own hair.

No, no, no.

Tamantha didn't know if she could do this. She had never gone out on her own before. She had never been truly alone.

She had to do it.

Tamantha pushed herself up off of the floor and walked over to the window. She gently opened it, trying not to alert anyone inside or outside of its opening. She took another deep breath.

She crawled out onto the fire escape, peaking at the ground. It was a long way down. Another deep breath. She searched for any sign of one of her Guardians patrolling the streets, but she had found none. Her outside Guardians were likely on break.

The stranger had planned it this way. He knew everything about the Guardians.

She trekked down the stairs of the fire escape, feeling no relief when she finally met concrete. She put her hair in a bun and put her hood on.

She never had to find directions to go somewhere. Someone always did that for her.

She whispered Sophia Academy to her telecrystal. She went to school there throughout her entire childhood, but she never thought about where it was in the city. She was walking into unknown terrain. The telecrystal glowed and pointed her in the direction she should go.

It was the last place she had seen Nolan before he died.

There were so many good memories at that school, but they

were all erased because of what the Academy was associated with.

She tried to remember the rules of the road. When was she supposed to cross the road? What part can she walk on? She always was delivered to exactly wherever she wanted to go, and she never ventured elsewhere.

Tamantha followed the glow to the Academy, almost making it with no issue. The strangers she passed by on the street barely glanced at her. The princess would not be out on the street by herself. It's just someone that looks like her.

She was no one right now.

Venturing out by herself should be exciting and freeing, but it wasn't. She was leaving one prison for another. The outside world was mute and uncaring.

Tamantha remembered meeting her best friends in this very school. Cole already knew her, but he enjoyed inducting Alessandra as part of the group. Sara and Davin didn't join until high school.

She looked up at the sky one last time, soaking in the blue color and the warmth of the sun. It might be the last time she would see it.

Tamantha approached the playground. She looked around, but no one was there. She gave up and sat down on a bench, waiting to see what would happen.

"Hello, princess," a voice growled behind her. She would have looked behind her, but she felt pin prick in her neck, watching the world fade to black.

Chapter Twenty-Four

When Tamantha Merope opened up her eyes, memories of the night of Nolan's death flooded into her. She looked at her surroundings, taking in the familiar blank canvas walls and the wooden bleachers.

"Are you finally awake?" a voice called.

Tamantha remained quiet, staring blankly at the source. It dawned on her what the last moments were before she woke up in this room. This man was wearing an owl mask. She had heard so many stories about this mask. She had so many tragedies occur because of it. She wanted to rip it off his face.

"Tammy! Why did you come?!" the voice of her red-headed best friend hissed. She turned to look at Cole, remembering why she was here. She had fallen into the trap of the owl mask.

"Hey, Cole. I couldn't just let you die. I'm so sorry," Tamantha whispered. She tried to reach out and wrap her arms around him, but she realized her arms were tied behind her back.

"You're such an idiot, Tammy. Now we're both going to die," Cole joked with bare teeth.

The man in the owl mask sat in a chair, staring at the two of them. Tamantha glared at him.

"What do you want? You got me here! Let Cole go, please! You can do whatever you want with me," Tamantha relented, tugging at the ropes. Cole shook his head.

"Your life is more important than mine." Cole was not letting the Crown drop off of her head.

"The throne will be able to replace me. I can't lose you," Tamantha whispered.

"I can't lose you either. We both lost our friends," Cole reminded, searching her ice blue eyes with his own chocolate eyes.

"Will you both shut up?" the kidnapper snarled, standing up. He grabbed Tamantha by the back of her shirt, causing her to squeal, and distanced her from her best friend.

"No!" Cole yelled. "Leave her be!"

The owl man stepped back, so both of them could look at him.

"I didn't really need you here, boy, but I needed the princess. How else do you lure her away from her Guardians?" the owl began to explain.

Tamantha felt her whole body shaking, fear coursing through her. This might be her last moments in this life. Everything that happened would be for nothing, but she would be free, right?

The man pulled out a syringe and approached Cole.

"No, don't!" Tamantha begged, trying to ram her body into the man, but she missed. Cole inched away, but he couldn't get far with his hands bound.

"I need a private conversation with Tamantha, and you're being absolutely too loud," the stranger growled, pricking Cole in the neck with the needle.

Cole passed out just as quickly as Tamantha had on the playground.

"Cole," Tamantha called, hoping he would wake up only seconds later, but he fell into a deep sleep, slumping onto the wooden planks of the gym floor.

"Now, Your Royal Highness, it's just you and me. Let us get to the bottom of the real issue at hand," the mysterious man announced, reaching for his owl mask. "I don't need this for now. This body has been useful to say the least, and I wouldn't want it to lose its life because of my actions."

The owl became a man.

"Thomas," Tamantha hissed, confused that such a strange Guard is behind all of this.

"Yes, this body's name is Thomas," he agreed, kneeling down in front of Tamantha. "It's been a long road to get to this point. I want to confirm my suspicions before I waste my energy."

"Why are you doing this?" Tamantha asked, tired of all the games.

"All I knew was one of the original Eklektos was in this life in a royal body. I don't care much if you're one of the seven sisters. They don't give me the essence I need," Thomas began.

"What are you even talking about?" Where was he going with all of this?

"My dear, you are a soul of the Creator," he stated, pulling out a knife and cutting her ropes apart.

He grabbed her wrist. Thomas ripped the bandage off, revealing the Gold color.

"Only the children of the Creator would have this. Silver means you have met the Creator, but Gold means you are of the Creator. Which soul are you? A sister, or the mother or father?"

"Let go!" Tamantha screamed, yanking her wrist away. She crawled away backwards.

"I once had a sister, but it just felt like any other regular soul.

I had another one recently too. Atlas is a bit harder to find and doesn't seem to give any more the rest of them, but Pleione is the sweetest one to taste. She keeps me alive," Thomas explained. "It is her powers that feed me."

Tamantha felt tears stream down her face. She really was going to die here. She peeked at Cole.

"Please just let Cole go. Whoever I am, you can have, but please just free him," Tamantha begged.

"We have a while before he wakes up, you know."

Thomas stood up and walked over to the typical painting of the Creator and her children. "These days, it's a little harder to get my hands on Pleione. She seems to be born further and further apart."

"What are you muttering?"

"The first time I drank her essence, she was just a little girl, a child of the Electra family. It was around the same time of the great fire. It had been an accident, but it made me realize how much more I would be capable of."

Tamantha was perplexed by what Thomas was going on about. Was he crazy, or was he being truthful? Tamantha crawled over to Cole while Thomas was looking away, fixated on Pleione in the picture.

Tamantha stroked Cole's face, brushing a red strand out of his face.

"Please wake up," she whispered, desperate for both of them to escape. She searched the gymnasium, wondering how quickly she could get to the door, but if she did that, Cole would die for it. They both needed to be awake for them to get away. There was no way she could drag him away fast enough before Thomas stopped her.

"Do you know how many people I had to kill to find where

Pleione is in this life? I'm so thankful your mark appeared. It gave me relief that I wouldn't have to take any more lives. The Merope family barely has any heirs left. At least, they have your cousin," Thomas noted.

"Who did you kill?" Tamantha questioned, trying to distract him long enough in hopes someone might rescue them, but how would the Guardians find them? Athan wasn't here to save her this time.

"Well, some of them were accidents. They got in the way while I was looking for Pleione, but the others I deliberately killed. I killed a lot of people over the years, Tamantha. You're not any different. I think I killed a Princess of the Maia, a Lady of the Taygete, and most recently of the royals, I killed a Merope prince."

"What?"

"Oh, yes, the last kill was in this very place. It's fitting you will die in the same place," Thomas chuckled, painting a bright grin on his face.

Tamantha furiously shook her head. "No, my brother died from the Curse of the Lost One!"

"Actually, I snuck in. He woke up from the Test. He was so relieved to have lived, but I took his essence. It was for naught. He did happen to be a sister though, somehow, so that helped a little bit while I waited for Pleione," Thomas remarked, wiping a bit of drool from the corner of his mouth.

"No, that can't be true!" Tamantha refused, standing up. Her legs felt like liquid from the medicine he injected her with, but she felt adrenaline coursing through her veins. She had to get both of them out.

"Your friends, your brother, they were all collateral damage, but I'm so sure this time. You must be Pleione!" Thomas approached her, grabbing her by the chin. "I suspected it when I took Clayton. I didn't realize who I had taken. I thought I was just entering another random person's body." He let go of her and gave her some space.

"You were the woman at the party. The one he said he last saw."

Thomas nodded. "Now you're getting it, Tamantha. I was indeed. It's just my luck I found a literal son of the Creator. The power that flowed through him. Guardians really are a force to be reckoned with. It's a bit hard to possess them though when they are already sworn to protect someone. It's nice he came with no strings attached. What a lucky break to feel the blood of the Creator flowing through my veins, but I couldn't hold onto him long. The Creator was sure of that.

"I decided to keep him around for a bit longer, entering the body of this 'Thomas' and then imprisoning the boy. I planted the seed to have him kidnap and torture you, but I didn't think he would go so far. I need you alive after all. I'm lucky that Athan boy found you," Thomas told her.

"Why are you bothering to tell me all this?" Tamantha prolonged the inevitable.

"Because I have lived a long time, Tamantha. Three hundred years, maybe? It's nice to tell my story every once in a while, even if you won't be alive long enough to hear it."

"When will 'The End' come? I am tired of playing this game with you," Tamantha said, accepting her eventual death.

"Let me have my fun. You were clever to tell the Guardians that you were planning on taking a long sleep. I wonder what they are thinking. They can probably feel the same turmoil as you now, but will they check on you or leave you be? You have given me so much time, my foolish princess. It's a shame you are a Merope. I don't like to kill my own."

Tamantha glanced at Cole, feeling sad she would have to leave him alone in this life.

"Your brother took a great fall and broke his neck, but somehow, he became okay. The Creator found you before I did, and She tried to protect you from me. She knows of what I have done to Her children, but was it enough? If you do live, maybe I could give you a reward. How about that?" he motioned, watching her carefully.

"Like what?" she eyed the knife in his hand. She wondered if she could wrestle it away and possibly wound him. It would be enough to take him down and get Cole and herself out in one piece.

"For your prize, I can tell you something about this body," Thomas promised.

Tamantha raised an eyebrow. Thomas was a nobody. Right?

"If you live, you can take this knowledge with you. Thomas is not just a guard. He is a Guardian of the Electra. His tie is weak, but it is there. The Electra family is alive somewhere, and I know who exactly the heir is." He watched her shock and awe.

"Wait, what?" Tamantha choked, searching the floor at her feet for answers. She remembered the article about the last Electra prince and his mistress. What if the Electra line really has survived? Who is the Electra heir that the Guardians are protecting?

"That's all I will give you, princess. Our dance shall end," Thomas told her, twirling the knife in his hand.

Thomas watched the princess squirm under his gaze. Her eyes traced the figure of her red headed friend. "Cole, wake up!" Tamantha sobbed. Tears were uncontrollably streaming down her face as she froze in the spot where she stood, a deer in the headlights.

"You are just part of the grand plan, and your friends were also part of it. I am sorry it had to be this way," Thomas said. He grabbed Cole's hair and dragged him further away. Cole did not stir. "I might have given him too much of a sleeping dosage."

Tamantha felt panic rise up in her chest. She had to get them both out somehow. She knew the Guardians could sense her distress, but it might be too late by the time the princess and the lord are found. All she could do was worry about Cole. He had no part in this. He was just the bait, and he would suffer for it.

Her ice blue eyes glared at Thomas, peering at his towering figure.

"It matters a great deal to me." Thomas grabbed a knife out of his guard belt. Tamantha screamed as he plunged it into Cole's chest.

"No! Cole!" Tamantha felt the tears flow freely from her. Thomas took the knife out. He let go of Cole and let her friend drop onto the floor hard. He backed away a bit, waiting to see what Tamantha was going to do. She broke free of the fear that rooted her in one spot. She ran over to her best friend, groping the fresh wound to stop the bleeding. Blood splashed onto her cheeks, creating false freckles. "Why?" Tamantha screamed at him. "Please no! Don't die, Cole."

Thomas sat down in the chair again, watching the princess grieve as the boy she cares so much for dies in front of her. He placed his chins on his hands, a pondering look on his face.

"Somebody, help!" Tamantha was desperate, knowing no one would hear her during the summer break. The school halls were empty. "Please don't die, Cole!" She slumped over and rested her head on his chest, still holding onto the gaping hole in his chest. She didn't care if the blood seeped into her hair.

A warmth passed through her as she tried to get the sleeping

Cole to cling onto his life. One of her memories of a past life drifted into her mind. Tamantha stood on a pier, staring out into the sea. She was waiting for someone, longing for her other half. The scenery around her was of a world that no longer is.

Tamantha then remembered another moment. She remembered staring up at a woman with silver eyes. The woman was smiling, but there was pain hidden behind those ancient eyes. Tamantha watched the woman fall to the ground, never to be risen again. She heard that same woman whisper into her ear now in the present day, "You are set free."

A light shone from her hands into Cole's bleeding wound. Tamantha lifted her head and watched in awe as the gaping hole began to close under her hands. She removed her hands and admired the fresh pink slit.

Thomas chuckled, a chuckle that became booming laughter as he looked up at the sky. He turned his eyes back to Tamantha who felt fear at this moment. "I have finally found you, Pleione!" He grabbed her by the shoulder, dragging her away from her now very alive friend.

"No, let me go! Cole!" Tamantha leaned as far away from him as she could. She only felt concern over the boy who had still not woken.

Cole should be dead.

"You should have paid better attention to the Creation story, Your Royal Highness. The Creator reached the continent of Prota. She lived on that land, but she eventually began to grow lonely. The Creator called out to the skies for some kind of comfort. The Creator felt a power grow inside her very being. Two beings emerged from her body. She named them Atlas and Pleione. All who live and breathe today with the blood of the Eklektos have descended from these two divine souls," Thomas retold the common story all children learned in their classes at the Creationist halls.

"It's just a fairy tale," Tamantha rebutted, trying to get away from him.

"Whatever you believe, princess, but the proof is right here. This boy is alive because of you. When Atlas and Pleione were in their original bodies, Atlas had the Creator's power of immortality, but Pleione had the power of healing, able to save people from the brink of death. Prota was not the immortal world it was when it first began. People could still die. Pleione eventually passed away of old age, but Atlas continued to live. He begged the Creator to take away his ability to live forever, so he could be with his beloved Pleione. Pleione still harnessed the gift given to her."

Tamantha felt the fear and panic take over again. She didn't understand how she managed to save Cole, but he was alive, for now.

"You are my Pleione. I am so happy to find the treat I have been looking for," Thomas announced. Tamantha yanked herself away, causing him to drop the knife. He didn't bother to pick it up, unconcerned and not needing the weapon.

Tamantha felt weak on her feet. She felt drained from what she had done to Cole.

"This will not hurt, Princess. You will be taking a nice long nap, and you will wake up in your next life. Maybe it will be a little bit longer before I find you again. It's such a pity you had to be born into this body. You would have made a great queen. I am sorry it had to be this way in this life, but I need you," the man soothed, stroking her cheek with a thumb, rubbing a tear away from her face. "At least, you won't have to wear the Crown anymore." She looked away, trying to focus on a spot on the wall. Her breath hitched.

He grasped her face with both hands, forcing her to look into his eyes.

Chapter Twenty-Five

Tamantha felt herself be pushed out the body she inhabited. She felt herself being ripped away. She saw herself slumped over on the ground. The body sat up, staring at the hands that were hers. Thomas fell to the ground, laying down next to her. "Damn it. Where did you go?" her own body growled out.

"Pleione," a female voice called. The room swirled around as she looked at a bright light standing next to her. "You are under my protection. He cannot harm you." Tamantha felt all of her fears and worries wash away.

"Athanasia?"

"It's been a while since anyone said my true name. Yes, I am Athanasia."

"I'm scared," Tamantha squeaked. The warm light enveloped her very soul.

"It will be okay. You have a mission in this life. You will end the Eklektos curse I created with the help of Atlas and Harmonia, but please do not shirk your duties as the Merope heir. The time will come when you are needed to complete the mission, but while you are waiting, become Queen and take care of Sophia. Atlas will hold the weight of the world, but you must be the one to help him. You must save everyone," the Creator directed. "I do not know how much protection I can give you, so please try not to get into too much trouble. I cannot always protect you from him."

"Who is he?"

"He is the one who killed my first-born child and my soul mate. He killed my precious Harmonia. He is the soul of the Electra king that helped destroy life on Prota. Do not look into his eyes. Use your powers and fend for yourself," the Creator commanded. "We will see each other again soon, Pleione."

Tamantha felt power seep into her, vibrating her entire being. "Athanasia!" Tamantha called.

"Fight, my child!"

Tamantha felt the world go black around her.

She opened her eyes, looking up at the ceiling of the gymnasium. She raised her hands, staring at them, focusing on the glittering gold that got her into this mess.

She heard the groan of a man next to her. She did not turn to look at him, remembering the Creator's words. She must not look into his eyes. She must not open the window to her soul to him.

How can she fight him? What good will the powers of healing do against anyone?

If she can heal, why can't she do the reverse?

Thomas sat up, rubbing his forehead. "What the hell was that? Whatever it was, I don't care! I must finish this!" He leaned over. His hand grabbed onto her shoulder, and the other one grabbed her chin. "Give yourself to me, Pleione!" Thomas commanded.

"Never!" Tamantha cried, putting her hands on his face, covering his eyes. She felt the power flowing through her hands, the same power that saved Cole. This time they did not glow the same warm yellow light. They were glowing a dark charcoal color.

Thomas screamed in pain.

Whatever she was doing was hurting him. It was working.

"Die!" Tamantha roared, pushing further and further up. She sat up as he tried to get away, clinging onto his face. He tried to pull her hands away.

"Stop it!" Thomas begged.

She felt his life slipping away. She felt him leaving this body. "You will harm no more! You will be the one moving onto the next life!"

The gymnasium doors slammed open, and people ran into the hall. She eyed the familiar blue that came straight towards her. Tamantha let go, and Thomas fell over, gasping for air. A couple Guardians surrounded him as he lay dying.

Tamantha ran everything that happened in the last few minutes. "Wait! Close your eyes!" she commanded, but it was too late. Thomas dropped his head on the ground with a loud crack. She watched as one of her Guardians swayed back and forth. The Guardian slumped forward. She recognized this Guardian as the oldest one she had. His name was James.

James straightened his back, staring at the sky. "This isn't over, princess," he announced. In lightning speed, he ran out of the gymnasium. The Merope Guardians were confused by James's sudden outburst.

"Go after him!" Tamantha commanded. Siberius sent one of Tamantha's Guardians after James, but it was impossible. James was one of the most experienced and powerful Guardians. James and the soul who took him were already gone. She hoped James would be freed and would come home someday, and this spirit would not permanently take him.

"Are you alright, Tamantha?" Elsabeth questioned.

Tamantha nodded, flabbergasted by the whole situation.

"Yes, I'm okay," Tamantha noted, glancing over at the mop of red hair on the floor.

"What were you thinking? Why are you here?" Elsabeth hissed, checking Tamantha over. Elsabeth checked her a million times, unable to let it sink in that something like this happened to Tamantha.

"How did you find us?"

"You used your telecrystal to find the school. Thank, the Creator, we have a trace on your telecrystal now," Elsabeth stated, shaking her head at the princess. Tamantha nodded, glad she did something to help the Guardians out.

Siberius nudged Thomas with a foot.

"He's dead," Siberius announced.

Tamantha heard Cole moan as he woke up from his deep sleep. Tamantha tried to crawl over to him, but Elsabeth stopped her by grabbing Tamantha's shoulder.

"I got it, Your Royal Highness," Siberius alerted, studying Cole, who began to slowly sit up. "He's okay."

Cole shook his head groggily, trying to shake off the deep sleep.

"What happened?" Cole wondered aloud, grasping onto his forehead.

"That's what I would like to know," Siberius muttered, checking Cole for any injuries.

Cole yelped in pain, clutching onto the fresh wound. "What is this?" he gasped, looking at the fading pink.

Tamantha was unsure of how she could explain all of this to them. She had learned so much from this event. She had witnessed so much. She had discovered her own soul. She met the Creator. She killed someone.

"I," Tamantha began, but the world faded around her, feeling it all finally take a toll on her.

Tamantha woke up, searching the high ceiling of her palace bedroom for rhyme or reason of how she got here. What was she doing back in this hell?

She was tired of waking up in random places.

She was tired of blacking out and losing sight of everything that came to pass. She did not want to do it anymore. She wouldn't let herself find herself like this again.

She was tired of always needing to be rescued.

She was tired of losing the ones she loved.

She tried to recall the last few moments before she woke up here.

It was all blank. Tamantha let out a long sigh.

"Tamantha?" Cole's voice called.

She sat up quickly as it all came back to her.

Tamantha has the soul of Pleione, and someone wants her dead for it.

She turned to look at Cole, who was sitting at the side of her bed. "Cole!" she cried out, hugging him tightly. He was alive. She didn't notice, but she was sobbing into his shoulder.

"It's okay, Tamantha. We're safe now," Cole comforted, rubbing his hand up and down her back.

"I was so scared I was going to lose you! You almost died!" she weakly answered. She choked on her own tears, gulping them and tasting the salt. He shook his head, putting both hands on the side of her head.

"We're both here. We're both alive. You can't rush in like that. You're so much more than I am. If I die, no one will remember me, and I will join Alessandra," Cole offered.

"I love you, Cole. You deserve to die peacefully in your own bed, not at the hands of a stranger," she said, brushing a red strand of hair out of his face.

His mouth burst open with a wide smile. "For Creator's sake, Tammy," he muttered, leaning his forehead on hers.

"Did they find James?" she asked.

He shook his head. "Hopefully he will turn up somehow," he stated, running his fingers through her pale blonde hair.

"So much happened, Cole," Tamantha reminded. "How did you even get kidnapped, Cole?"

"Well, this Thomas dude called me. He said he has my little brother and would kill him if I didn't come. My brother was crying on the telecrystal. I couldn't let him die," Cole explained.

"I'm so sorry," Tamantha whispered.

"The Guardians are helping right now to find where he put my little brother. My parents are so furious that any of us got caught up in this mess. They almost don't want me to marry you. They say you're bad luck," Cole chuckled. "You really are."

Tamantha rolled her eyes. "I'm sure they will find him. Don't worry, Cole."

"What happened while I was was out, Tamantha? I have this weird scar," Cole noted, rubbing on his chest.

Tamantha nodded, sniffling the last of her tears away. "Thomas is not Thomas. I don't know how to explain that, but the person inside him is a different person. This person can jump into any person. He claims to be three hundred years old, back to the time of the Electra demise."

"But no one can live that long, not since the ages of Prota." Cole frowned, stroking the back of Tamantha's hand.

"I know. He's still alive. I almost killed him, but he escaped right into James. Poor James. He doesn't deserve it."

"It still doesn't make sense. Why did he want you?"

"I am Pleione." Cole froze up, searching her ice blue eyes.

She offered her golden tattoo. He traced it with his finger, admiring the shimmer. "I've never seen this color before."

"It is the color of a Child of the Creator. Only Pleione, Atlas, the seven sisters, or whatever physical child the Creator has will have it. Because of this mark, it confirmed Thomas's suspicions. I harbor the soul of the Mother of us all," Tamantha announced, pulling her wrist away.

"It was silver before," Cole remarked.

"It was. I think whatever seal the Creator put on me blocked my soul from being known, but the seal broke completely. It became Gold after I gave my love to Athan," Tamantha mentioned, remembering the tender moments she had with the silver eyed boy. She could still smell his musk, unable to let go of his scent. She shook the thought away.

"So, what is this mark?" Cole wondered, poking at his chest.

"Thomas stabbed you, and I healed you. I don't know how I did it. All I know is I wanted to save you. I couldn't lose you too. I drew on the powers of Pleione and used them to save you," Tamantha explained, staring down at her hands. She wondered how she could access those powers again. She wondered how she managed to reverse the powers to take life away from Thomas.

Tamantha concentrated on her hands, trying to get them to do the same thing. A faint white glow appeared for a brief second. Tamantha and Cole both gasped.

"I don't know how I did that. It could be useful, right?" Tamantha said, trying to give any excuse to exercise her newfound powers.

Cole shrugged. "Maybe, but let's work on it later. I believe your father wants to know when you've awoken."

Tamantha sighed, not ready to step back into her real life, but she had to face the inevitable. "Okay."

Cole stood up from his chair and went to the bedroom doors, opening it a crack. He spoke to the Guardian outside her door and closed it again.

"Life will never be normal," Tamantha whispered to herself. She stepped out of bed and put on a robe to cover her night gown. Cole returned to her side.

"You really do got to stop being kidnapped, Tamantha. It's not good for anyone's mental health or your physical health," Cole joked.

Tamantha snorted, lightly hitting him on the arm. "Shut up, Cole. You did it too."

Cole laughed. "Thank you for saving my life, Tamantha," Cole said gratefully. He took her hand and kissed it lightly.

"You're welcome. Now don't go doing it again," Tamantha scolded, poking him on the forehead.

He rubbed his forehead. "I'll try."

Tamantha heard a knock on her door. "Come in!"

The door flung wide open to reveal the face of her father. "His Majesty, the King!" Siberius announced. Tamantha curtsied, and Cole bowed.

"Don't let anyone in, Siberius," the King ordered. The tall Guardian bowed and shut the door behind them.

"I'm sorry for any trouble I have caused you, Father," Tamantha apologized, bowing once more.

Alvyn shook his head. "I am sorry we could not protect you better, Pleione."

Tamantha watched in shock as her own father bowed to her. "Papa?"

"You are the Mother of us all. You are the Mother of the royal bloodlines. We would not be here without you, Pleione," Alvyn said as he rose up.

Tamantha shook her head. "That may be who I once was, but that is not who I am now."

"Regardless, it is why the Creator wanted you on that fateful day. Because of your soul, you saved your brother's life after he broke his neck. Because of your soul, you will be ending our curse," Alvyn revealed.

"You know?"

"Yes, I know. Athanasia told me of her plans before she left this world." Alvyn eyed the mark on her wrist. "She had me bring you to her, and then she sealed your identity away to hide you from the world. You are the one of the most well-known souls in the world inhabiting the body of a princess in line to the Sophia throne. It was too much power for one person."

"But, papa," Tamantha interjected.

"She found the souls of Pleione and Atlas, and she sealed both of you away. She gave you her soul, so you would be safe. It was never enough though. All we can hope for is that you end the difference between Eklektos and Anaxios."

"Atlas?"

"Yes, her own blood son is inhabited by Atlas. You know him well," Alvyn announced.

"Athan?"

The King nodded. "It's such a shame you can no longer be together in this life. Not as you both are now."

Tamantha stared at her hands again. "The seal has been broken."

Alvyn pursed his lips, nodding reluctantly. "The seal meant to protect your identity is broken, yes, but you are ready for so much more than before."

Cole looked at both of them over and over, unsure if he is meant to be here.

"I will protect you, Pleione, for as long as I can. The three of us in this room will not reveal your true identity to the world. It will be between all of us. But once it gets out, it will be out of my hands."

"Father, this Thomas man told me some things, and I must tell you them."

"Alright, my darling. What is it?"

"First, the Electra royal family is indeed alive. Thomas was an Electra Guardian, right underneath our noses. He says he knows who it is, and he said the link was definitely there. The Electra Guardians are harboring this secret from us," Tamantha noted first, noticing Alvyn's face was unchanged.

"I know that it was likely the Electra are still alive, but now we have evidence that it is true they are still alive. I will have to have the Guardians investigate and possibly interrogate some Electra Guardians to confirm who the heir to the Astrapi throne is. Could they be keeping them off throne to protect them, or is it for their own political gain as an Electra Guardian acts as President of Astrapi?" the King wondered aloud. "Continue, Tamantha."

"Secondly, whoever was inside Thomas has been killing others besides my friends. He has killed countless royals. Papa, he killed Nolan." Tamantha watched the King's mouth drop open.

"But he died to the Curse of the Lost One?" Cole asked, butting into the conversation.

"He didn't. This man took him from us," Tamantha said, watching her own father falter.

He shook his head, fighting away any tears. "Regardless, I am glad you're safe. You're alive. Please stop doing this to your mother and I. I don't know how much she or I can handle the stress."

Tamantha bit her lip and nodded. She approached her father, faltering. Would this man allow her to hold him? Was he king or father? He opened his arms to her. She smiled, embracing her father. He tenderly rubbed her back and held her for so long.

All the things that had happened over the last year, she lost loved ones. She wondered what good came out of all of it. Some powers? Pleione's soul? None of it mattered to her in this life. She wanted to let it all go in exchange for her friends to be returned to her. For her brother to come back her.

Tamantha let go, and Alvyn patted her on the head, ruffling her head. "I know it's a lot, kid, but I know you can handle it. You're so brave. Things might not have gone the way you want it, but life is unpredictable. Getting up every time you fall is the most important thing you can do as Queen."

"Thank you, Papa."

The King stepped back. "Cole, your brother is safe."

Cole took a sigh of relief. "Thank you, Your Majesty. I am so deeply sorry for getting Her Royal Highness mixed up in it."

Alvyn shook his head. "No, Cole. You are not at fault. It is the one who wishes to hunt Tamantha's soul and harm all those in his way. I am hopeful they are able to find James in one piece."

"Papa, where is Mama?" Tamantha questioned, peering around him at the door.

"She has gone out of the country to Thalassa. She decided to take a vacation from all of the stress. She wanted to be here, but since she knew you were safe, she decided she needed time. She's so afraid of losing you. It's been so much for us, Tamantha," the King explained.

"I understand, Papa. I'm glad you're here at least."

The King smiled at her. "I will always be here for you, even if we were nobodies. You are my daughter in this life," the King stated.

"Why were you so afraid to tell me of the truth?" Tamantha asked.

"The Creator made me promise to wait until this moment comes. She did not want to risk your identity being known. She was afraid he would find you when you were so young. Your soul is Her own child. She does not wish to see Her children suffer, and She wishes they may all live happy, long lives without worry of the past," the King marveled on it. It was a direct order from someone higher than a King himself. The Creator had decreed, and he had to follow.

"What about Athan? He's out there somewhere. This man will be hunting him too, most likely," Tamantha wondered, dreading what might happen to Athan,

"We will do our best to protect him, but our main concern is you, my princess," he explained. "It is unfortunate you have been exposed, and it very likely there will be consequences. It won't be long before the public learns the future Queen of Sophia is the one true Mother of the Eklektos."

"Don't worry, Tamantha. You're not any different to me," Cole announced, slapping a hand on her back.

"Cole, I have to ask you something," King Alvyn stated. Cole froze in his spot.

"Yes, Your Majesty?" Cole said, his lip beginning to quiver.

"Because this has finally come to light, I must ask you something that will affect your entire life from this point on."

"I will do anything for Tamantha. She's my best friend," Cole answered.

The King nodded. "Then you will marry my daughter."

"I will."

"Wait, wait, wait. What? This is going too fast, Dad," Tamantha noted, in disbelief her father would be rushing for her marriage after her betrothal failed.

"It will slow down your reveal as Pleione. It will give us enough time to deal with any ramifications, and this way you are marrying someone you love. It will also give us an heir if there may be an untimely death. Your title and your soul together risk the very throne. I'm sorry, my dear," Alvyn explained, putting a hand on her cheek. He stroked his thumb over a faint scratch she got in the skirmish with the Stranger.

"Tammy, I promise I will do my best as your husband if you will take me," Cole pleaded.

Tamantha bit her lip, pulling away from her father. She stared at the ornate walls, trying to focus on a single spot. Just months ago, she was engaged to another man. Now, she would be marrying her best friend.

Most people in an arranged marriage would prefer such a situation, but the love of her life is who she wants. She wants to be in his arms like she did on that fateful night he disappeared.

"Cole, you have to understand, being married to me could lead to your own death, as it already almost did. It will come with so much responsibility to be husband to the Queen of Sophia. Look at my mother. She practically runs the nation for my father when she is needed. Is this something you will really want?"

"I do, Tamantha. You are my best friend. I've already faced my own death, and I'm not scared. I want to help you. I want to protect you. You're all I have left in this world. Alessandra is gone. Sara is gone. Davin disappeared. We are all we have left of our old circle."

Alvyn watched them both curiously.

"I knew this day would come even when I was with Alessandra, and she knew it could happen too. It comes with the last name. The Baldwins are a source of spouses. The Baldwins have always served the Merope family in this way, and it will happen again even after we are gone. I love you, Tamantha. We can do this together."

"Alright. Let's do this, Cole. At least now that I have these new powers, it's very unlikely you will die when I'm around," Tamantha joked with a tongue in her cheek. Cole grinned widely.

Tamantha stared down at her hands. She healed Cole, but she killed Thomas. What else could she do with these powers?

First, she needed to learn to control it.

Chapter Twenty-Six

Tamantha sat in front of her vanity mirror, brushing out her long platinum blond hair. Her mother would be returning today. She sighed, staring at the face in front of her.

She could barely recognize herself. She didn't look the same as she did almost a year ago.

She tore herself away from the gaze, standing up. She hesitated, feeling a twinge of pain in her knee. Everything she had been through had scarred her. She sat back down, tracing the pink skin. She wondered if she could do something about it.

Tamantha thought back to the moment in the gymnasium. How did she heal Cole? She closed her eyes, trying to draw on that same feeling.

Maybe she could heal away the scars.

It felt odd. Nothing was happening. She opened her eyes, hoping to see the gold glow. Nothing.

A knock on the door caused the princess to straighten up. "Come in," Tamantha hummed.

A maid entered the bedroom, holding a tray. "Hello, Your Royal Highness. I've brought your lunch. The chef ordered me to bring it to you," the maid announced.

Tamantha nodded, pointing towards a table nestled in the corner of the room with a large window. "Please place it over there. I'll eat soon."

The maid bowed her head and took it to the desired location.

Tamantha stared back down at the scarring on her leg, frustrated. She just wanted one little glow, holding her hand over it.

She paused, wondering why she had not heard the door open and shut again. She looked up at the maid in the corner of the room.

"You may go now," Tamantha ordered, glaring at the pesky presence lurking in her domain.

"It doesn't work that way, you know," the maid noted, pointing towards Tamantha's hand.

"Excuse me?" Tamantha responded, wondering what this woman was talking about. Why was she still here?

"Well, Pleione could never heal herself. To use the healing powers, it would draw on her own life force. It would be pointless if Pleione draws her own life force to heal herself." Tamantha froze.

"Excuse me?" Tamantha repeated herself, feeling her own breath hitch.

The maid sighed, bowing. "Anything else, ma'am?"

"What did you just say?" Tamantha glanced to the door for a split second. Her Guardians could be in here as soon as she screamed.

"I didn't say anything, Your Royal Highness," the maid insisted.

Tamantha shook her head, unsure if she was losing her mind amongst all the stress. "Never mind. You may go."

The maid bowed walking towards the door. She paused, putting her hand on the door. "Tamantha, are you sure you're hearing things?"

Tamantha watched the maid turn around. The same eyes were staring back at her that had tormented her over the last few days. "Get out before I call the guards."

"He will come back someday," the maid announced.

Tamantha raised an eyebrow. "Who?"

The princess felt her ice blue eyes pulsing, yelping and clasping onto her head.

"You may have Athanasia's protection, but her spell will break. Your soul and Atlas's souls will be mine!" Tamantha felt a voice screaming in her head. "Hear me, Pleione! I will have the gift that belongs to Prota!"

"Get out of my head!" She groaned, standing up. She watched a disheveled maid cowering in the corner.

"What's happening, ma'am?"

Tamantha couldn't call the Guardians, could she? How could they fight what they can't see.

"Leave now, please," Tamantha begged, turning away and facing the wall.

"The longer you trap me in here, the more I crack away at the wall She built," the voice whispered in her ear. "I will have you, Pleione."

"Go," Tamantha coughed. She fell to her knees. She heard a shuffling in the background, and the door slammed open.

"Somebody help! The princess needs help!" the maid yelled as she ran down the hallway.

Tamantha's breath hitched, grabbing onto her dressing table.

"Let go, Pleione. It will all be over soon." Tamantha shook her head. She felt like someone stuck in a pickaxe in her skull.

Someone put her hand on her back. "Your Royal Highness, are you alright?"

Tamantha retched, feeling nothing come up. It was Siberius. She shook her head, closing her eyes.

"Yes, Tamantha, leave me in here. Your soul will be mine."

Tamantha felt something drip from her nose onto her hands. Dark red blotches covered the back of it.

She fell backwards. Her ice blue eyes met the same eyes that had cared for her all these years. "Siberius, look away."

It was too late. The headache subsided, and she breathed a sigh of relief.

Siberius caressed her cheek.

"Siberius, what the hell are you doing?" a Guardian yelled at him.

"I will always be here, Tamantha. I am the Guardian near you. I am the maid. I am the stranger passing you by on the streets. I am your friend or your family. I am anyone. You cannot escape me, Tamantha," Siberius stated, letting her go. He turned around, looking into the stern eyes of the next Guardian.

"I am him." The voice came from that same Guardian. He turned around and peered into the eyes of the next target.

"You cannot escape me," the voice came from Elsabeth. A sly grin curled on her face. The smile did not match the same blue haired girl she knew.

Elsabeth looked back into Siberius's confused eyes.

Siberius turned back to Tamantha. "When Atlas comes, I will be ready for him. The protection the Creator gave you can easily be broken. Atlas is the biggest prize."

"Why?" Tamantha hissed, standing up.

"Because he is now immortal," the voice was inside her head this time. Tamantha shook her head, clasping onto it again. She heard a scream. It was her own.

"Leave us!" the voice of a woman cried out from inside her. The Stranger was expelled from her mind. She didn't know where he went, but she knew he wasn't gone. His spirit was bouncing around the palace, easily ready to enter the next body he could find.

"Tamantha, what's wrong?!" Siberius begged, unsure of what to do.

This was an enemy the Guardians could not fight. What could she tell them? How do they save her from what they cannot see or know?

Tamantha shook her head, wiping the blood away from her face. "I'm sorry. I don't know what just happened. I guess I'm not okay," the Princess diverted. They heard the voices though, the voices coming from those in this room.

"Elsabeth, get the doctor. The princess needs to be checked on," Siberius ordered. Elsabeth nodded, running down the hallway.

Tamantha closed her eyes, feeling the room spinning. "Carry me to the bed please."

Siberius picked her up in a swift motion and gently laid her down. "Tamantha, what just happened?"

"I can't." She can't add her own paranoias to the Guardians' own worries. They would trust no one, not even themselves. It would cause the chaos the Stranger needed to break back into Tamantha's mind.

Tamantha peered into the eyes of those around her, searching in each one. She was afraid of where the Stranger might appear. Who could she trust now?

"Darling!" her mother called out, rushing into her bedroom. "Are you alright?"

"I'm okay. I just panicked. I guess I'm not okay after all that happened in the last few months," Tamantha offered.

Clarisa sat down next to the princess on the bed, feeling her forehead. "Are you sure?"

Tamantha nodded, feeling the tears well up in her eyes. She rested her forehead in her mother's bosom, trying to take solace in this single moment. "I'm scared, mama."

The Queen ran her fingers through her daughter's silky hair. "I'm here, my child. It's alright now," she whispered. She hummed a song as she held and rocked her daughter.

It was a distant lullaby, one sung to the children of the royal families. The song told the tales of the Creator and Prota. It was a reminder to the children of what would be on their shoulders.

No one knew the weight could be so heavy on Tamantha's shoulders right now. She did not have only the crown to hold, but she had the fate of Pleione and Atlas crushing down on her. She didn't know what that would mean to her later on, but she was scared of where it would take her.

The people of Atlantis are taught to cherish their past lives, but to live the lives they have now. They must look forward to the future and carry on, knowing there will be more after life is over.

Tamantha's past life has intertwined into this life, endangering her once again as she fights the Stranger. Pleione would never have a simple life. She and Atlas were doomed to face the past the Creator had given them.

She wondered if Athan was okay, wherever he is. She knew she loved him with every part of her being. She understood now why he had to go. She would try to keep him safe as long as she can. Every fiber in her being wants to run to him, but she can't.

Tamantha had to become strong, for all those she had left, for her entire country and even the world, and mostly for herself. She couldn't be a scared little girl anymore who expects everyone to fight for her. She had to fight her own battle.

Tamantha pulled away from her mother. "Mama, thank you. I think I'm okay now," she reassured her mother. Siberius was hovering in the background, watching her. She wasn't okay, and he knew it.

"As a queen, you won't have anyone to cry on anymore. Your tears will have to hide from the world, and the only one who sees it will be your most cherished person. I've seen your father's own tears. I'm sure your fiancé will be there for comfort too," Clarisa consoled. She meant Cole.

"Papa told you?" Tamantha sighed. She was so afraid of how much danger she would be putting her best friend in, but she knew it was the only logical choice.

"Yes, the Symvoulio is arranging the marriage contract as we speak. We hope for a wedding in the very near future," the Queen revealed. Tamantha froze, but she threw on the stereotypical mask her mother always wears.

"So soon? I guess it's how it's supposed to be," Tamantha muttered. Her mother patted her hand.

The doctor rushed in with Elsabeth. "Took you long enough! Doctor Slycroft, my daughter is in need of care, and you are slacking," her mother hissed.

The doctor bowed profusely to the Queen. "Your Majesty. Your Royal Highness, let me check you over. I need to know the cause of this episode," the doctor requested.

Clarisa stood up at that moment. "Make sure you don't miss anything. This is the future Queen of Sophia. It is best you make sure she is in tip top shape and ready to rule a country, or I will have your medical license," Clarisa threatened, plastering a sly smile on her face. She turned to her daughter and kissed her on the forehead goodbye. "We shall discuss wedding plans soon."

The Guardians and doctor bowed to the Queen as she left. Princess Tamantha let out a breath she didn't know she was holding. "I think I'm okay now, doctor," she noted.

The doctor shook his head profusely. "Nonsense, I must examine you." Tamantha groaned, relenting to him.

He found nothing and only recommended rest for the weary princess. How could he find what could not be seen? She nodded her head, but she knew there was no rest for her now. "Thank you, sir," Tamantha said, ending the exam.

The doctor bowed and left the room.

Tamantha looked out the large windows overlooking the gardens. She remembered running through those same gardens with Cole and Alessandra as children. She remembered walking with Sara and Davin, giggling about stupid boys and girls in school. She remembered kissing Athan, the lips that she feared she would never feel again.

This little country she would inherit would be ready to stand for her in war and peril. The Guardians would die for their Queen and fight till their last breath, but this battle was hers to fight. She had to fight what could not be seen. All the armies in Atlantis could not conquer this monster. She would have to dig deep inside her. She would have to unleash the thousands of years her soul had existed. The Creator trusted her to put an end to it all.

Tamantha rose to her feet. "Siberius, I have a request."

"Yes, Tamantha?" Siberius stood at attention. It was only she and him.

"I need your help. Train me to fight. Train me to draw a sword. Train me in hand-to-hand combat. I must learn how to fight my enemies. I cannot fall into the wrong hands no longer. Siberius Gagnon, Guardian of the Crown Princess Tamantha of

Sophia, will you assist me?"

"Absolutely, my lady." There would be no questions. "There will be a lot for us to cover. Let us begin, Tamantha Merope."

Tamantha raised her hands and looked at it, conjuring the glow of Pleione. She would be ready when he comes again. She is Tamantha Merope, Crown Princess of Sophia, the soul of Pleione Prota, and no one will take it from her.

* 9 7 9 8 9 8 8 9 0 6 8 0 3 *